Also by Claudia Gray

EVERNIGHT
STARGAZER
HOURGLASS
AFTERLIFE
BALTHAZAR

FATEFUL

SPELLCASTER
STEADFAST

A THOUSAND PIECES OF YOU

SORCERESS

A SPELLCASTER NOVEL

CLAUDIA GRAY

HARPER TEEN

An Imprint of HarperCollinsPublishers

HarperTeen is an imprint of HarperCollins Publishers.

Sorceress

www.epicreads.com

Library of Congress Cataloging-in-Publication Data
Gray, Claudia.
   Sorceress : a Spellcaster novel / Claudia Gray. — First edition.
      pages cm. — (Spellcaster)
   Summary: "Teenage witch Nadia must defeat the evil sorceress
Elizabeth before Elizabeth gathers enough power to summon
the One Beneath and destroy everything Nadia has worked to
protect"— Provided by publisher.
   ISBN 978-0-06-196124-3 (hardback)
   [1. Witches—Fiction. 2. Magic—Fiction. 3. Horror stories.]
I. Title.
PZ7.G77625So 2015   2014026693
[Fic]—dc23   CIP
                                                             AC

Typography by Torborg Davern

15   16   17   18   19   PC/RRDH   10   9   8   7   6   5   4   3   2   1
❖
First Edition

1

"THE ULTIMATE WEAPON IS FORGED FROM HATE."

Nadia watched Elizabeth reach into the glowing woodstove in the corner, the one burning with a flame that did not come from wood. Although Elizabeth's fingers had to be singed by the heat, she never flinched. Did you become immune to pain when you became a Sorceress, sworn to serve the One Beneath?

Soon Nadia would find out, because she was now sworn to Him too.

She hadn't made that bargain freely, out of the lust for power that drove Elizabeth, the four-hundred-year-old witch who now served as her teacher. Nadia had been forced to swear herself to the master of hell in order to save the people of Captive's Sound from Elizabeth's terrible curse. Now she was trapped, learning the darkest magic the Sorceress had to teach.

Elizabeth continued. "People try to pretend that hatred is . . . debris. Just the wreckage of something else." She withdrew her hand from the stove, her fingers reddened from the heat; Nadia saw her holding something small that glowed with an unearthly, beautiful light. Even as Elizabeth's skin smoldered from the heat of what she held, she brought it closer to her face. "But hatred has its own power. Its own role to play in the world. To understand dark magic, you must understand hate."

Nadia's mother had told her that sacrifices, too, had their own power. That was when Nadia had learned that Mom hadn't simply abandoned her family, with no thought for Nadia's training or Dad's heart or poor little Cole. Instead, Mom had sacrificed her love for them—her very ability to love—in an attempt to protect her daughter from the One Beneath. Nadia had been born as the child of two witching bloodlines, one perfectly created for the casting of dark magic; that meant she was precisely the kind of servant the One Beneath most wanted.

However, her mother's sacrifice had been for nothing. The One Beneath had found a way to trap Nadia anyway.

Now she could only hope her own sacrifice would have power. Nadia had given herself to the One Beneath to save the people of Captive's Sound—particularly her family, her best friend, Verlaine, and Mateo. Always Mateo. Maybe, in time, that would be enough to save her from darkness.

Otherwise, she would be trapped in the service of the One Beneath forever—and trapped into helping Him cross

2

into the mortal world, destroying it completely.

They sat together in Elizabeth's house, in what had been witched to look like any normal living room—practically a page out of the Pottery Barn catalog. But Nadia, now possessed of the magic allowing her to see through Elizabeth's glamours, knew the room was a ruin. This ramshackle wooden house had been Elizabeth's home for at least a century and probably more; the floor was littered with broken glass, every corner laced with cobwebs spun by spiders that would do Elizabeth's bidding. Patterned paper put up long ago now hung from the walls in ragged strips, and the few pieces of furniture were bent with years, hardly more than the rotten frames of the chairs and sofa they had been. Nadia and Elizabeth sat near the stove, which burned . . . no telling what, something never meant to be used as fuel. That was all Nadia knew for sure.

I can't end up like her, Nadia thought, clenching her hands so tightly that her fingernails dug into her palms. *Elizabeth's hardly even human anymore. There has to be a way out for me. There has to be a way to stop the One Beneath.*

As long as she was sworn to the service of the lord of hell, Nadia had rules she was forced to follow. Her only chance to learn how to defeat Him—and Elizabeth—was by pretending to be a loyal student of dark magic.

No, Elizabeth wasn't fool enough to believe that. But if Nadia acted the role of a perfect student, Elizabeth would have to pretend to be a perfect teacher. The rules of service to the One Beneath imprisoned them both.

"Is there any defense against it?" Nadia asked. "Against the perfect weapon, I mean. Against hatred."

Elizabeth didn't answer right away. She continued holding the glowing ember between her fingers, though by now small tendrils of smoke snaked up from her fingertips. Her flesh must have been burning, and she must have felt the pain, but she didn't care. Nadia would have been impressed if she weren't completely grossed out.

Finally Elizabeth let the ember drop to the wooden floor; it sizzled against the old, warped floorboards, a brief glow of red before it went dark. Only then did Elizabeth lift her face to Nadia's. She was fair where Nadia was dark, with freckled cheeks, chestnut curls, and an oval face that looked sweet to those who didn't know better.

"Love," Elizabeth said. "Love is the only defense against hatred."

Nadia tried to keep her expression impassive, but inside she seized this, clutched it close. Finally she had a reason to hope. *Love defeats hate—of course it does. How could it be any other way?*

Elizabeth smiled, as though she'd overheard Nadia's thoughts. Maybe she had. "But love doesn't last forever. Hatred endures."

"Nadia?"

Mateo knew only that he was looking for her. She seemed to be the only thing that mattered in the world.

Not that he seemed to be in the regular world any longer . . .

Where am I?

He wasn't sure, but he was beginning to believe that he might . . . he might be in hell.

Mateo lifted his head, trying to understand his surroundings. Despite the darkness, he could tell that he stood inside a cavern—but one illuminated from outside by some light so powerful that it shone through stone with the red glow of lava. Heat and moisture surrounded him, made him feel sticky. Mateo had to struggle to catch his breath. A deep thump-thump, thump-thump *could only have been the beating of his frightened heart.*

In the fitful crimson light, Mateo could make out only the faintest outline of the shape around him. He saw sloping walls, a slightly bowed roof overhead, and vast curving arches around him—harder, darker lines within the stone—

They weren't stone. They were . . . ribs.

A shudder rippled through Mateo as he realized he wasn't inside a cave; instead he was inside a living thing, vast and terrible. The heart he heard beating was not his own. It was as though he'd been swallowed whole, or eaten alive.

But somehow he wasn't alone inside the beast. He could hear groans, shrieks, cries of pain, all of them echoing within this creature's flesh but far away—until someone screamed just next to him.

Mateo turned around to see Nadia wearing black, her eyes wide with tears, as she hung in midair. But the scream had come from Verlaine, who clung to Nadia so she wouldn't fall. Verlaine's gray hair streamed out behind her as though they were in a whirlwind, one Mateo couldn't feel even as he reached out for Nadia—

He jerked awake, hands scrabbling for his blankets,

but—once again—he wasn't in his own bed. Tonight, Mateo's sleepwalking had taken him to the edge of the pier, almost into the water of the sound.

Someday I'm going to wake up just in time to drown.

Mateo tucked his bare feet under him; the early-December chill was harsh, way too cold to be outside in just boxers and a T-shirt. At least the snow from two days ago had melted. Otherwise he might have woken up with frostbite, too. Shivering, he started to get up and hurry back to his house before Dad realized he was gone—his father was already worried enough.

But then he saw the water, really saw it, and went still.

Anyone else who looked at the sound right now would see a seashore on a cloudy winter night: sand turned silver-gray by the moonlight, the dark surface of the water almost too smooth, the distant lighthouse sweeping its one pale beam around and around.

Mateo, however, was Nadia's Steadfast. That meant he helped strengthen her magic; any spell she cast when he was near her was far more powerful. Steadfasts also gained the ability to see magic at work around them. Thanks to Elizabeth, magic was tied into the very framework of Captive's Sound, visible everywhere, twisting and dark.

Which meant that Mateo could see the town was on the verge of falling apart.

A viscous, roiling substance arched overhead, like a dome blocking Captive's Sound from the stars; its light was fever-ish, tinted red. Deep lines in the earth seemed as though they were on the verge of crumbling in, collapsing into vast sinkholes. Worst of all, out in the water, something stirred fitfully, as if it were preparing to surface. By now he knew that was the place where Elizabeth was breaking down the barrier between the demonic world and the mortal one—the gate she was preparing for the One Beneath.

Mateo clenched his fists as he stared at it, wishing there was something, anything he could do to make this stop—

A strange pulse ran through his body. It wasn't painful, exactly, but it jolted him. Around his limbs, Mateo thought he saw a bluish light . . . but he couldn't be sure. It faded fast.

Just your Steadfast powers messing with you, he told himself, even though the powers had never done that before. *Stop making yourself crazy and go inside.*

Mateo forced himself to turn away from the nightmarish scene. The whole way back to his house, he kept his head down, looking only at the pier and the sand beneath his feet, which were reddened with cold. By the time he slipped back inside, he was almost numb, and he fumbled with the door . . . but luckily his father remained sound asleep.

As far as his dad knew, Mateo had begun "having seizures" in the past several weeks. That was how he'd been diagnosed by doctors who couldn't see the signs of magic, and what his father stubbornly insisted on believing. But everyone else in town knew what the real problem was, even people who had no idea that magic existed. Otherwise-reasonable people in Captive's Sound still believed in the Cabot Curse.

It was part of the town's folklore by now: In every

generation, one member of the Cabot family went violently and irreversibly insane. Mateo's mother had been the last. Like all the others, she had become convinced that she could see the future through increasingly disturbing dreams. Like too many of his ancestors, she had chosen to end her own life.

Mateo's dreams had begun this summer. Ever since then, he'd been spiraling further and further from "normal"—whatever the hell that was in this town. Everybody at school had always treated him strangely, like they were just waiting for him to lose it one day.

So, doing crazy stuff like waking up all around town, disheveled and ranting about whatever he'd just seen? Really not helping.

Mateo paused, remembering his terrible dream of the girl he loved in the belly of hell. His mind remained full of that nightmarish vision of her, weeping in grief and fear.

By now he knew that the dreams sent to him by his curse really did come true.

Another beautifully screwed-up morning in Captive's Sound.

Verlaine was up early, determined to swing by the *Guardian*'s office before she went into school. Usually people around here were all too eager to ignore the weirdness around them, but after what had been going on the last few weeks—complete with mystery illnesses and a brief quarantine by the Centers for Disease Control—surely everyone was going to come to their senses.

Coming to their senses might mean actually paying attention to the town newspaper, which was why Verlaine, world's-most-glorious-and-yet-unsung intern, was headed there now.

Okay, I might not have Steadfast powers, but even I can tell this town is at dangerously high levels of Not Okay. She brushed a stray lock of her brilliant silver hair out of her eyes as she stood in the town square. The town hall still had a couple of windows boarded up from the near-riot a few weeks ago, when Mrs. Prasad had briefly, and unfortunately, been given the power to see demons and gone after everyone around her with an ax. A few quarantine signs still hung on local businesses; the quarantine had been lifted, but people who were recovering from Elizabeth's witchcraft—*excuse me*, she thought, *the phrase for the newspaper is "mystery illness"*—hadn't necessarily gone back to work or school. Not everyone bounced back as quickly as her uncle Gary had.

The other sign of disquiet Verlaine saw was subtler; it was more something she didn't see. Normally, when she stopped in at the newspaper before school, she crossed paths with a few dozen other people: Mateo's father, Mr. Perez, on his way to get La Catrina ready to open; bank employees in their business clothes; various other people who had reason to be at work crazy early. Today, there was almost no one. The coffee shop was open, but instead of waiting in the usual long line, Verlaine was able to walk straight up to the counter.

Now, as she sipped her latte from a Hello Kitty insulated cup, she stared at a nearly deserted town square. It was almost eerie, how empty the place felt. If they were out West, she figured a tumbleweed would blow through.

It was like people could sense what was coming.

Which they couldn't. The populace of Captive's Sound would have had to be both a whole lot more knowledgeable, and possibly psychic, to guess that their town was about to become ground zero for the impending apocalypse.

She fished her keys from her backpack; they jangled against the door as she let herself into the *Guardian* office. This was basically one medium-sized room, which smelled of old books, atop a basement filled with file-cabinet archives. The printing technology was so out-of-date that she'd once found some iron letters in a drawer, left over from a type-setter they'd gotten rid of only a few years ago. Nobody else was around, which was hardly unusual. The owners saw the newspaper as an excuse to print classified ads and super-market circulars, with the actual news serving mostly as a garnish, kind of like the parsley on a restaurant platter. If the town was going to get any actual information, that was pretty much up to Verlaine.

She walked to the desk, shuffling through the few papers she found there, wondering idly whether her bosses had left a note for her, one with actual instructions. (Email and tex-ting were much too modern for them.) As she did, though, she heard the quiet scrape of the door opening behind her. A soft heat warmed her back, her legs, like a tropical sun had suddenly risen over a Rhode Island December—except the heat came straight from hell.

Verlaine smiled.

"You know," she said, without turning around, "if I'd realized I was going to be stalked by a demon today, I'd have put on something fancy."

"At least you wore shoes you can run in."

"Always do. Around here, it pays off more often than you'd think." Verlaine finally looked over her shoulder to see Asa.

He didn't look like a demon, at least not the kind that showed up in horror movies or Renaissance paintings. Instead he looked like another kind of Renaissance painting, the ones that always had titles like *A Youth* and showed impossibly gorgeous young men with dark curls and meltingly beautiful brown eyes. To be specific, he looked like the late Jeremy Prasad, who had been a grade-A dickweed in Verlaine's class at school until Elizabeth had killed him and given his body to her own personal demon servant. Asa was meant to help Elizabeth every step of the way as she brought the One Beneath into the mortal realm, bringing about the end of the world as they knew it.

Which made Asa a slightly inconvenient guy to fall for. But Verlaine had fallen anyway.

Asa strolled in, his black jacket outlining his tall, wiry form. "Today's Converse are an unusual yet delightful shade of blue."

"Tiffany blue," she said, lifting one foot and twirling her

ankle around to show off. "They were a limited edition a couple years back."

"Sounds expensive."

"Not necessarily. They don't have eBay in hell, do they?"

"No. Another of the many luxuries the place lacks."

Verlaine turned to face Asa. She tried to pretend she wasn't completely overcome by him, but who was she kidding? Inside she felt like she was melting, and probably she looked like it, too.

Asa was the first guy she'd ever cared about, the first one who had ever cared back. Nobody else ever had, or ever could. Years ago, when she was only a baby, Verlaine had been robbed by Elizabeth. In order to protect herself from being discovered as the supernatural evil she was, the Sorceress had stolen not only Verlaine's parents (who'd died in their bed), but also something far more ethereal than that.

Elizabeth had stolen Verlaine's ability to be loved.

Verlaine wasn't the only one Elizabeth had stolen from; over the centuries, she had stolen dozens of people's lovability, leaving them terribly, permanently alone. Meanwhile, Elizabeth cloaked herself in all that love—which made everyone in Captive's Sound ignore her odd appearance, forget her bizarre behavior, and adore her no matter what.

Meanwhile, Verlaine had nothing, and almost no one. Nobody besides her dads, Uncle Dave and Uncle Gary, truly loved her. Even they would have been unable to if they hadn't already known and loved her before Elizabeth's theft. Her whole life, Verlaine had been either viciously bullied or completely ignored. Nadia and Mateo were her only two friends, because they'd been given glimpses through the dark magic done to her; however, they had to constantly remind themselves to think about Verlaine and take care of her. Nobody could overcome that kind of magic completely . . .

. . . except for a demon.

Asa saw her. And it was obvious, from the slow smile on his face as he took a step forward, that he liked what he saw.

"As for the rest of this look"—he cocked his head—"I'm guessing you're going for a late '50s feel, sort of a sexy secretary vibe, am I right?"

Verlaine nearly always wore vintage, or at least vintage-inspired clothing. Today she had on a dark blue pencil skirt, white shirt, and belted periwinkle cardigan that she had one hundred percent intended to create a late '50s feel. But she ducked her head. "I'm not a secretary. I'm an intern."

"A sexy intern vibe, then. Whatever it is, I approve."

"Didn't do it for your approval." If she waited for people to like what she did, Verlaine knew she'd be waiting forever. And as good as it felt to see Asa, as eager as she was to repeat their one perfect kiss, it was time to stop flirting and deal with the facts. "You shouldn't be here."

"I know," Asa said quietly. "But we'll see each other in school later today, and I thought—I thought maybe we should get it over with."

"What, you thought it would be easier like this?" Verlaine tried to smile, but it felt crooked and fake. "It's not going to be easy no matter what."

"No. It's not."

They stood there for a few long moments, knowing they should come no closer, but unable to turn away.

Asa was a demon. That meant he wasn't a willing servant of the One Beneath; instead, he was enslaved to Him, and by extension, to Elizabeth. Verlaine had realized that Asa usually didn't like obeying the evil orders he was given, but he had no choice in the matter. In the struggle ahead, when Verlaine fought alongside Nadia and Mateo to try to stop the end of the world, Asa would have to fight alongside Elizabeth to bring about the apocalypse.

They would battle each other, and only one side would survive.

"Have you learned yet?" Asa said.

Verlaine toyed with her one loose strand of silver hair. "Learned what?" she said, although she already knew.

His voice was hard as he answered. "How to kill a demon."

"Of course not. It's not like you can look that up on Wikipedia, you know." Verlaine stared down at the loop of hair around her finger, unable to meet Asa's eyes. "And you can't tell me."

"If I tell you how to kill me, I'm telling you how to destroy one of the weapons of the One Beneath. Which would be an act of disloyalty to my master. Which would lead to permanent exile to . . . a hell within hell, a place so dark I can't even describe it to you."

Asa had been to that place once before, for only a few days—but days that had felt like centuries. It had been his punishment for helping Verlaine escape harm. He'd endured that for her.

Leaning against the doorframe, doing a good job of acting casual again, Asa added, "I mean, I'm fine with you killing me so that I go to hell. I've been in hell for a few centuries now, and I know I have to return to it. But I'd rather not piss off the devil right before I meet him again."

"I'm trying to learn how. I'm looking." What a crappy thing to have to promise—that you'd kill the guy you were crazy about. Even worse was being that guy, knowing that no matter what, there was no way out for you.

"Keep looking," Asa said, and vanished.

He didn't go *POOF* or turn into a ball of smoke or anything like that; he'd explained that he could simply move much faster than the human eye, which gave him the ability to seemingly disappear in the blink of an eye. Verlaine walked to the place where he'd stood; the heat of him still emanated gently, like a warm shadow he'd left behind.

Then, just in case he was still near enough to listen, she called out, "Next time, shut the door!"

The crow circled in the sky over Captive's Sound, higher than birds were meant to fly. The air was thin under its wings, light in its lungs, and yet it kept on, unknowing. Its eyes were grayed over, as though covered by cobwebs.

From her place below, where she sat by her woodstove, Elizabeth saw what the crow could not. Shimmering around her was the vision of everything surrounding the bird . . .

by now, the clouds. They were heavy and fat, deeply cold, waiting to shed snow.

There would be no snow in Captive's Sound today, and probably never again.

She folded her right hand around her left; on her left middle finger was her ring of jade. Touching it, grounding her spell, Elizabeth summoned the ingredients:

Going without food when there is plenty.
Staying awake when it is time to sleep.
Withholding love though it burns within.

Then she brought up the specific memories that would fulfill those ingredients, remembering each so fully that it was like living them again.

"You won't have any? Are you sure?" Her mother, holding out a cup of a stew that smelled so delicious that hunger seemed to claw within Elizabeth's empty belly. But the child Elizabeth shook her head, thinking that if she just kept refusing to eat, they'd realize coming to the New World had been a terrible idea and get on the next ship back to England.

Knowing it was midnight, knowing she would have to rise with the dawn to help care for her nieces and nephews, but sitting up by the fire anyway, because only then would she have the privacy for her first tentative efforts at black magic.

"Come and give us a kiss, then." Aunt Ruth smiling at her on Elizabeth's wedding day—a marriage she hadn't wanted, to a man she despised, just because her family couldn't afford to support her

any longer. Elizabeth normally hid her true feelings, but that day she'd turned her head sharply away from her aunt, pretending not to see the hurt in her eyes.

It was done. The clouds around the crow subtly changed. They went still in a way that defied the winds, almost as though they were painted instead of real.

When the time came for them to burst forth, it would be with a deluge that would serve Elizabeth's bidding, and mark the beginning of the end.

2

ISAAC P. RODMAN HIGH SCHOOL HAD HAD ITS SHARE OF problems since the school year began. A group of juniors had been caught cheating in AP Calculus. Someone had vandalized Mr. Crane's van. The football team was finishing their season with two wins, eleven losses. A chemical reaction gone wrong in Mrs. Purdhy's classroom had caused a number of students to lose their inhibitions, creating a scene that led to chaos, a follow-up session by school counselor Faye Walsh, several parent-teacher meetings, and, on a brighter note, the formation of Rodman's first LGBTQ Student Alliance group. Mrs. Purdhy, former homecoming queen Riley Bender, a student's father, and any number of students had all collapsed from the mysterious illness that had swept through town in November, two of them on school grounds. This same illness had led to class cancellations and an extremely high absentee rate. Then, just before Thanksgiving, a minor earthquake had caused further academic disruption and damaged most of the AV equipment. And the school had been turned down as host of the regional show choir championships yet again.

Had any single teacher or student been asked their opinion, they would have said it might be better for Rodman to start over fresh in January. But time, tide, and AP exams would wait for no man.

They had to make up for a lot of lost ground. So, for the remaining three weeks before Christmas, class was back in session.

Nadia shouldered her backpack as she walked inside Rodman High. Maybe it was stupid to feel more nervous about coming back to school than she did about facing down Elizabeth, but she did.

She couldn't let herself freak about Elizabeth. So she ended up channeling all her fear into high school. Nadia hadn't seen Mateo since the horrible day everything fell apart—or Verlaine, or Faye—and she wasn't exactly sure how to handle that. Act casual? *Hi, how have you been since I was ensnared by the forces of evil?*

As soon as she reached her locker, she saw Verlaine standing nearby, waiting. To her surprise, Verlaine smiled. "Hey. I was wondering if you'd show."

"Kinda have to. Dad doesn't know about—" Nadia's voice trailed off as she thought of the many secrets her father didn't and couldn't know, because the First Laws forbade even telling him that magic existed in the first place.

"—about your extracurricular activities," Verlaine finished for her. "So, you get to return to the unparalleled joy that is Rodman High just in time for the nonstop adrenaline rush of exams."

Nadia smiled crookedly. "Thanks."

"For what?"

"Acting like everything's normal."

Verlaine shrugged. "Hate to break it to you, but dark sorcery ruining our lives right and left? That pretty much is the new normal."

"I wish you didn't have a point."

At least her best friend was still with her. Nadia hadn't been sure of that when they parted, but Verlaine had simply needed a couple of days to get her head together. *She's stronger than I realized*, Nadia told herself. *Verlaine doesn't let this weirdness affect her. She'd never let herself get carried away with any of this.*

Yet it was hard for Nadia to truly believe it. Darkness separated people from the world; already, she could feel it. Sooner or later Verlaine would feel it, too.

And then . . .

She didn't see Mateo come in. Didn't hear his voice among the dozens around her in the hallway. Instead she felt his presence, like electricity racing along her skin.

It was as though she knew he would embrace her from behind even before she felt his touch. When he did, Nadia leaned against him, relishing the strength of his arms and the feeling of his strong chest against her back. The only times she felt safe now were the moments she was with Mateo.

"Hey," he murmured, before kissing her on the cheek. "Missed you."

"Missed you, too," Nadia said, turning her head sideways toward his. They couldn't be around each other as much now; as her Steadfast, Mateo multiplied her magical power tenfold just by being near. This had been wonderful when he was supercharging her good spells. Now that he had the potential to do the same for the destructive spells she had to cast with Elizabeth? Not so wonderful. Nadia was still figuring out exactly what that meant for both of them.

It couldn't mean being apart from him always, forever. That was impossible; it had to be.

Verlaine cleared her throat. "Three o'clock."

"Huh?" Nadia straightened up slightly; Mateo, finally realizing Verlaine was there, flipped her a quick wave.

"Three o'clock," Verlaine repeated in a stage whisper, then stood up straighter as someone else walked directly toward them.

"Gage!" Mateo let go of Nadia to step slightly in front of her, placing his body between her and Gage.

Which was totally unfair in some ways, because Gage Calloway was friendly, funny, and about ninety-five percent less neurotic than the rest of the populace of Captive's Sound. (Though, Nadia figured, growing up in a town completely inundated with black magic was pretty good reason for neurosis.) Even now he was grinning, his backpack slung over one shoulder as he walked up to say hi.

But they knew something about Gage he didn't know about himself. Gage was in thrall to Elizabeth Pike.

According to Mateo, Gage had always had a crush on Elizabeth; obviously they'd never told him the truth about who and what Elizabeth really was. Nadia had never dreamed Elizabeth would misuse Gage's feelings by seducing him and putting him in her thrall—which meant that, at any moment, Gage might stop being himself and start doing absolutely anything Elizabeth told him to do, no matter how evil. Afterward he wouldn't even remember it.

Just like he didn't remember trying to kill Mateo last week.

"Hey, guys, what's up?" He slugged Mateo on the shoulder—not hard, just as a joke, but Nadia winced. Gage didn't see it. "You feeling better?"

"Yeah, totally," Mateo said. "Just, uh, had to get back on the meds."

"Good, glad to hear it. And hey, Verlaine, your dad was one of the people who got sick, right? How's he doing?"

Verlaine lit up merely from being remembered by Gage—by anyone. "Uncle Gary's great. He still has to eat really boring food, like toast and chicken broth, but aside from bitching about that, he's never been better."

"Awesome." Gage nodded, then seemed to realize how awkward the mood was. "Huh. So. Mateo, catch up with you in American History?"

"Definitely." Mateo watched his friend go before turning

back to Nadia. "How can we let him go on like that? Isn't there anything we can do?"

"Maybe. I don't know yet. I might be able to find out from Elizabeth." The more Nadia thought about the idea, the more encouraged she felt. It would seem as though she were asking Elizabeth about dark magic—like she was starting to come over to Elizabeth's side, really falling under the sway of the One Beneath. Elizabeth wouldn't think to suspect Nadia of worrying about Gage; she never thought anybody really cared about anyone. "Tonight. I'll ask her tonight."

Mateo's face fell. He must have wanted them to get together tonight.

Nadia took his hand. "Maybe after I come by La Catrina?"

He smiled—but Verlaine interjected, "Hate to be the . . . word that rhymes with 'rockblocker' here, but I actually really need to talk to you later on, Nadia. Think we could fit it in right after school?"

"Sure. Of course." Nadia mostly felt irritated; she'd already promised to play with Cole that afternoon, which felt like enough on top of what she already had to deal with. But that's just the black magic around Verlaine, she reminded herself. Trying to make you push her away. Don't let it win.

"So, I'm going to head on to Novels class, where the hot demon sits in the next desk over." Verlaine tucked a long lock of her hair behind her ear. "Let me know if you need anything, okay?"

"Okay." Then Verlaine's words sank in—a couple of

seconds late, as they often did. Nadia frowned. "Wait. Did you say 'hot demon'?"

Verlaine's eyes widened. "Um, I meant literally. Literally hot. Asa actually heats stuff around him, remember?"

"Oh yeah. Right," Nadia said. Mateo shook his head and smiled as Verlaine hurried away. More quietly, he said to Nadia, "Even Verlaine wouldn't do anything as weird as date a demon."

Nadia nodded, but there was something in the way Verlaine had become so flustered. And Asa did try to manipulate them all by promising what they wanted most.

She knew what Verlaine wanted most in the world was for someone to truly love her. Anyone.

Even a demon.

Verlaine knew Nadia really, truly did not want to hang out after school. By now she was good at picking up on the signs that people didn't want to be near her.

Well, too bad, Verlaine thought. The conversation she and Nadia had to have this evening was too important to postpone.

Still, the battle against the forces of evil wasn't the only thing on her mind. When her lunch hour rolled around, instead of going to the cafeteria, Verlaine smuggled her sandwich out to the parking lot and slid into her car. The enormous old land yacht had a great heater, which would have her feeling toasty in no time.

Besides, she had some temptation to fight. And probably lose.

Verlaine knew she wasn't supposed to open the college recommendation letters from her teachers. But when they left the envelopes so invitingly unsealed—when the paper was right there winking up at you, letters almost visible—how could anyone resist?

With a grin, Verlaine slipped the notes from their envelopes.

And read.

And wanted to cry.

Instant karma, she thought. *This is what you get for breaking the rules. A slap in the face.*

But maybe it was better she'd done it. Because these letters? Were not good.

Oh, they weren't bad. Nobody came out and said *Verlaine Laughton is a serial killer in the making, also possibly a cough syrup wino*, or anything similarly awful. She almost wished they had. At least being terrible was interesting, and hey, maybe Ivy League schools had a sociopath quota they had to fill. These letters were worse than bad. They were boring.

Verlaine Laughton participates in class discussion. Ms. Laughton satisfactorily completes all course assignments. School records indicate perfect attendance before a brief illness in October. And so on.

"Perfect attendance?" she muttered as she sat in her front seat, envelopes scattered across her lap, top half of her body freezing, bottom half seared by the volcanic heat spewing from the land yacht's vents. "The nicest thing you can say about me is that I don't skip?"

The thing was, Verlaine knocked herself out at school. She did more work on the school news site, the *Lightning*

Rod, than the rest of the staff put together—including her journalism teacher. Every single extra credit assignment in every class. Volunteer activities, extracurriculars at the *Guardian* and a hiking club, AP History and Calc, even one dismal semester as hall monitor—Verlaine had done all these things hoping that at least her teachers might see she had something to offer.

They hadn't.

By now she knew the reason for this was black magic. It was amazing how little knowing that helped.

I can't get into Yale with recommendations like these. I'll be lucky to get into URI with these. Verlaine had always hoped to go farther away for school, farther than that for grad school, as far away from Captive's Sound as she could possibly get. But Elizabeth's evil had even stolen that.

With a groan, she leaned her head against the steering wheel, her gray hair falling around her like a curtain that shielded her from the world.

Look on the bright side, she told herself. Chances are the world's ending soon. So it's not like you'd be going to college in the first place.

Nope. That didn't help either.

"Tell me how to kill a demon."

Nadia shot Verlaine a look, then nodded her head toward the living room of her home, where Cole sat in front of the television. Luckily he seemed enraptured by *The Penguins of Madagascar*, so she just whispered, "Keep it down, all right?"

"Oh, come on, he'd only think we were talking about a video game or something." Verlaine was a lot more impatient than usual—not to mention more homicidal. Her hands were in fists at her sides. Nadia was just glad Verlaine wasn't mad at her. "I have to know how to take Asa out. You can't do it anymore, right? If you killed a servant of the One Beneath, it would backfire on you somehow?"

"I think so," Nadia said, though she wasn't entirely certain. "But Asa's hardly our top priority. Elizabeth's the real problem. Why are you so hot to take him down all of a sudden? Has he done something to you?"

Verlaine took a couple of steps backward, hugging her arms around her as she leaned against the kitchen wall. "No. But—we're kind of headed into the home stretch here, right? If I might have to do this, I need to know how."

There was more to this than Verlaine was saying. Always, before, she'd stuck up for Asa, defending him so fiercely that even Nadia had doubted her own contempt for him. Demons were evil, but enslaved; Asa had no choice but to do the One Beneath's bidding. When he wasn't trying to screw with their heads, he could be almost . . . interesting.

Still, Verlaine was right. Soon they might all be called upon to exceed their own limits, or to act in desperation. Even to kill. Verlaine was the most powerless of them all; she lacked Nadia's witchcraft or Mateo's ability to glimpse the future. She deserved whatever chance Nadia could give her.

At least this proved Verlaine wasn't crushing on Asa. Nadia

was relieved; she should have known Verlaine wouldn't get that mixed up.

Nadia leaned out of the kitchen and called to Cole. "Hey, buddy, Verlaine and I are going to hang out in the attic for a while. Is it okay if we play with your cars a little later?"

"Right after *Madagascar!*" Cole said, his eyes never leaving the screen.

"You bet," she said. He probably had two or three episodes on the DVR. That would give them plenty of time to search through Goodwife Hale's Book of Shadows.

Goodwife Hale had been a powerful witch who'd lived around the same time Elizabeth had been young; Nadia and Mateo had rescued her centuries-old spell book from the place she'd hidden it, deep under the water of the sound. The magic it held had protected it from the damp, made it glow in ways only Mateo's Steadfast power revealed. That was what happened with Books of Shadows that belonged to powerful witches—they gained their own magic, even something close to sentience.

Like Elizabeth's terrible book, which once had tried to kill Nadia . . .

She shook off her chill as the wooden ladder to the attic rattled down. Together they climbed upward into the space Nadia had claimed as her own. The large Victorian house the Caldani family had moved into a few months ago was as rickety as it was romantic, but Nadia loved it. How else could she have ended up with such a great space for her magic? A few oversize pillows and a small jar of chocolates made the space comfortable—and hopefully made her dad think it was nothing but a place to hang out, on the few occasions when he stuck his head up here.

He never hung around long enough to pull back the cloth draped over her jars of spellcasting materials. Never realized prisms were hung in the windows and the ceiling painted blue for a reason. Never pushed aside Nadia's paperbacks to reveal the Books of Shadows hidden beneath.

As Verlaine sat cross-legged next to her, Nadia took up her own Book of Shadows first and pressed her hand against the cover—her way of saying hello. It was important to acknowledge your Book of Shadows, to connect with it. Only then did she pick up Goodwife Hale's spell book —

"Ow!" Nadia pulled her hand back as the book tumbled onto the floor. Her fingertips stung, as though she'd been shocked. That couldn't be right. The only electrical sockets up here were several feet away. "Is there—broken glass on the floor?" Although Nadia didn't remember breaking anything, maybe Cole had sneaked up here.

"No. Nothing." Verlaine picked up the spell book and turned it over. "Did a spider bite you or something?"

"I hope not." With a shudder, Nadia remembered the thousands of spiders living in Elizabeth's home. "Here, I'll—ow!"

The Book of Shadows shocked her again, worse this time, and Nadia jerked back. When the truth sank in, she felt it cold and heavy in her gut.

Verlaine looked down from Nadia's face toward the spell

book, then up again. "What's going on?"

"The Book of Shadows has rejected me. It knows I'm working with Elizabeth."

"It's a book. How can it know that? No, wait, how can it know anything?"

"It knows," Nadia repeated.

The spell book knows I'm bound to evil.

"Wow. Awkward. Whole new area of awkward." Verlaine bit her lower lip. "Are you still going to be able to use it?"

Nadia took a deep breath. She had to be smarter than a mere book, however supernatural it might be; she had to remember her goal, to get to a day when she could break her bonds to Elizabeth and the One Beneath, permanently. "I can still use it, but only through you."

"Through me?"

Maybe Mateo could have used it, too, but Nadia still wasn't sure what effect a male Steadfast might have. So she simply nodded. "You take it. Read your way through. You might not understand all of it, but all you have to do is look for any reference to demons."

Verlaine peered at the hefty, overstuffed tome in her lap. "I guess an index is too much to hope for."

"No index." Nadia had already combed through the book backward and forward, taking what notes she could and learning her way around. Working with a handwritten spell book that old was like memorizing paths through a forest without using a map. "I know there's nothing in there directly about killing demons, because I looked as soon as Asa showed up. But there are probably hints we can put together. Just write it all down, and come back to me."

"You mean you want me to take the Book of Shadows home?"

"Not like I can do anything with it here. Actually, take them both." Nadia pointed toward the other borrowed spell book she had, the one that once belonged to Faye Walsh's mother. She hadn't found time to explore that one yet. "I doubt either of the books wants to have much to do with me. Just be careful with them."

"No using the ancient, priceless spell books for coffee coasters. Check." Verlaine grinned at her, and Nadia managed to smile back.

But as the evening went on, and she played cars with Cole, and stir-fried veggies for dinner, Nadia could only remember the terrible sting against her hand as the book had rejected her. The physical pain had been slight, almost meaningless. What hurt worse was the knowledge of how much she was changing. Her own Book of Shadows still responded to her, because it reflected Nadia herself; as she became darker, so did her spell book. Magic had changed for her, probably forever.

Not dark magic, though. It still loves me.

Nadia decided not to think any further about magic, dark or otherwise, until the time came for her to obey Elizabeth's summons later that night. Already she could feel the pull—the strange, unearthly undertow that was Elizabeth's way of calling Nadia to her side. She would have to go soon.

She texted Mateo that she couldn't come to La Catrina—even though she desperately wanted to see him. But if she saw him, she would have to tell him what had happened, and right now she didn't think she could stand to speak the words.

Instead Nadia sat through a family dinner, nodding when her dad spoke and laughing at her little brother's silly jokes, keeping everything she really felt on the inside. No matter what she heard or said, the voice in her head just kept repeating, *You can never be what you were before.*

Never again.

"Mom? Dad? I'm going out!" Asa called.

The Prasads were not his parents. They had been the parents of a boy named Jeremy, who had been arrogant, sexist, spoiled, and cruel. Asa knew this had not given Elizabeth the right to murder him and then hand his body over for Asa's use. But the guy had been so nasty that Asa didn't feel too bad about it.

He made a good Jeremy, in his opinion. Better than the original. Already Asa had pulled up Jeremy's GPA, despite having to balance homework with his service to the One Beneath. (Teachers were unlikely to accept excuses signed by the lord of hell.) Although Jeremy's old friends had mostly dismissed him as "no fun anymore," virtually everyone else Asa interacted with seemed happily surprised by his transformation from a raging asshole to . . . well, okay, to a demon dedicated to the destruction of the world they knew, but a *polite* one.

As Asa slipped into his black jacket, Mrs. Prasad appeared in the mudroom, affectionately petting his shoulder. "You'll be in by curfew?"

Jeremy's curfew was absurdly late—and yet Asa had the impression it had been observed more in the breach. "Sure. Of course."

She beamed. "While you're out, I might make some snickerdoodles. You used to love those when you were little!"

Apparently Mrs. Prasad felt nothing but love for him—and it was at moments like this when the guilt threatened to creep in. Thinking of this new family and the way Mrs. Prasad adored her son reminded him of the sister he had lost so long ago that he could hardly remember her face. . . .

"Cookies would be great," Asa said. He forced himself to smile back. "Thanks."

It was a relief to finally be out on the streets, walking through Captive's Sound. Although the trees were almost entirely bare of leaves now, their naked branches clawing at the cloudy sky, there had been no snow since Thanksgiving. Asa was one of the very few people who knew that had happened for a reason.

Soon they would all know, he thought. Not even the most skeptical human in Captive's Sound could fail to recognize what was about to come.

When he reached Elizabeth's house, she already had the spell prepared, which was just as well. Asa didn't like seeing her kill things. Not that he liked looking at crow entrails either, but better the aftermath than the event. He only hoped she'd been quick about it. As he stepped over the bird guts on the floor, he said, "Love what you've done with the place."

Elizabeth ignored this. She was immune to humor, he thought, like virtually every other human emotion. "Nadia should be with you."

"Was I supposed to pick her up? Nobody told me about the car pool."

"The summons should be as clear to her as it is to you, but she has not answered." Instead of being ticked off, though, Elizabeth seemed oddly . . . satisfied. *Now what's that about?* Asa wondered.

Then he heard Nadia's footsteps outside, and she hurried into Elizabeth's house, cheeks flushed, as though she'd run here. She lifted her chin as though in defiance, but stopped when she saw what was left of the crow.

Elizabeth's eyes narrowed. "You ignored my call?"

"Of course not. I'm here," Nadia said. "But what—what are we doing with that?"

"Death provides the ingredients for some of the work we do. You should know that by now." Elizabeth sat on the floor, in what seemed to be the only area free of broken glass and dust. With his boot Asa kicked away a clear spot for himself; as Nadia made her own place, Elizabeth continued, "These sorts of spells are delicate. More complicated than you might think."

Nadia hesitated. She was flustered, Asa noticed. For a girl her age, Nadia was uncommonly self-possessed. But there was something about her this evening—fear, loneliness, and

34

longing, too: Demons could almost smell that kind of need.

Which made him think of Verlaine glancing over her shoulder at him, and of the one and only time they'd kissed . . .

His train of thought was broken as Nadia took her place in the circle. "What kinds of spells? Dark magic?"

"No. By now you must have realized much dark magic is simple. Elegant." Elizabeth smiled. "Spells to influence the weather are not inherently dark, and they can be far more complex."

"The weather? This is all about the weather?" Nadia looked as though she wanted to laugh. Had she understood the work ahead, Asa thought, she would not have been so amused.

Serenely, Elizabeth looked up at the ceiling—exposed boards and rotting plaster, laced with countless cobwebs— and held out her hands. Asa took one of them; Nadia the other. When he and Nadia joined their fingers in turn, they exchanged a swift glance. She looked bewildered; he tried to look sympathetic.

"We are going to command the winds," Elizabeth whispered. "We are going to still the sea. And then, we will summon the rain."

3

THE RAIN CAME DOWN, AND DOWN, AND DOWN.

Endless sheets of it, sweeping like silvery curtains along the street. Nadia hugged herself as she stood with Asa and Elizabeth on Elizabeth's porch, watching the gutters turn into small rivers, and the puddles in every yard welling wider.

"You could at least have told us to bring raincoats," Asa said.

Nadia stifled her smile, but Elizabeth was, of course, unmoved. "If you can't endure getting wet, the days to come are going to be beyond you." She glanced sideways at Asa, her eyes cold and flat. "But we already knew that."

Asa turned away, casually, as though he hadn't heard. But Nadia saw the tension in his shoulders, remembered how his expression had always darkened whenever they reminded him that he was "on Elizabeth's leash."

I think he hates this as much as I do.

"You can leave," Elizabeth said to Asa, then turned away from him as though he were already gone. "Come, Nadia. You and I have more to do."

Nadia followed Elizabeth back inside the house, casting one glance behind her to see Asa's reaction—but he was already gone. Probably he'd clapped his hands together and stopped time in the eerie way he had, then strolled home while dodging the raindrops hanging around him in midair.

As they walked back into Elizabeth's main room, Nadia said, "The days to come—what will they be like?"

Elizabeth turned back toward her with a smile on her face that looked almost genuine. "After the One Beneath walks into this world? Glorious. The bridge between the demonic realm and the mortal realm will allow the demonic realm to triumph."

"Will they become the same? Like, just one place?" Nadia couldn't wrap her head around the idea of the whole world becoming hell.

"Not exactly. Humans will still live here. They will have the same feelings, the same wishes. But they will inhabit a transformed world. One that answers to no natural law, one where they will forever know the One Beneath in all His power and caprice. As He wills it, so shall they suffer, and from their suffering He will grow even stronger. His reign will be eternal."

The image in Nadia's mind showed a world devastated and terrifying, but still itself. Like *The Walking Dead* except worse. As terrible as that seemed, she almost felt relieved. No matter how dangerous this world became, no matter how much pain people endured here, it had to be better than hell.

"About time you started asking questions," Elizabeth said. "Is there anything else you would like to learn tonight?"

She thought of Asa, making jokes before he walked out into the rain. He looked like any other guy. Spoke like one. It was hard for her to remember that Asa was under Elizabeth's control, that he could become a weapon at any moment. Verlaine was right. They had to protect themselves. "How do you kill a demon?"

Elizabeth halted midstep. She turned, looking over her shoulder at Nadia; the orange glow from her stove painted the lines and shadows of her face sharply, and strangely. "Why do you need to know?"

"I don't." Nadia shrugged. "I want to know."

"Do you hate him?" Elizabeth said, a hint of a smile playing on her lips. It was the way any other girl would say, *Do you like him?*

The lie came easily: "He's supposed to serve you, right? To serve us. Sometimes I think he forgets that. I ought to know how to deal with him if he gets . . . ahead of himself."

Elizabeth took her usual seat on the floor, amid all the broken glass that glittered in the dim orange light. "It involves the use of his real name, which can be powerful in certain contexts. Demons' names are important. Also you'll need the blood of the sea, and a dagger consecrated to white magic." The confusion on Nadia's face must have been obvious, because Elizabeth smiled. "So many things you have yet to learn. But you can learn the details later, when we get into darker magic. We cannot worry about mere nuisances when there is serious work to be done. For now, Asa is a necessary tool."

She nodded, like that was okay with her. Inside, though, Nadia could only think, *Darker magic?* Darker than working toward the end of the world? So she made her next question direct. "What's the next step for the One Beneath?"

"For us as His servants, you mean." Elizabeth's eyes narrowed, and Nadia realized she should push no further tonight. "Next we draw Him forward. Each spell we cast toward His power will bring Him closer to the surface. Others will attempt to undo our work here tonight. We must prevent them from doing so."

"Undo our work? You mean, they'll try to work against our spell? Other witches?" Weren't all the other witches in Captive's Sound defeated by now, or too terrified of Elizabeth to act? Nadia had always thought she had to stand against Elizabeth alone.

Elizabeth shook her head. "I mean the works of man. They can be stopped. What we have to cast is a spell for falling apart."

"Falling apart? I never heard of a spell like that."

"Of course you haven't. The spell is of my own creation."

Nadia went very still. Creating your own spells was the highest form of witchcraft—something she had never attempted, something her mother had never mastered. It was a gift not one witch in a thousand could claim. Why wasn't she surprised that Elizabeth was the one? "What does the spell do?"

"On its own? Very little. But it enhances the magic we've already done. Intensifies its impact."

Could she stop Elizabeth from casting this spell? Not without giving herself away, Nadia figured. Anyway, this was only adding onto the spells they'd already cast, which so far only affected the weather. Besides—she couldn't help feeling curious. What would an original spell feel like? How much power had Elizabeth unlocked?

"Grounded by agate." Elizabeth wore an agate ring, a milky-lilac circle around her left little finger. Nadia's agate charm dangled from her bracelet, and she clasped it quickly as Elizabeth began to recite the ingredients: "Three things are needed. A woman weeping for something lost forever. A time when you were cruelly betrayed. And a time when you cruelly betrayed another."

The memories drawn upon for dark magic were never pleasant ones. Nadia closed her eyes, felt the ripple of magic around her as Elizabeth began, and summoned up her own version of the spell to combine with Elizabeth's.

Verlaine crying in the front seat of her car as she talked about the magic worked on her, the magic that had stolen her ability to be loved by anyone.

Her mother saying, "It's better this way," before walking out the door to leave their family forever.

Standing on the small island with Elizabeth, swearing her allegiance to the One Beneath, while Mateo shouted for her to stop.

Nadia jerked her head upright, feeling a shock wave ripple through her—unlike any kind of magic she'd felt before. The sensation was uncomfortable, not painful but queasy and wrong.

"You chose poorly," Elizabeth said with her eyes still shut.

It was true; she had. Nadia had felt betrayed when her mother walked out, but now she knew the truth behind what Mom had done and why; that had actually been Mom's deepest sacrifice for her family. And she'd had no choice but to swear allegiance to Elizabeth, to save the lives of dozens of people.

Elizabeth couldn't know which memories Nadia had chosen—but obviously she had felt the spell's failure. Nadia felt embarrassed despite herself. *You know you're too much of a perfectionist when you're upset that you weren't good enough at being evil.*

Elizabeth's smile was thin, yet satisfied. "You need more experience with betrayal."

Mateo had known something was up when Nadia texted him that she couldn't come by La Catrina. He'd worked his way through his shift, his thoughts so confused that he'd delivered burritos to the table that wanted tamales—and vice versa. Eventually his dad had drawn him aside. Not for a lecture. No, worse: Dad was worried that the "seizures" were affecting his ability to concentrate.

"That's not it. I swear. It's Nadia. She's upset about something, and I don't know what, so I can't stop wondering why." It was a relief to be able to tell his father the truth for once.

Dad folded his arms. "Maybe I should be relieved it's just hormones like any other guy your age. Don't worry; you two will work it out. Talk to your girlfriend later. Now? Concentrate on what you're doing."

Mateo nodded and tried to concentrate on his tables. Still, he didn't feel right.

The second he was free, though, he grabbed his phone—and it buzzed with a text from Nadia just as he picked it up. *Can you come get me? It's raining.*

Mateo hadn't even heard the rain before, not over the mariachi music playing in the front of the restaurant. Sure enough, drops were pattering against the window in the back room. *Of course. Where are you?*

Elizabeth's.

A chill shivered along Mateo's skin, but he punched his arms through the sleeves of his coat and headed out.

Elizabeth's house glowed a sickly, feverish red on the horizon as he sped toward it on his motorcycle. His Steadfast powers showed him the magic within that house, the twining, twisted evil that clung to it like ivy. The heat of it beat at him even through the December cold, so fierce that he almost expected the rain to evaporate before it fell—like it would sizzle into steam.

Mateo had braced himself to walk up the steps or even

inside to get Nadia if he had to. But even as he brought his motorcycle to a stop, she dashed out to him, holding the collar of her coat over her head. From his glove box he fished out his waterproof jacket—the one he would normally wear when riding his cycle in this kind of weather but had saved for her tonight. As Nadia wrestled it on, Mateo saw Elizabeth looking out the door at him, leaning against the jamb with a slight smile on her face.

Last month he'd tried to convince Nadia they should try to kill Elizabeth. She'd talked him out of it at the time. He still thought it wasn't a bad idea.

Nadia spoke not a word. Not as she put on his spare helmet. Not as he sped her to her house. When he stopped, though, they got off the bike together and ran to her porch, their feet sloshing through mud puddles side by side. Only when they sat on the wood steps of her porch—him half-soaked and shivering, her in the bright orange reflective jacket, did he break the silence.

"Why didn't you come by earlier?" he asked.

Nadia shrugged. "I was upset." Her voice barely carried over the pattering of the rain.

"Why? I mean, why particularly. Besides the apocalypse."

"Oh, yeah, besides that." She had to smile then, and Mateo knew it was all right to cover her hand with his. How did she manage to look beautiful even in an orange reflective parka? "I tried to look through Goodwife Hale's Book of Shadows and it—rejected me. Wouldn't let me even hold it."

"How did that happen?"

"It knows I've sworn myself to the One Beneath." Nadia's wide eyes sought his. Her hand beneath his palm was chilly, like someone who'd awakened from a bad dream. "The evil I'm working with—it's becoming a part of me."

No, he wanted to say. *That's not true.* And yet there was a kind of dark fire about her now, a feverish quality to the light in her eyes. Maybe that was what allowed her to glow despite the darkness, to remain warm despite the cold . . .

Quit it, he told himself. *She hasn't changed. Your mind is playing tricks on you, that's all.*

"Stop it right there." Mateo gripped her hand more tightly, rubbing his thumb back and forth along her skin. "You said it yourself. You're working with evil right now, because you don't have any choice, and because it's the only way to stop Elizabeth. You know that as well as I do."

"The Book of Shadows doesn't know that."

"Exactly. Because it's a freakin' book. It's just—just—it's a tool you can use, right? A tool. Nothing more than that. Right now, you're using a different tool. You just can't hold them both at the same time. That's all there is to it."

Nadia stared into the distance for a few seconds, and he studied her profile—the delicate slope of her nose, her stubborn little chin—until she said, "Do you really think so?"

"Absolutely. If working with Elizabeth is the better tool right now, then you're doing the right thing." He lifted her hand to his and kissed it. "You usually do."

She turned back to him, and her smile took away all the cold, all the dark. Mateo leaned in to kiss her. The moment their lips met, his heart seemed to jump inside his chest—which was the moment a small voice crowed, "They're kissing!"

They broke apart to see Cole up against the front window, grinning because he'd caught his big sister in the act. The thump of footsteps inside revealed that Mr. Caldani was coming to snag Cole out of the way—but that, too, kind of killed the mood.

Instead Mateo leaned his forehead against Nadia's and murmured, "The next time you're feeling lost, don't avoid me. Call me."

"And then you'll find me," she whispered. "You always do."

Nearby, from a shadowed place between two trees, Elizabeth watched them. Rainwater trickled down her face, plastered her hair to her scalp and shoulders, and soaked her dress through. She didn't pay attention to the rain, didn't even wipe her face, as she stared at Nadia and Mateo kissing on the porch. Nadia's mouth was open against his; Mateo's hands ran through her thick black hair. *Passion*, Elizabeth thought. For her it was an abstract concept.

Once, long ago, she had been in love, but she hardly remembered it any longer. Had it made her so easily distracted? So vulnerable?

Perhaps it had. No matter.

Nadia needed to commit herself more fully to darkness. Right now she served the One Beneath by obligation; what

He truly wanted was her devotion. Elizabeth intended to give Him precisely that.

The love Nadia and Mateo shared would serve as just one more weapon in her hands.

In a whisper, Elizabeth repeated the words she'd said to Nadia earlier that night: "You need more experience with betrayal."

As the rain pattered comfortingly against her bedroom window, Verlaine sat on the floor, her cat curled next to her, and flipped through Goodwife Hale's Book of Shadows. She'd been trying to outline the thing—even opened a file for it in Scrivener—but had given this up as futile about half an hour before. Now she was just scanning each page, looking for any mention of the word *demon*.

And there were lots.

Lists of demons filled the pages, too many for Verlaine to have any reasonable guess as to which one of these (if any) Asa might be. (At least ten of the names started with the letters *A-S*. Didn't narrow it down lots.) These demons were blamed for any number of weird events: blights on crops (whatever a blight was), sick livestock, sudden turns in the weather, that kind of thing. Verlaine would have written this off as the superstition of ye olden days if she hadn't personally known a demon—though Asa didn't seem interested in blighting anything.

Still, there was no doubting that demons played a role in black magic, and Goodwife Hale had been very, very interested in how to stop them.

"The demon's name has more power in hell than on earth, but even here it can be used against him," Verlaine read in a whisper, leaning forward as she traced the scrawled handwriting. Time had faded the ink to sepia brown, and deeply yellowed the page, but she could make it out. *"Mark him in the Word of God. Mark him in the words of the Craft. And Mark him in that which he himself possesses. Pierce these and the demon will perish, returning to hell forevermore."*

Mark him? Pierce these? The demon's name?

"What is any of that supposed to mean?" she asked her cat. Smuckers blinked up at her, then stuck one leg in the air and began to lick his privates. Verlaine sighed. "Helpful *and* classy. Way to go, Smuckers."

"Honey?" Uncle Dave called. "There's a roll of slice-and-bake cookies in the fridge calling your name."

Verlaine loved cookies as much as the next right-thinking human being, but . . . "I've got homework!" This ought to count as an assignment, right? Analyzing "historical documents"? Maybe she could get extra credit.

"I hear that, but you're a seventeen-year-old girl, so if you bake cookies on a weeknight, you're just being a normal kid. If I bake the cookies, as a supposed adult person, then I'm a pathetic slob with no self-control."

She laughed despite herself. "Okay, hang on, I'm coming." Cookie emergencies couldn't be ignored. It wasn't like she could transcribe the entire Book of Shadows tonight anyway.

But quickly Verlaine flipped open Mrs. Walsh's spell book, because she could have sworn she'd seen something about "the demon's true name" in there when she'd scanned it the first time. *Where is it, where is it . . .*

There.

With his name and with this you will conquer him. The words were written beneath a wickedly edged drawing of an ornate dagger. There was no explanation of what the dagger did, but—come on, it was a dagger. Pretty obvious what that was for.

I couldn't hurt Asa in any case, she thought. The relief that settled over her went deeper than she'd known it would be. *That is definitely a very specific kind of dagger. Not just some knife at your local Walmart. So Asa's safe, because I don't have a dagger like that or any idea how to find one . . .*

Which was when she realized she'd seen a dagger exactly like that. It was the knife Mateo had taken from his grandmother's house, the one with an intricate design set into the hilt.

Just like in this drawing. Exactly like it.

The tool to kill Asa was at hand, and it had been all along.

"The same knife?" Nadia said the next day in gym class, as they waited for their turn on the leg-press machine. "Are you sure?"

Verlaine gave her a look and breathed out sharply, blowing aside a lock of her silver-gray hair that had escaped from its PE bun. "What, based on my expert knowledge of demon-killing magical weapons? I don't have any idea if it's the same one. But—it looked like it to me. Do you still have the knife?"

Nadia nodded. Mateo had promised to return it to his grandmother eventually, but he hadn't yet been able to face returning to her grand house on the Hill, or her unending disapproval. "It's in the attic."

Their eyes met, and then neither of them knew what to say.

"Laughton!" Coach Pang called. "You're up!"

It took Verlaine a moment to follow the coach's instructions. Nadia hugged her arms around herself as she thought about what they were doing. It was one thing to research ways to kill a demon—another to take hold of a real, literal knife and think about murdering Asa.

Verlaine seemed to feel it even more.

And when did the dagger become consecrated to white magic? A long time ago, Nadia suspected—witches hadn't used the term white magic much in the past couple hundred years. Maybe she shouldn't have been so surprised that at least one of Mateo's cursed ancestors had figured out what was happening and at least tried to defeat the supernatural and break the curse.

After Verlaine got done, Nadia took her own turn on the weight machine—hamstrings burning as she pushed through the reps—then joined Verlaine in the line for the bench press. Nadia muttered, "I'm not sure you're just supposed to stab Asa with it."

That won her a raised eyebrow. "I'm supposed to use a

dagger to kill a demon, but not to stab him?"

"I said, not *just* to stab him. You said—let me get this straight—that the Book of Shadows said to mark his name three times and pierce him."

"Um, pierce means stab."

Nadia shook her head. "I think it means to pierce his name first. The book said the name had power, right?"

"How am I supposed to pierce the name?"

Ever since Verlaine had texted her the info late last night, Nadia had been thinking about this, and finally she thought she had it. "Remember, in witchcraft, books are powerful. The written word matters. I think you're supposed to write his name three times, then pierce the three papers with the dagger. Once it's been anointed with whatever the hell Elizabeth was talking about. Then the knife is ready."

Verlaine's eyes widened. "Marking means writing? And on the Word of God—that means in a Bible, right? Or a Torah, or a Koran, or any other religious text, because holy is holy, right?"

"Probably." The gears were turning now, showing Nadia more and more. "The 'words of the Craft' obviously means writing his name in a Book of Shadows. That which he himself possesses—probably that's anything belonging to him here. A notebook, even."

"Not hard to get." Verlaine looked so sad.

"We still don't know what 'the blood of the sea' is—"

"Seawater." When Nadia stared, Verlaine just shrugged. "It's obvious."

"It's too bad you're not from a witching bloodline. You'd have been great at the Craft."

For the first time that day, Verlaine smiled.

Now it was bench press time. Nadia gritted her teeth as she managed to pump the bar upward. Usually she hated gym class, but right now, the distraction was welcome. It felt good to only exist in her body for a few moments, where she couldn't worry about anything but how freakin' heavy this was.

When they moved on toward the free weights, Verlaine muttered, "I can't believe we're supposed to worry about building muscle tone while we're fighting the apocalypse."

"Don't get distracted. If we head to my place after school, do you think you could remember the drawing well enough to tell for sure if the Cabot family dagger is the right one?"

Shifting her weight from one foot to the other, Verlaine didn't quite meet Nadia's eyes. "I don't know. Maybe I should go get that Book of Shadows from my house. It would be okay as long as I'm the only one who touches it. But then, maybe it shouldn't get wet?" The heavy rain hadn't stopped, not once.

Nadia said, "I know you don't want to think about— hurting Asa."

"Killing." Verlaine finally looked straight at her. "Let's skip the euphemisms. We're talking about killing him."

"Excuse me?" Kendall Bender glanced back at them. She was Rodman High's one-girl gossip amplification system; while she wasn't actually all that bad, Nadia thought, there was no such thing as keeping a secret anywhere in her vicinity.

So she improvised quickly. "We're talking about a—role-playing game. Online. Multiplayer."

"With orcs." Verlaine caught on right away. "Tons of orcs. Plus dwarves and elves and fighting unicorns."

Kendall rolled her eyes as she turned from them. "You guys are such geeks."

Although Verlaine grinned, like, *That was close,* Nadia knew they needed to stick to the subject. "You realize there's no reason for you to go after Asa, right? Not yet, anyway." In the final battles to come, there was no telling what any of them might be called to do. "If Asa gets killed, Elizabeth might summon another demon to take his place, and that one might be even worse. So I don't know why you're so fixated on taking Asa out right now."

"I have to be ready. That's all."

That couldn't be all.

Nadia had taken comfort from Verlaine's determination to kill Asa, assuming that meant she wasn't too attached. But what if it was the exact opposite?

They aren't—they can't be—

"Uh, Coach Pang?" Kendall piped up. "Is it, you know, flooding in here?"

People giggled and skittered to the far side of the room as water began pooling in one corner of the weight room. Coach Pang looked more annoyed than anything else. "I told them building in the basement was—never mind. Come on, guys, get some towels. Let's keep this contained if we can."

Before Nadia could say a word, Verlaine hurried for her locker. *Probably to get some pictures of the "news story" for the Lightning Rod*, Nadia thought. Most of her classmates ran for towels. Nadia remained where she was, watching the gray puddle swell on the concrete floor, its curved outlines slowly, inexorably expanding outward.

It was just a puddle, now. But later . . .

Nadia's eyes widened as she realized the rain Elizabeth had called down wasn't just some random trick, or cover for something else she meant to do. The rain was the whole point.

No, not the rain, Nadia thought. *The flood.*

USUALLY MATEO LIKED THE OCCASIONAL RAINY NIGHT, because it meant fewer customers to deal with. (Of course, that meant fewer tips, not to mention lower profit for Dad, which was why he only liked them occasionally.) Also it gave him a chance at free salsa and chips, and tonight he got to share them.

"People are crazy," Gage said as they hung out in the corner booth, just beneath the faux–Frida Kahlo mural on the wall. "I say, anybody who lets a little falling water keep them from Mexican food? They don't *deserve* Mexican food."

"Agreed." Mateo glanced out the nearest window at the still-heavy rains. Honestly, he could see why people wouldn't want to go out in this.

Between crunching chips, Gage added, like it was no big deal, "Might run by and see Elizabeth after this. That's another thing this rain's not going to keep me away from."

"Okay." Had that come out calmly enough?

Apparently not. Gage leaned over the table, his forehead furrowed. "Are you sure you're all right with this?"

Mateo was definitely not all right with this, but he couldn't tell Gage the reasons why. "I'm not jealous. I'm not interested in Elizabeth that way. Bring me a Bible; I'll swear on it."

"We don't have to go dragging Bibles into this. But I know I violated the Bro Code pretty seriously here."

Why can't we tell him the truth? Mateo pushed the frustration aside. "We're cool. Okay?"

"Okay."

Surely there was some way to warn Gage about Elizabeth without either revealing witchcraft or sounding jealous— but before Mateo could think of one, he realized table eight was finally ready to pay their ticket and go home. "Be right back."

Then it was all *how was everything, glad you enjoyed it, see you back at La Catrina soon*—but while Mateo was running the credit card through, he saw Gage suddenly stand up from his booth. His movements were jerky, and too fast, as he started for the door.

For one moment Mateo thought Gage still felt awkward about their conversation, but no, that wasn't it. The glazed look in Gage's eyes, the way his body didn't even seem to be wholly under his own control: That could only be Elizabeth's work.

She had taken Gage under her thrall again.

The last time this had happened, Gage had tried to kill Mateo. Apparently this time Gage had been programmed with another agenda, but what?

Mateo hurriedly finished up with table eight, then went to his father. "Can I leave?"

"You've got another hour and a half on your shift."

"Dad, nobody's coming in. Nobody. I mean, look at the weather out there. And if anybody did come in, which they won't, Melanie could handle it."

"Fine, fine," Dad said, giving Mateo a look. "But you give me back an hour and a half this weekend, all right? We need to do inventory."

So much for his Saturday morning, but a deal was a deal. "Got it."

Mateo threw on his waterproof gear and went outside; Gage was still visible, barely, a dark shape moving farther down Captive Sound's main street. He had no umbrella, no raincoat, not even boots; Gage trudged through the downpour and the puddles, oblivious. Elizabeth's thrall outweighed anything else.

Although he hated to leave his motorcycle behind, Mateo decided to follow Gage on foot. As he ran along the sidewalk, trying to catch up, he noticed how fat the gutters were with rain; already the puddles rippled over the sidewalks in some areas. A few of the lower-lying roads would wash out by morning if the rain didn't stop . . . and if Nadia's suspicions were correct, the rain wouldn't stop anytime soon.

What does Elizabeth have to gain from this? Mateo wondered. By now he knew very well that Elizabeth did nothing that wouldn't benefit her, or at least the One Beneath. But he couldn't see how rain did anything except make everybody wet.

Finally he got within a dozen feet of Gage, and Mateo stayed back, watchful and cautious. Probably the thrall wouldn't let Gage notice Mateo any more than he noticed the rainfall, but Mateo was in no hurry for a repeat of their last brutal fight. Gage was a big guy, and only luck had saved Mateo before.

Luck and something else, he thought. When he and Gage had struggled, something had flashed through Mateo—something related to magic, though he didn't know how. That was what had snapped Gage out of the thrall, turning him back into himself once more. What was that? Mateo still didn't know. He kept meaning to ask Nadia, but they'd had bigger things to deal with. Like Armageddon.

Gage suddenly turned away from the main street, up toward one of the town's smaller hills. Through the gloom, Mateo could just make out a broad, cast-iron gate in the distance, and he shivered.

They were walking directly toward the cemetery.

He pulled the hood of his waterproof jacket more firmly around him and followed Gage up the slope, along the winding path that led into the graveyard. Although the gate indicated that, once upon a time, the town had tried to keep visitors out except at certain hours, the fence around the perimeter had fallen into disrepair decades ago. It existed now mostly as a trellis for ivy, all of which was brown and dead now in wintertime; the small shriveled leaves shook from the raindrops, making whispery sounds Mateo hoped would cover his footsteps.

Not that Gage seemed to be listening, or paying any attention to his surroundings at all. He weaved through a gap in the ivy, then kept on straight toward the graves. Mateo trailed several steps behind him.

Should I try to wake him up? They say if you wake up a sleepwalker they'll die—which is probably fake, but I don't know—and I don't know if this is anything like sleepwalking. Was there anything constructive he could do? Finally Mateo took his cell phone and started recording Gage; whatever this was, he wanted Nadia's take on it.

Gage's halting steps ceased when he found what he'd apparently been looking for—a tombstone, one of the older ones, small and thin, curved at the top, tilting to one side. Mateo crouched down low behind the newer tombstone of a *Tiffani Montgomery* and kept recording, even as Gage dropped to his knees and started . . . digging in the mud?

Even the mud against Mateo's knees was sharply cold—just above freezing—so he could only imagine how cold Gage's hands must be. But Elizabeth had put Gage in a state where he couldn't feel it even if he got frostbite. Gage dug deeper and deeper, and Mateo's stomach turned as he realized the goal was the dead body beneath.

Not a dead body. Gravestones like that—they're usually

at least two hundred years old. Bodies rot long before that. There won't be anything left but—

Gage stood up, clenching slivers of white in his hands.

Mateo swallowed hard. Nothing left but bone.

His errand not yet complete, Gage began to walk toward Elizabeth's house. No doubt, tomorrow, Gage would think he'd had another hot date with the girl of his dreams. He wouldn't have any idea what he'd done, or what had been done to him.

Mateo stopped filming and watched Gage go; if he couldn't bring Gage out of his enthralled state, then there was no point in following him farther. Besides, he wanted to investigate the old grave. Once Gage was out of sight, Mateo walked to the tombstone and used the flashlight app on his phone to shine a light on the aged granite. The carved letters had been worn down by wind and rain over the years until they were almost nothing but shadows on dark stone. But as Mateo leaned close, he was able to make out the name:

Eleanor Anne Cabot.

One of Mateo's ancestors—and another bearer of the Cabot Curse, to judge by the brief lifespan noted there. He shuddered as it sank in: Elizabeth was collecting his family's bones.

Mateo couldn't help wondering whether she wanted his, too.

That night, Mateo dreamed of Nadia.

She stood wearing a cloak of flame; her skin seemed as brilliant and soft as molten gold. Nadia's dark eyes blazed as she came close to him, slid her warm arms around his body. His hands clasped her beneath her cloak, and felt only bare skin.

"No one will stop us now," Nadia whispered. She kept kissing him—his lips, his throat, the exposed skin at the V of his T-shirt. Mateo shuddered as she pressed her body against his. Laughing softly, she continued, "No one will ever stop me again."

Mateo wove his fingers through her thick hair. It seemed to be floating around her, as though they were underwater, but he knew they weren't. Where were they? Alone together in some vast darkness where there was no up, no down—nothing else but the two of them together.

Why did she look so strange to him, and yet so familiar? Nadia smiled, even more radiant in the gold and the flame—and Mateo remembered.

This is what Elizabeth looked like the first time I saw her as a Steadfast. This is what a Sorceress looks like. What evil looks like.

Nadia's grin only widened. "Wait until you see what I do to anyone who tries to take you from me."

Then she kissed his mouth, and Mateo knew she was evil, that she was going to consume him alive, and still he didn't want to pull away.

When he awoke—in his own bed for a change—Mateo couldn't stop shaking. He didn't think that had been a vision, just a plain old nightmare.

He hoped so, anyway. If he were wrong, then Nadia was walking down the same path Elizabeth had, and she wouldn't stop until she was as cruel and twisted as Elizabeth had ever been.

And still, still, he wanted her.

Vintage clothing stores never carried raincoats. And retro umbrellas? Forget it. As long as the rains kept coming, Verlaine would be stuck hiding her red floral '40s swing dress under a raincoat and galoshes that made her look like the Gorton's Fisherman.

They held a meeting of Team Not Evil at lunchtime, even though the cafeteria was overstuffed and loud. With the outdoor picnic tables useless in the rain, everyone had no choice but to cram themselves in. *Cliques collide with cliques,* Verlaine thought, providing color commentary in her head. *Will the jocks survive their proximity to the mathletes? Only time will tell. Meanwhile, only our valiant heroes are trying to save the lives of mathletes and jocks alike.*

What made it even weirder was that the school counselor had come to sit with them.

"Lots of spells require bones," Faye Walsh said. "Not just black magic, either."

Mateo made a face. "You mean, good witches dig up people's bones?"

"It's not like that," Nadia explained. "Well. It's like that, but usually it's one of your own ancestors; in every spell I learned, you looked for the bones of another witch, someone in your own bloodline. It was a way of drawing on your family's strength. Any witch would be fine with her descendants doing that. I mean, they're just bones."

"They're 'just bones' until it's your own family," Mateo insisted. "Anyway, the spells you're talking about—that's not what Elizabeth is doing."

Nadia shook her head. "No, but I have no idea what it is."

Oh, come on. Verlaine just managed to hide her impatience. "I thought the whole point of you going to work with Elizabeth was so you could find out what she was up to."

This won her a sharp look. "Actually, the point of my working with Elizabeth was saving everyone in the hospital."

Which was totally true, and one of the lives Nadia had saved was Uncle Gary's. Sheepishly, Verlaine said, "Sorry. It's just—I didn't think Elizabeth would keep hiding things from you even after you signed on to destroy the world."

"The world won't be destroyed," Nadia said, "just completely overrun with demons under the rule of the lord of hell."

Verlaine rolled her eyes. "Same difference. Anyway, why would Elizabeth still be hiding things from you? I mean, yeah, really you're on Team Not Evil, but Elizabeth doesn't know that—does she?"

Nadia tugged at the end of her ponytail. "Elizabeth's not stupid. She understands I'm only working with her because I have to. I think she trusts me only because there are a lot of ways I can't defy her—not while I'm sworn to the One Beneath."

"Then that means—" Mateo's eyes widened. "That means

anything she's hiding from you is something you have the power to prevent. Or work against, defeat, whatever. If you were powerless to prevent whatever it is she's doing with my ancestor's bones, she wouldn't bother hiding it at all."

"Maybe," Nadia said, brightening.

"So, all you have to do is get the info from Elizabeth," Faye said. Verlaine's eyes widened in surprise, because Ms. Walsh was talking like that would be so easy, instead of potentially fatal.

Nadia went very still. Despite the roar in the cafeteria, Verlaine almost could have believed everything around them became hushed. "It's not as easy as asking Elizabeth. Her answers aren't—straightforward. She teaches by example." Slowly Nadia added, "But—maybe I could try her Book of Shadows."

Mateo and Verlaine shared a look as Faye said, "Didn't her Book of Shadows try to kill you?"

"Not kill," Nadia said. "It tried to trap me, with cobwebs and all the—all the spiders." A tremor passed through Nadia, and Verlaine didn't blame her. She had refused to shower in her own bathroom for two weeks after she'd seen a cockroach in her tub; if she'd been Nadia, literally cocooned in webs spun by hundreds of spiders, she probably would have had to go into therapy afterward. "Elizabeth would've killed me after she found me there."

"That's not reassuring." Mateo took Nadia's hand. "I told you about Gage just to find out what was going on. That's all. I don't want you to do anything dangerous on my account."

Nadia shook her head, her dangly earrings swinging. "All of this is dangerous. We have to do what we have to do. That's all."

"Wait, okay?" Mateo pleaded. "Let me watch Gage a while longer. Maybe it was a coincidence that it was one of my ancestors. Maybe she just needed bones."

Nadia gave him a look. "Mateo. Come on."

Mateo gripped Nadia's hand tighter, and his eyes were wide. To Verlaine, he looked less concerned, more . . . desperate. "Maybe you shouldn't have Elizabeth's book."

"It would be dangerous," Faye agreed. "If her Book of Shadows is as aware as you say it is, it wouldn't want to leave Elizabeth. God only knows what that thing could do on its own."

"That's not what Mateo meant." By now Nadia was sitting upright, almost rigid. Her words were clipped. "You don't think I can be trusted with it, do you?"

That idea hadn't even occurred to Verlaine, but when she saw Mateo's cheeks flush, she realized Nadia was onto something. Quietly he said, "It's dark magic I don't trust. Not you."

Nadia's expression remained stormy. Verlaine found herself imagining the kind of Sorceress Nadia might be if she really meant it . . . which was a terrifying thing to think about.

"You have to trust me," Nadia finally said as she shrugged on her backpack to go. "And I have to trust myself."

Verlaine nodded, even though she knew they didn't

exactly have any other choice.

But if she wanted more information in the near future, she might have to ask someone else.

Asa knew he shouldn't have responded to Verlaine's text. If she was smart (and he thought she was), this might well be her setting the stage to finally kill him. If she was being foolish—if she simply wanted to see him—then his best move would have been not to answer, and definitely not to agree to meet her near the remains of Davis Bridge after school.

But apparently I'm foolish, too, he thought as he parked his car near the bridge.

Verlaine's old maroon car was a few feet away, not too far for a mad dash through the rain. Asa felt lazy, though, and his umbrella was in the backseat, so—

He clapped his hands together, and instantly, time froze. The raindrops hung in the air, thousands of steel-gray, glittering spheres. Some of them were stopped midsplash, tiny sprays of water rising from puddles, logs, the hood of Verlaine's car. Carefully Asa opened his car door and wove through the raindrops, making his way to Verlaine.

She sat in the driver's seat, and for a moment Asa simply stood there amid the hanging raindrops and looked at her. Verlaine wore a red dress with white flowers, cheerful and bright, like the only spot of color in a world gone drab. Her silvery hair was pulled up into an adorably messy knot, with just a few tendrils escaping to frame her long face. His magic had caught her in the middle of applying pale pink lip gloss, so her mouth was slightly parted, her dark eyes focused on her reflection in the visor mirror. Asa would not touch her when she was like this—it would be a violation—but he couldn't help staring.

Are you trying to make yourself lovelier for me? Or is the makeup just a shield you wear, like the elaborate clothes—one more way to keep the world from seeing how vulnerable you are? With a sigh, Asa opened the passenger side door, slid in, then clapped his hands again.

Verlaine jumped as—so far as she could see—Asa instantly appeared by her side in the car. "Holy cats!" She made a face; when she'd startled, she'd smeared pink lip gloss across her cheek. Asa resisted the urge to wipe it away with his thumb. As she scrubbed at her face with some Kleenex, she said, "Do you always have to do that?"

"The alternative involved getting extremely wet. I thought I'd skip it." Asa leaned back in his seat, trying to make himself feel as casual as he looked. "So what's this about? My demise?"

She jerked back. "Wait. You thought I asked you here to kill you?"

"Let's say I knew it was a distinct possibility."

"And you came anyway? Do you have a death wish or something?"

Various sarcastic comments came to mind, but Asa made none of them. "I guess I do."

Verlaine stared.

Asa breathed out, a sharp sigh of frustration. "No, I don't

want to die. But I don't want to be responsible for killing you, and if I live long enough, that's what I'll have to do, eventually. That said, I don't mind not dying today. Have you at least learned how to kill me yet?"

She sat there wordless, eyes wide, for so long that he had his answer.

"Good girl," Asa said, grimly satisfied.

She scowled, an expression that should not have looked as adorable as it did. "Stop that."

"Stop what?"

"Talking to me like—like I'm your student, or something."

He grinned. "Aren't you? I'm teaching you how to deal with darker forces, with matters so far beyond your ken that you're only beginning to understand how deep they go. You need a teacher, Verlaine. The only other one you'd find is Elizabeth, and . . . let's say her discipline is much harsher."

His arms ached with the memory of pain, the long cuts Elizabeth had made in his flesh to work some of her magic. Demons were more than evil henchmen; they were a body and a soul in service, there to stand in for any spell a Sorceress might need to cast, no matter how painful.

"That's actually why I wanted to see you," Verlaine said, her fingers tapping nervously on the steering wheel. "Turns out Elizabeth's up to something that she hasn't explained to Nadia. I wanted to see if you could tell me what's going on."

How short-sighted they still were. Elizabeth was "up to" countless spells and enchantments she wouldn't share with

Nadia or even with Asa. Dark magic so consumed her life that nearly every action she took was in some way connected to her work for the One Beneath. "What worries you in particular?"

"You know how she has Gage Calloway in her thrall?"

Did he ever. He had a class with Gage Calloway and had had to listen to him talking about how amazing Elizabeth was—well, twice now, but that was two times too many, enough to bring Asa to the point of nausea. "If you're asking me if I can free Gage, I can't. That's not the kind of magic a demon can perform."

"Oh, I hadn't even thought of that. Well, damn." Verlaine shook her head. "No, the thing is, Mateo followed Gage the other night when Gage was zoned out, or whatever you'd call it when Elizabeth's the one in charge. Gage went to the cemetery and dug up the bones of one of Mateo's ancestors. Which is creepy regardless, but given the whole Cabot Curse thing, has the potential to be seriously bad. What is she doing with those bones? Do you know?"

Asa didn't have any idea. He hadn't even suspected Elizabeth might be attempting to manipulate that curse. "No. But I'll try to find out. Probably that's something I can tell you about without violating my service to the One Beneath." Depending on what it was Elizabeth was up to—anything involving curses was as dark as dark magic got.

Verlaine's face lit up. "I knew you'd help."

"How could you have known that? I keep reminding you, Verlaine, I'm a demon."

Her smile never changed. "For a demon, you're a pretty nice guy. Better than most of the real guys I've known, anyway. Most of the bad stuff you do, you can't help."

"I can't help," he whispered, scooting closer to her in the car, "serving the greatest evil that has ever existed. I can't help what I'm called upon to do, and if at any point it endangers you, I still have to carry it out, no matter how much I might . . ." Asa caught himself. "You need to be afraid of me. Very afraid."

They were only a few inches apart now, so close he could smell the strawberry gloss on her lips. "I am," she whispered, but her eyes met his so easily that it couldn't be true. At least, not in the way she should be afraid.

No, Asa realized, the fear she felt was the same as the fear within him. The fear that you'd do anything—give up anything, go against what you knew had to be true, all for the sake of someone else—the fear that part of you belonged to another, and you'd never, ever get it back.

You have to stop this, he told himself, even as he leaned closer to Verlaine, even as she tilted her face up to his. *You have to stop—*

Asa kissed her. He'd told himself he would never kiss Verlaine again, that their one embrace in the snow had to be the only one they would ever share. Yet here he was kissing her again, then again, folding her into his arms. Verlaine made a small sound—hungry and happy both—and he was lost. They tangled in each other, kissing faster, almost frantically.

It had always felt good to have a human body again, but

this—how could he have known it could feel like this? His skin blazed with warmth every place she touched him; he could feel her body pressed against his as he leaned her back in the car. Inside it was both as though he were dizzy—completely overcome—and yet more focused than he'd ever been. Asa could take in everything about her at once, from the way her breathing quickened to the taste of her mouth opening under his, and know her completely.

He tugged at the elastic holding her hair into a knot, and it came loose around his fingers. Verlaine's silver hair tumbled down over his hands, framing her face. She pulled back from him slightly, just enough to whisper, "This is a really bad idea, right?"

"Terrible. I would say disastrous."

"Right," she said, and kissed him again. Asa didn't even try to fight it.

Serving the One Beneath wasn't like an after-school job; Nadia didn't have a set schedule, hours when she was supposed to show up, anything like that. When she'd tried to explain it to Mateo, she'd said, *I know when Elizabeth wants me there. It's not like she takes me over or speaks to my mind, nothing like that; I just know, and then I need to go to her as soon as I can.*

Tonight, she knew she had to go.

Dad had cooked this evening, under their new agreement where she'd let him make dinner at least twice a week. He still wasn't good at it, exactly, but turkey tacos were pretty hard to screw up. When he cooked, she did the dishes, which was why she was elbow-deep in suds when suddenly she understood that she'd have to go to Elizabeth's as soon as she could.

Nadia powered through the rest of the dishes, then walked into the living room as she dried her hands with a towel. "Dad? I was going to run over to Verlaine's for a while. Can I borrow the car?"

"You're going out in this?" Dad looked up from his book; Cole, playing some game on the iPad, didn't even glance at her. "Looks nasty out there."

"It's just rain."

"Still, a couple of the roads on the west side of town are washed out. Couldn't you guys talk on the phone? But kids don't even do that anymore, do they? You can Skype or something. Or Snapchat. What is Snapchat?"

She managed not to laugh. "Come on, Dad. Verlaine's house is nowhere near the washed-out roads. It's not far." Elizabeth's house was even closer; Nadia had walked it in better weather.

"All right, then. But you text when you get there and when you start back home. Hear me?"

"Loud and clear."

While Nadia drove the few blocks to Elizabeth's house, she took a good look at everything around her. Every single yard had deep puddles; all the gutters were thick with rain. How did it work, the magic they'd cast? Were clouds from all over being drawn toward Captive's Sound? Nadia could hardly believe there was so much rain in the whole world.

"When does the rain stop?" Nadia said as she walked into Elizabeth's front room, instead of hello. She began to shuck her raincoat, then realized water was trickling through the decrepit building's roof, all the way down to the ground floor. The water wasn't puddling—mostly because the floorboards leaked as badly as the roof—but the entire place was musty and wet. The raincoat stayed on.

Elizabeth paid no attention to the water, or to Nadia's question. "Would you like to know how to move water?"

"I know that spell, actually."

"Good." She smiled up at Nadia; her tattered white dress was gray with damp, but none of it seemed to touch her. "Then I can help you make it stronger. Together we can direct the currents. We'll even own the sea."

Was this about clearing the One Beneath's pathway to their world? Nadia knew the sound itself was important, for that. Yet she sensed this was something else.

And how was she able to sense that?

I'm tuning in to her magic more, Nadia realized. *I'm starting to understand this on a whole different level.*

Was that understanding dangerous? Or was it the only way for her to ever conquer Elizabeth? Both things might be true.

Either way, there was nothing for Nadia to do but to sit beside Elizabeth, nod, and say, "Let's begin."

5

I'VE GOT IT BAD, VERLAINE THOUGHT. IF YOU'RE MAKING out with a guy and you actually hear music? You have to be completely, totally in . . .

"Wait," she gasped, pulling back from Asa. "My phone."

"To hell with your phone." Asa kissed her throat, just beneath her jaw.

"Uncle Gary. He's only been out of the hospital—"

"I know," Asa groaned, but he loosened his embrace around her and even grabbed her purse, placing it in her lap.

Verlaine scooted back into her seat—not that she'd actually left it, but there had been some sprawling—and grabbed her phone. Since this was the first-ever time she'd made out with a guy, she would have blown off any other text; however, this song was Uncle Gary's tone, and if he was in trouble, she had to help him if she could.

As she caught her breath, she saw the message. *Are you at the* Guardian?

"I interrupted making out for a parental panic attack?" She rolled her eyes.

Asa laughed and kissed her forehead. "Go on and tell him you're alive. The last thing I need is to be accosted by a protective father with a shotgun."

Uncle Gary with a shotgun: absurd. Verlaine quickly typed back, *Not there yet. Headed that way.*

"Headed to the newspaper? Already?" Asa's fingers tangled in her hair as he pulled her close again. "Are you sure I couldn't persuade you to stay?"

It wasn't like Verlaine had forgotten that hooking up with a demon was a really terrible idea. But the voice inside her head reminding her of that had gotten very, very quiet during the last half hour. She smiled up at Asa. "I meant, I'm headed there . . . eventually."

"Like, a couple hours from now? Or tomorrow?" His lips traced along her neck, making her shiver deliciously. "How long can I talk you into staying here with me?"

Verlaine never found out, because her phone chimed again in her hand. *Don't go anywhere near it! Apparently the newspaper offices are flooding.*

"Oh, my God." She scrambled back from Asa, all the adrenaline coursing through her instantly turning to panic. "The *Guardian* is flooding. We have to get there."

It took Asa a moment to catch up. He ran one hand through his rumpled hair, trying to refocus. "Verlaine, it's dangerous. What is it you think you can do? The rain won't stop."

"The archives." She cranked the car, and the aged motor rumbled into life. The windshield wipers began *slap-slapping* back and forth. "Those records—I digitized some of them, but there are whole decades that are print-only. Those are the only existing copies. If they're lost in the flood, they're lost forever!"

"Come the apocalypse nobody's going to care about—"

"Screw the apocalypse. The One Beneath is not going to win, okay? We're going to stop Him."

Her words were empty and she knew it. Maybe they'd win; maybe they wouldn't; she wasn't going to be the deciding factor either way. But when Asa smiled at her, Verlaine felt as though what she'd said wasn't so empty after all. "You amaze me," he said. "Your bravery—but surely there are tests enough for your courage. Saving some moldy old newspapers isn't worth endangering yourself."

Verlaine shook her head. "They're not 'moldy old newspapers.' They're records of how people lived, who they loved, and how they died. Everything that's human and normal and right about Captive's Sound—that's what's in the *Guardian*. That's what we have to save. Besides, if there's anything in Elizabeth's history that's going to trip her up? That's where it's going to be. Now, are you with me or not?"

"I am," Asa said.

She put the car in drive.

Whenever Asa found himself helping Verlaine, Nadia, or Mateo, he felt the strain of his bonds. Literally: It was as though he could sense the One Beneath's hold on his soul like straps across his chest, biting through his skin, making it harder for him to draw breath.

Once, when Verlaine's life had been in danger, he had deliberately worked against the will of the One Beneath. The price had been a brief time back in the furnaces of the demonic realm, suffering torments that still gave him nightmares. Worst of all, Asa knew the day would come when he would be ordered to hurt Verlaine, and he would not have the power to defy.

But this task, this moment: This was something he could do for her.

They parked a couple of blocks off the town square, because the police had already sealed off one of the streets. Together Asa and Verlaine ran toward the *Guardian* offices, leaving umbrellas and raincoats behind; they were about to get so wet a few raindrops couldn't make any difference. Although the puddles on either side of the streets were so wide they nearly met in the middle, the square itself didn't seem to be flooded. Waterlogged, sure—but not flooded.

As soon as Verlaine unlocked the front door of the *Guardian*, she cried out in dismay. The entire front half of the main room was about three inches deep in water that had flowed in from the street.

"We move the archives to the higher shelves?" Asa said, getting ready to do some heavy lifting.

Verlaine shook her head. "First we have to get everything we can out of the basement."

"This place has a basement?"

"It's little, and it's old, and most of the records there are more recent, but if there's this much water up here, how bad must it be down there?" She ran toward the back, her Converse sloshing through deeper water, and opened a door. "Oh, no!"

Asa went to her, or tried to; already Verlaine's footsteps were thumping down metal stairs. He got to the doorway to see her almost to the bottom of a spiral staircase, which led to a basement room that had to be at least a foot deep in water.

Only one bare bulb in the stairwell burned, dimly illuminating the scene below. Verlaine sloshed down into the water, the skirt of her red-and-white dress darkening as it got splashed. Around her, various file cabinets stood, swaying slightly in the current. One of them had already tipped against the wall. What worried Asa the most was that water continued flowing into the room. The level of flooding was going to rise, and quickly.

Verlaine remained undaunted. "Come carry some files!" she shouted up at him. "The ones in the lower drawers—it's too late already—but we can get a lot of the rest out if we work fast."

Asa felt the straps holding him back again—putting his mortal life in any risk, even the slight one presented by going into the flooding basement, verged on the limits of the freedom allowed him by the One Beneath.

But he wouldn't abandon Verlaine even one second before he was forced to. Until then, he stayed by her side.

"Coming!" he shouted, as he went into the water and the dark.

"Again you've chosen your ingredients poorly," Elizabeth said.

Nadia only barely managed to conceal her frustration. "I haven't been around as long as you." That was putting it lightly. "I don't have the same number of memories to choose from."

"You interpret events too literally, then." Elizabeth's smile was that of a queen on her throne—distant, unruffled, unchangeable. "We have weapons beyond experience, you know. We have nuance. Double meanings. The many shadows and possibilities tied up in what might have been."

Nadia frowned. Her mother had told her this much, of course—but she had also warned Nadia against doing this too often. "Mom said that twisting memories twists up your mind, in time. She said it makes you dishonest, and dirties your magic."

"We're playing dirty," Elizabeth said. "Haven't you realized that yet?"

Nadia's cheeks flushed, and she stared down at the floor. When her mother had taught her about magic, she'd always stressed how smart Nadia was, how much she could do. Learning from Elizabeth was all about learning her limitations—and being made to feel small.

She thinks I hardly even know what I'm doing, Nadia thought. *I'll show her.*

"Choose your memories again." Elizabeth's green eyes flicked up to Nadia's, almost teasing. "Try again. See if you can sense the current this time."

How was she supposed to darken this spell? It was a cheerful one, hard to twist. Nadia's eyes shut as she called the memories forth:

The love of a child.
A living thing rising from the earth.
Hope through grief.

Each one would have to be turned dark in some way—

Cole sobbing against the door right after Mom had walked out, hitting it with his little fists, and the pure hatred Nadia had felt for her mother at that moment.

The seaweed that had tangled around her limbs the night she dove for Goodwife Hale's Book of Shadows, the living green stuff that had captured her and attempted to drown her.

Hoping that her mother would be glad to see her during her last trip to Chicago, and the terrible disappointment when Mom had opened the door and felt only annoyance—when Nadia had seen that there was no love left in her at all.

And she felt it—the current of the waters, surging through her as powerfully as her own heartbeat.

At La Catrina, Mateo froze, knife in his hand, half-chopped tomato on the cutting board.

What was that?

It had felt like . . . an electric shock? No. The sensation had lasted too long for that. Whatever it was, it had coursed through his entire body, strong and insistent, just at the verge of pain.

Mateo knew the sensation was related to magic; this was like the shadow of what he felt when he helped Nadia by strengthening a spell. In its wake it left behind sorrow, and guilt, and fear. Those emotions weren't his own—they couldn't be—but he knew they were related to whatever Nadia had just done.

In an instant, he saw a face, pale and frightened as it got caught up in the wake of what had just happened. Someone who was now in danger.

He sucked in a breath and whispered, "Verlaine."

Hurry, hurry, I've got to hurry—

By now the water was up to Verlaine's rib cage. She had taken on basement duty—wading through the floodwater to grab the most important files, then handing them off to Asa, who had stair duty. He'd grab an armload of files from her and hurry upstairs, depositing them safely, before running back down to help her.

They were working as fast as they could, but the flood was rising faster.

All these papers, Verlaine thought despairingly. She didn't think of them as newsprint and wood pulp; she thought of them as the lingering traces of people who had lived here, real human beings who didn't want to be forgotten any more than she did. *They're being destroyed, and I just can't move fast enough.*

The metallic ringing of Asa's footsteps made her look up as she struggled back to the stairs. He was breathing hard; by now he would have made at least thirty trips up and down, if not more. "Come up," he panted. "You need to come up now. The water's too deep."

"I can go a while longer," Verlaine insisted. "A couple more handfuls means a couple more years of records making it out."

"This is taking historiography too far." But Asa held out his arms, and she shunted the next pile of papers to him.

As he made his way upward, Verlaine pushed off from the metal rail of the staircase; by now, the water was deep enough that she needed extra energy to move through it. *This dress is ruined,* she thought; it was one of her favorites, a '40s original that still had all its original color and swing. But she'd have sacrificed more than a dress to save as much of the *Guardian* as she could. The weight of her waterlogged clothing seemed to drag at her as she walked—in what felt like slow motion—back to one of the last filing cabinets she hadn't dealt with. Verlaine pulled open the top drawer, filled her arms with papers—

—and that was when the waters surged.

The current quickened, intensified, maybe even doubled. Verlaine squeaked as she staggered backward, dragged off-balance by the sudden torrent of the water around her. Before, it had felt like struggling to walk through a swimming pool;

now it was like being caught in a storm-swollen river. She could hardly remain upright . . .

Then she couldn't. Verlaine lost her footing and fell.

The water closed over her head, cold and fast. She had managed to close her eyes in time, but she could feel the flotsam and debris as it scored her skin—grit, gravel, and all the other detritus the flood had picked up. Although she tried to grip the files in her hands tightly, the currents were too strong. The folders were torn from her, and though Verlaine tried to reach for them, they were lost.

Bracing herself against the floor, Verlaine pushed herself to the surface to breathe—but just as she gulped in air, the current knocked her feet out from under her. Immediately she went under again.

It's okay, she thought, trying to ignore the panicky fluttering in her chest. *You're all right. Just reach the staircase, and Asa will help you.*

Then she couldn't seem to get her feet under her, and she wasn't sure which way was up, and if she could have taken a breath, she would have screamed.

"There," Nadia said in satisfaction as she sat back. "You can't complain about that."

"No, I can't." Elizabeth looked more pleased at Nadia's success than expected.

Only then did it hit Nadia: *I successfully cast black magic. I made myself get better at it. I made myself useful to Elizabeth.*

How could she have been so stupid? She'd let pride goad

her into doing Elizabeth's work more perfectly. She'd gotten so caught up in her own petty irritation that she had completely lost sight of the goal.

What have I done?

"Don't punish yourself," Elizabeth said. "It's only natural. Falling prey to easy temptations of ego—it's how most practitioners of black magic begin."

Being seen through so easily hurt even worse. "Most?" Nadia said, trying to cover her own horror. "Not all? I guess that means, not you."

"Not I." Elizabeth's smile was a small, secretive one, like a girl thinking about her crush. "I knew exactly what I wanted all along."

I've got to get her out of there, Asa thought as he hurried back down the stairs, leg muscles aching. He had been able to stop time for a few of his trips down, allowing him a moment to rest, but by now even the rest breaks didn't cut it. And now he felt Elizabeth and Nadia's dark magic at work, strengthening the chaos around them. *The crusading-reporter thing only goes so far. This is the last trip, the absolute last.*

He rounded the final curve of the spiral staircase to see everything submerged even deeper, the flood surging into the basement so quickly the water ran white, as though they were in the rapids. Verlaine was nowhere to be seen.

"Verlaine!" he shouted. No one responded, of course— but amid the bubbles and currents Asa thought he caught a glimpse of swirling silver hair just beneath the surface.

Instantly Asa dived into the water. The shock of the cold hit him anew—his legs were used to it by now, but not the rest of him—and it took his demonic heat a moment to compensate. He opened his eyes despite the sting of dust and debris and saw Verlaine struggling feebly beneath the surface. With a hard push of his feet against the floor, he propelled himself toward her, managing to hook one arm around her waist.

Together they surfaced. Verlaine gasped for breath so desperately that he knew she'd been under too long. "Asa?" She clung to his shoulders. "We have to get out of here."

"As a wise man once said, no shit."

The water was surging past his ability to overcome it. Asa struggled toward the staircase, but already he was in danger of losing his footing. And his breath shortened as the straps around his chest tightened, punishing him for risking his mortal vessel for an enemy of the One Beneath. Maybe— maybe he could get the better of it, if he just stopped time—

To do that, he had to clap his hands together. To clap his hands, he would have to let go of Verlaine. That would mean letting her go under the water again. Panting and exhausted as she was, Asa thought she would be in danger of inhaling water—going from in distress to actually drowning even faster than his demonic powers could act.

I won't let go, he thought. *No matter what.*

Then the current strengthened yet again, and Asa and Verlaine both cried out as they were knocked off their feet and slammed against the filing cabinets. Asa tried to protect her as best he could, wrapping both arms and one leg around her, but she was in danger of being ripped away at any instant.

That was when he heard, "Hang on!"

Asa looked up to see Mateo Perez, running down the last few steps of the staircase. How had he known they were in there? No telling—and at the moment, it didn't matter. One person's help might make the difference in saving Verlaine's life.

Obviously Mateo realized that plunging into the water himself would just mean three people at risk instead of only two. Instead he went to the bottom of the stairwell and hung onto the railing with one hand—allowing the current to pull him a little deeper into the basement. By now less than two feet remained between the surface of the water and the ceiling.

With his other hand, Mateo reached out as far as he could. "Grab on!"

Could Asa make it? He had to, for Verlaine's sake.

But just as he thought this, Verlaine clutched one of his hands and pushed herself forward, making the leap for Mateo herself. Mateo had to reach for her, but somehow they managed to hang on to each other. Then Verlaine shouted, "Let go! I've got you!"

"I came down here to save you!" Asa protested, but there was no point. Every once in a while, a guy had to let himself get saved instead.

He let go of the file cabinets, and the current caught him, hard—but he and Verlaine held on to each other. Mateo grimaced as he towed them in, but slowly he managed to get Verlaine back onto the steps, and then the two of them helped Asa. Once he had metal under his feet, he felt a little better.

And yet, exhausted. He'd had no idea a human body could ache like this, and he had extra strength to call upon from his demonic side. Verlaine had to be on the verge of collapse, and even Mateo would be weary.

"Upstairs," Asa gasped. "We have to get out of here."

Verlaine groaned—no doubt still mourning all the lost records, all the forgotten realms of the past—but she started making her way up. Mateo followed, and Asa brought up the rear . . .

. . . until the moment the staircase pulled free of the wall.

Verlaine screamed. Mateo shouted. Asa didn't know what sound he would have made, because he almost instantly fell back into the water, which rushed into his mouth and made him cough for breath.

The currents have torn the metal staircase from its moorings, Asa realized. *If we don't have the stairs, how do we get out?*

In one more instant, he had the answer: *Maybe we don't.*

"What did we just do?" Nadia asked. Her panic deepened, dizzying her. Every sound beyond her own breath seemed to have been muffled. "The current—the water—what's happening?"

86

Elizabeth shrugged. "The specific and immediate conse-quences are almost irrelevant. We have brought this weather upon the town to do the work of rain, which is never accomplished in a single night. Its destruction is slower—but inevitable."

This made no sense to Nadia. No, she hadn't napped all the way through the geology unit of natural sciences; she knew rainfall was one of the most powerful forces on earth, tearing down mountain ranges by a millimeter a year until they turned into sand. But that took hundreds and thousands of years.

They don't need to wipe Captive's Sound off the earth entirely, Nadia realized. *They just need to break things down—which is already happening.*

And I'm helping.

Elizabeth had played into Nadia's impatience, her insecu-rity, even her hatred to make her do exactly what the One Beneath wanted. Worst of all, when she'd worked that dark magic—when she'd twisted her memories of her life into their darkest, bleakest form, staining them forever—it had felt good. Amazing. Like she'd been hungry her whole life and not even known it until the moment she bit down on the richest chocolate cake ever. Yet instead of being full, now she was even hungrier. Now she knew what she was missing.

Nadia shoved herself away from the circle and got to her feet. From her place on the floor, Elizabeth watched, impas-sive and amused, as Nadia said, "I'm going. I have to see what—what we've done."

"I told you," Elizabeth said. "It doesn't matter."

She made no move to stop Nadia as she dashed out of the old house, into the rain.

Mateo had learned the same stuff about water safety that any kid learned when they lived on the shore. One of the first lessons: *Don't attempt to rescue somebody if you can't see it through, because the last thing you need to do is put two people in danger instead of just one.*

Should've remembered that, he thought as he grabbed for the metal stair railing, grasped it—and felt it come loose from the wall. Now it was only heavy metal dragging him down.

His head plunged beneath the surface of the water; Verlaine's body collided with his as she fell. Now all three of them were tangled in one another and the spiral staircase, hardly able to move. Mateo fought past his panic as he tried to get to the surface, pushed his face above the water just long enough to grab a breath, then slipped under again.

The staircase was the problem, he realized. If they'd just been stuck in a fast-rising flood, with their only exit several feet above their heads, they could probably have treaded water long enough to reach the doorway, or at least until more help arrived. The stairs were now nothing more than a spiral of twisted metal that thrashed in the current, banging and bruising their limbs, pushing them down, and turning the last space in the basement with any air into a deathtrap.

Mateo managed to push himself above the water again just long enough to see Asa trying to pull Verlaine up—managing to do it—and then tumbling back under himself. The water churned around them violently, and water splashed into his nose and throat, making him cough.

Verlaine screamed, "Help!" Wow, she could seriously scream when she wanted to. But Mateo knew that if somebody wasn't already searching the *Guardian* offices, nobody would be able to hear them no matter how loudly they yelled.

This might be it, he thought. *We might die.*

The knowledge of it felt different than he'd thought it would. He'd been in danger before but there had always been something he could do, some action he could try even if he failed. Now all three of them were helpless, unable to do more than desperately claw their way upward for breath. This felt less like panic, more like an incredible weight pressing on his chest, and the narrowing of his thoughts down to nothing but how long they might have.

A metal step slammed into his gut, and Mateo slipped underwater again. He found himself thinking of that time he'd had to rescue Nadia—how he'd had to breathe into her mouth for her, giving her air, to keep her alive—

Maybe his life was starting to flash before his eyes.

Then a strong hand closed around his upper arm and yanked him up. Mateo surfaced, gasping for breath, to see that Verlaine had taken hold of him while Asa helped brace her against the wall. He wanted to thank her, but he didn't have the breath.

Then he heard a shout from above. "We've got people down here!"

Thank God! Mateo looked up to see Gage. He wore a fluorescent yellow safety vest over his clothes; he must have been one of the people pitching in to help the cops. As Gage leaned through the doorway, he braced himself and yelled, "I'm gonna throw down a rope, okay?"

None of them could answer, but when a nylon rope dropped into their midst, they all let go of one another and grabbed on. The rope had plastic toggles every foot or so, which kept it from slipping out of their grasp. Mateo knew there was no way Gage could possibly tow them up on his own—and the metal staircase still slammed against them, back and forth, with the brisk current. But just being able to keep himself above the surface was something.

From above he heard various shouts; apparently the other rescuers were coming to help, now that Gage had raised the alarm.

"This isn't right," Verlaine said, half-dazed. Wet strands of her gray hair framed her face. "Something happened during the flood. Something changed it."

Asa gasped, "Black magic."

That was what Mateo had felt—the darkness of the magic transforming this flood into something murderous.

He also suspected the magic had belonged to Nadia.

Nadia drove toward the sound of sirens. *Dad is going to kill me if he ever finds out,* she thought as she swerved around orange plastic cones meant to keep her out of the most dangerous area.

When she pulled into the town square, she saw a few police cars and both of the town's fire trucks, their lights beating red and blue flashes onto the otherwise darkened square. Where was everybody? The cops, the firefighters? Nadia frowned—then remembered how many houses and stores here had basements. For storage, mostly. Her fear dimmed slightly as she thought, *They're just trying to protect people's property. I didn't put anyone in danger. It's okay . . .*

Then she saw that a group had gathered in front of the *Guardian*.

"Verlaine!" Nadia ran from the car, rain spattering down on her face and hair as she dashed toward the newspaper office. Her breath caught in her chest, and a stitch ached in her side, but she pushed herself to run faster. If Verlaine was in there, and she had to do magic in front of every man in the world to save her, then that was how it had to be.

As she reached the building, a fireman saw her and held out his arms. "Miss, you shouldn't be in this area."

"Verlaine!" Nadia yelled, or tried to yell. She could hardly breathe. "My friend—is she—"

At that moment, Gage emerged from the doorway with Verlaine leaning against him, one of her arms around his shoulder. The paramedics immediately wrapped her in a shiny-looking thermal blanket, and Verlaine sank down on the sidewalk, almost too exhausted to even sit up.

Asa stumbled out afterward, waving off any attempts at assistance. His eyes met Nadia's, and he smiled mirthlessly. "Well done."

Nadia winced.

The paramedics swarmed around him, obviously eager to tend to him—but Asa brought his hands together. Everyone and everything froze, even the rain, and Nadia alone could still perceive what was going on.

"Can't let them take any vitals," Asa said, weaving his way through the paramedics to stand at her side. Raindrops hung in the air around them like thousands of tiny glittering jewels. He wrung water from his sweater and grimaced. "They'd think I had a fever no human could actually survive. I'd just as soon avoid any trips to the emergency room. The doctors will be busy enough tonight."

"Who else has been hurt?" Nadia said. "Nobody's been killed—have they?"

"How should I know? It's not our business to tally the deaths. Only to do the bidding of the One Beneath." His eyes narrowed as he studied her, as though he'd never really seen her face before. "You're good at this, you know. Better than I thought you'd be."

She didn't answer. She couldn't.

Asa walked past her, and a few moments later she heard his hands come together—and the rain and movement began again. For a moment the paramedics were startled, looking for the patient they'd seen just an instant before, but then a fireman helped someone else outside.

"Mateo!" Nadia cried. They tried to hold her back from them, but Mateo held out his hand to her, and she was able to grab it. As the paramedics worked on him, she knelt by his side, refusing to let go. "I'm so sorry—I'm sorry—" she kept repeating, the words coming out of her in a rush.

"I know," Mateo said. She knew he meant to sound understanding, but all she heard was that he understood exactly what she'd done. His stare was hard, and Nadia found herself pulling back from him.

Even the guy she loved could tell the evil was getting to her—slipping into the cracks, wearing her down, just like the endless rain.

Elizabeth splayed her hands in front of the stove's glow, feeling the warmth penetrate through her flesh, down to the bone. To her it seemed as though the strong currents flowed around her hands and through her fingers. When Elizabeth closed her eyes, she could even imagine herself in a great river at its mouth, where freshwater met salt. The waters would rush over and around her, and her feet would sink into the silt at the bottom; the current would be strong enough to move even the mud, to make the earth itself begin to move.

All this I have done for you, she thought, thinking of the One Beneath. *We are so very close now, my only love, my only master.*

He did not reply in words. His orders and emotions came to her in different forms: powerful sensations that washed over her, and the knowledge of His thoughts, more vivid to Elizabeth than mere speech could ever be. The One Beneath rejoiced in her strength, strained impatiently at the last bonds that kept Him outside the mortal world, and—wanted more.

Not the world Elizabeth had laid before Him. Already the One Beneath knew of her gifts and gloried in them. His desire was for His other servant to join in Elizabeth's work fully and joyfully.

Still, even now—He wanted Nadia.

I gave her to you, Elizabeth thought, forcing herself to remain calm. *She is your servant, sworn to you.*

But Nadia's heart was not entirely in her work. Not yet. Already Elizabeth had cast Betrayer's Snare—a spell meant to deflect some kinds of witchcraft, to turn their powers back on the witch who had cast them. Were Nadia to try to directly go against Elizabeth, casting spells to harm or kill her, those spells would work on her instead. If the girl thought she could turn against Elizabeth without paying a price, she would be very deeply sorry.

Soon, though, Nadia would be loyal.

Elizabeth filled her mind with the image of Nadia's face as she had looked just before she dashed out of the house. Yes, there was hatred there, and despair . . . but also self-knowledge. Darkness had crept into Nadia's magic, and thus into Nadia's soul. She could not resist it much longer; she wouldn't even want to. As for the bonds of love that kept Nadia tied to the mortal world, well, those were already strained. Soon they would snap.

"Not long now," Elizabeth whispered.

6

MATEO HAD THOUGHT ESCAPING FROM THE FLOODWATER had been tough. Dealing with the resulting parental over-reactions? Possibly tougher.

"You went in to help. I understand that." Dad didn't look understanding. He looked like he was trying really hard not to get mad, because he knew he should be proud. His eyes were shadowed, though, and in them Mateo could glimpse how badly scared his father had been. "But you have a medical condition, *mi hijo*. You can't take certain risks right now."

"I know I do." The paramedics had walked Mateo over to La Catrina, where he now sat in one of the booths; Dad had draped his own fleece jacket around Mateo's shoulders, and put a bowl of garlic broth in front of him to heat him up.

The chill wouldn't have gotten to Mateo half as much if Nadia had been here. But she'd drawn away, apologizing, as the medics had surrounded him.

"You look worse." Dad put his hand to Mateo's forehead like he was a seven-year-old kid again, trying to play sick to get out of school. "You never should have gone down there. How did you even know Verlaine was in trouble?"

Mateo figured he'd better skim past that question. "I'm sorry, Dad. Believe me, if I'd realized just how bad it was going to get, I'd have called for the cops or the fire department right away. Since they have the best deputies." He smiled at Gage.

Gage grinned. "Death-defying rescues, at your service."

Thank God Gage had come back to La Catrina with him. Dad only stopped being upset with Mateo long enough to admire his friend. "Since when do you volunteer with the fire department, Gage?"

"Well, you remember the haunted house fire at the Halloween carnival, right?"

"Right," Mateo said; that would have been his last day on earth, but for Nadia.

Gage continued, "After that, I thought I ought to get some emergency training. So I could be useful when something like that happened, instead of just taking pictures and putting them on Instagram, you know? I signed up for the next Red Cross class, which was Disaster Assistance. The fire department texted everybody from the class this afternoon and told us to come in, which is how I got this awesome outfit." He gestured to his fluorescent yellow plastic vest.

"Looks sharp." Mateo managed to smile at his friend, grateful to be with Gage—the real Gage—and to erase the memory of him lost in Elizabeth's thrall.

This is the person he really is, the person he's meant to be. How do we fix it so Elizabeth can't screw with his head anymore? As Mateo thought about it, he remembered their one terrible battle—and the way some strange force had traveled through Mateo, into Gage, for one instant setting him free.

"You must be cold, too," Dad said, patting Gage's shoulder. "You want some broth? Hold on. I'll get you a mug."

"Sounds good," Gage called after him. "A beer would sound better!"

"Don't push it!" Dad's voice vanished into the depths of the kitchen.

Mateo shook his head. "I can't believe you asked my dad for a beer."

"I just helped save his son's life. You'd think that would be worth a brewski."

"But not worth our liquor license."

In his rush to get to the *Guardian*, Mateo had forgotten his cell phone. Good thing, too, or else he wouldn't have one anymore. He looked down at his messages, knowing he should contact Nadia. What was he supposed to say, though? *I know you didn't mean to nearly kill us?*

Then he thought of Nadia's stricken face and realized it didn't matter what he said. She needed to know that he still loved her no matter what.

Quickly he tapped out, *Are you okay? I'm thinking about you. If you want to call or talk or anything—let me know. Love you.*

Nadia had managed to get upstairs without her dad seeing how soaked she was. She knew she ought to go downstairs and talk with him and Cole, but instead she sat on her desk chair, swaddled in her thick robe, hardly able to think, much less move.

How could I let Elizabeth taunt me into doing something that terrible? How?

And the way Mateo had looked at her outside the *Guardian*—if he hated her now, she couldn't take it.

Don't be stupid, she told herself. *Of course Mateo still loves you.*

If she talked with Mateo, maybe she'd feel better. First she'd test the waters with a text. Grabbing her phone, she typed, *I'm sorry I ran off like that. Everything is scary, and I feel so mixed up. Can we talk tonight? I need to talk to you.*

Nadia pushed Send, feeling as though she'd just been tossed a life preserver. Now someone would tow her back to shore.

Elizabeth sensed the opportunity, and struck.

As Mateo tapped out his message to Nadia, Elizabeth watched him through Gage Calloway's eyes. His father called to him, asking him to change into dry clothes. His message, not yet complete, remained unsent. The moment he was gone, she used Gage's hand to pick up the phone.

Through him, she sent magic that would destroy any messages sent or received that night, plucking them out of the electronic ether if needed, to ensure they never found their recipients. Back in the day, the spell used to make letters burn within their envelopes. Now? Elizabeth had no idea how cell phones worked and did not care to learn.

She knew how magic worked, and that was enough, because magic itself would know how to make sure Mateo and Nadia would not reach each other tonight.

When Mateo came back to the table, Gage was munching on chips and salsa. "Helped myself," Gage said. "Since I'm kinda familiar with the layout."

"You should work here," Mateo said. He finished his message, hit Send, and waited for Nadia to reply. Surely she'd get back to him right away.

But she didn't.

Nadia stared at her phone's screen for the better part of an hour before she accepted that Mateo wasn't going to reply.

Maybe he fell asleep. He had to be exhausted.

Try as she might, Nadia couldn't convince herself of that. Mateo just—didn't want to talk to her. Wasn't ready.

Maybe she could believe that much. That he just wasn't ready.

That night, Mateo was so exhausted and miserable he didn't even bother taking his usual Tylenol PM. His worry about Nadia had escalated to fear, but there was nothing he could do—not if she wouldn't even talk to him. The hopelessness dragged him down even further, until all he could think about was going to sleep. He showered to get the weird musty smell of floodwater off him, then passed out almost the moment he collapsed into bed.

But he wasn't too tired to dream.

Mateo's hands rested on the thorny halo around his head. Usually the dark, twisting thorns were something he could see only in the mirror because of his Steadfast powers, but now they were real and tangible. One of the thorns pricked his skin, and when he pulled that hand away, a single bead of red blood welled in the center of his palm.

"Don't take it off," Nadia pleaded. She stood next to him in what looked like a room in an abandoned house—cobwebs in every corner, windows gray and opaque with dust, and bits of old paper strewn on the scuffed floor. "You can't take it off."

"I have to." Mateo could feel the thorns pressing through his scalp, as though the halo was digging itself into his flesh. But the pain wasn't the reason he needed to rid himself of it. He couldn't remember the reason right now, but he knew it was the most important thing to him in the world.

Nadia shook her head. Tears welled in her dark eyes. "Then wait. If you wait just a little while longer—"

"Wait for what?" He tried to turn to her, but she never seemed to be in the same place from moment to moment. Although Nadia never took a single step, she was near him, far, in the corner, at the door, right in front of his face—in the strange, changeable way of dreams. Why would she ever tell him to wear the thorns? "Nadia, why do I need to wait?"

"You need to wait because of these."

She held out her wrists, and he saw, to his horror, that she wore shackles. The metal was newly forged, glowing with heat, and the cuffs were burning into her skin. Through her flesh, down to bone.

"Nadia—"

Mateo woke up, looked around, and thought, *Shit. Where am I this time?*

He lay on someone's back porch—out of the rain, although he'd obviously gotten soaked on the way there. At this rate he was going to forget how it felt to be dry. Shivering, Mateo pushed himself upright and glanced around.

From the looks of things he had wandered more than half a mile inland from the beach, to the porch of someone's yellow house. Yellow with dark green shutters: Wasn't this the Bender place?

Great. I walked straight to the house of the loudest mouth in Captive's Sound. If Kendall sees me, she'll tell everyone.

Not that almost everyone hadn't already written Mateo off as hopelessly insane—but mostly he just wanted to get home before Dad woke up. Apparently it was just past dawn, although the sky was so cloudy and dark Mateo could hardly tell. When was the last time he'd seen the sun? Seemed like days.

He was so cold. His feet and hands were numb. Mateo pressed on his toes—no frostbite, thank goodness—but the walk back in the rain was going to suck.

As he stood up, he saw the Benders' garden shed. Maybe Mr. Bender had a Windbreaker or gardening gloves out there. Galoshes. Something that might help. Mateo could sneak by later and put back anything he borrowed, probably before anybody knew it was gone . . .

"Mateo?"

He turned around to see Kendall Bender standing at the back door, staring at him through the glass. She wore an oversize pajama top and held a cup full of something steaming and warm, probably coffee. At any rate, she was definitely awake enough to remember this later on. It took all his strength not to swear out loud. "Uh, yeah. Hi. Sorry. I was, um, sleepwalking again. You know."

Kendall just stared.

Mateo hated it when people thought he was crazy. He hated it most when it felt like they might be right. Standing there on the Benders' porch, with Kendall staring at him, he felt weirder and lower and closer to the brink than ever before. Probably she would call the police at any second.

"Do you want some coffee?" Kendall asked. When he didn't answer right away, she lifted her cup. "It's, like, this special blend or something from South America, or maybe Central America, but it just tastes like regular coffee."

". . . Sure."

He stood there shivering until Kendall returned, pushing the door open and bearing a souvenir mug from Epcot. "Here you go. Do you want a jacket? My dad is way bigger than you, but it's not like anybody will see you. Besides me. And I'm seeing someone, so it's not like you have to show off for me."

"Kendall—why are you being so nice to me?"

She sighed. "Listen, like, I was talking to my mom who was talking to my dad who was talking to all these people in town, about all the freaky stuff that's been happening, with the sickness and the fire and the flooding and all of that? And at first you think it's bad luck, but then you start to go, like, there is a pattern here. This isn't right. People are starting to catch on."

Mateo couldn't quite follow. "Catch on to what, exactly?"

Kendall put down her coffee mug and folded her arms. "Supernatural stuff. The occult. Oh, my God, catch up."

He had no idea what to say.

"So I was thinking, you know, everyone says your family is cursed, which I think everybody meant more like a metaphor but is starting to make sense," Kendall said. "Mateo, do you think you act all freaky like this because, like, a witch put some kind of spell on you?"

Did she say . . . "A witch?"

"Or some kind of voodoo or something, although I don't know who around here would do voodoo. Maybe that weird Vera Laughton girl, I don't know. People were just saying, that's all. It makes sense. Do you maybe think that's what happened to you?"

If she'd said nothing, or accused him of madness, Mateo would have lied his way out of it. But hearing the truth—hearing something like understanding, from Kendall of all people—it seemed to break him open. The words poured out. "That's what happened. To my whole family."

Kendall's eyes widened. "Ohmigod."

"A witch cursed us more than two centuries ago." Even now, Mateo knew better than to accuse Elizabeth. "That's why we go crazy, you see? We really do have dreams about the future. But you can't understand them until—sometimes until it's too late. I never know exactly what the dreams mean until too late, and I wake up all over town, and it makes people think—"

All the pent-up hurt from a lifetime of ostracism welled up. It was too much to take all at once. Maybe if he hadn't been cold, and freaked out, and scared to death for Nadia—

"Hey," Kendall said. Her voice was softer than he'd ever heard it before. "Your coffee's getting cold."

Coffee. Right. Coffee is good. He took a couple of sips, and the hot coffee in his belly seemed to steady him. Within a few moments, Mateo felt almost like himself again.

Kendall finally said, "You could've told us, you know. Like, you could've just explained."

"Would you have believed me?"

"Not back in sophomore year. But after the past couple months, yeah." She acted like discovering the world of the supernatural was just one more bit of gossip she'd learned. "So, are you crazy right now? Because if you're not, I'll give you a ride home."

"Not crazy at the moment. And—thanks for the coffee."

She padded back into the kitchen, apparently to get her shoes. Then she stopped. "Just FYI? If you're cursed, we still have to treat you like you're dangerous."

Mateo hated to admit it, but—"That makes sense."

"But we'll understand."

"That helps."

Nadia awoke still wearing her bathrobe. She'd curled into a ball on top of her bedspread, too miserable and freaked-out to even get ready for bed. Groggily she turned over to grab her phone from its charging dock. Still nothing from Mateo . . . until the phone buzzed in her hand.

Mateo's message didn't accuse her, didn't comfort her. He just said, *Dreamed again. Went wandering again. Woke up on Kendall's porch.*

Another volley of gossip from Kendall was the last thing they needed. But then she read Mateo's next text.

Kendall realized I'd been cursed, for real. Apparently everyone in town is talking about witchcraft. Are they just being superstitious or do they actually know something??

Eyes wide, Nadia pushed herself upright as she continued to stare down at the screen. It wasn't like she'd had no warning this could happen. There had been weird scenes in town for months now, setting everyone on edge—and Verlaine had told her how a few people had begun talking about the supernatural during the terrible "epidemic" in November. Nadia had hoped that was nothing but panic, people losing it because they were scared for a moment.

Now, as the rain kept coming, people were even more afraid. And in their paranoia, the mob had hit on the truth.

They know. The Craft has been exposed.

Nadia shuddered—then told herself that couldn't be right. Okay, people in Captive's Sound suspected witchcraft. This didn't mean they had any idea how witchcraft actually worked, who the witches around them actually were. Nobody in this town had any facts. Only suspicions, hysteria, and conjecture.

Wasn't that even worse? Nadia didn't mind the idea of a torch-wielding mob chasing Elizabeth out of town. That was what they would do if they knew the whole story—which they didn't. Instead, people were going to start turning on one another. Suspecting their friends and neighbors . . .

No. People never turned against their friends first. Nadia had learned that from her mother, and seen it for herself by studying how people around the globe were still persecuted for witchcraft (mostly without any real cause). When people went looking for a witch, they didn't look at the people closest to them. Certainly they didn't look at the beautiful, beloved Elizabeth Pike, a teenager who seemed to be a friend to all. Accused witches were loners. Outsiders. The people already cast out from society, and looked down upon. Old women, or the disfigured, or those who had already experienced bad luck: An accusation of witchcraft was always made against the most vulnerable first.

The people who can least defend themselves, Nadia thought, the fear within her deepening. *The ones who've already suffered enough.*

How many more victims would Elizabeth claim before the end?

"How come we moved away from Chicago?" Cole whined.

That is a damned good question, Simon Caldani thought but didn't say. "First of all, it's not 'how come.' It's why."

"Then why did we move away from Chicago?"

"Because I got a new job, and I thought we all needed a fresh start." Some fresh start this was. He sighed as he drove the car toward Cole's kindergarten, trying to find a route where none of the streets were waterlogged.

Cole kicked at his car seat. He hadn't been able to burn off energy by playing outside for days now, and Nadia seemed to have a lot on her mind, so she hadn't had as much time for her brother. Simon's little boy was restless and uneasy; he knew how that felt.

"I don't like it here. Only bad things ever happen here," Cole said.

"Hey, that's not true," Simon said. "Remember how you love having a backyard?"

"I can't play in the yard until it stops raining."

"Well, that's true. But it can't rain forever."

Cole peered out of the car window. "I think maybe it can."

Simon turned a corner to see yet another washed-out street . . . and a car that had apparently stalled trying to drive through it. A woman in a waterproof jacket too large for her was peering under the hood, clearly unsure how to get out of this mess.

"Hey, buddy, we're going to help one of our neighbors for

a few minutes. Stay in the car for me?" When Cole nodded, Simon got out of the car and called, "Looks like you could use a hand!"

When the woman turned, he recognized Archana Prasad. She held one hand above her eyes to block the rain as she smiled. "Mr. Caldani! Never have I been so glad to see anyone."

Simon went to her car and gave her the most reassuring smile he could manage in the cold rain. "Couldn't get the police out here?"

"The police are too busy, with all the flooding. Every business downtown with a basement has water damage, and some are washed out entirely." Mrs. Prasad shook her head. "My husband is on the town council, you know. They're having an emergency meeting, so I couldn't reach him, and I didn't want my son to be late for school."

Cole was going to be late for school, but Simon doubted he'd mind. "Come on. You get in and put the car in neutral, and I'll push."

He sloshed into the knee-deep water, thinking that he really ought to buy a pair of hip waders—but the store was probably completely out by now. As Simon began pushing the car forward, another passerby waded out to help. He turned to give the guy a smile, then tensed slightly as he recognized Tony Bender.

The last time they'd met, Mr. Bender had been seriously, nearly criminally losing his temper—taking a swing at Alejandro Perez that had nearly hit Nadia. Simon tried not to hold it against him, because his daughter had been sick at the time and God knew that could mess with a man's mind. Still, it didn't seem like the start of a beautiful friendship, either.

Once they got the car to higher ground, Mrs. Prasad put it in park and Simon started emptying the water from her spark plugs, so she might be able to drive again. Instead of helping, Mr. Bender started talking to Mrs. Prasad. "My family and I got to talking this morning about what's been going on in this town. How things around here aren't right."

"It's just rain," Simon said, a little too forcefully. People in this town couldn't leave a bad situation alone; they had to add superstition to the mix.

"Just rain?" Mr. Bender lifted his chin, as though preparing for a punch. In the distance, Simon saw a Weather TV van rumble by—which made Mr. Bender's point for him. "Was it just rain that made a fire start in the middle of the Halloween carnival, even though nobody's been able to find a single candle or old cigarette or bad wire that might've set it off? Just rain that made my little girl sick last month, and all those people, too? And forgive me for mentioning it, Archana, but it wasn't just rain that made you lose sight of reality that night at the Town Hall."

"Don't remind me. I'm so ashamed." Mrs. Prasad hung her head, but her dark eyes looked to Mr. Bender's for reassurance. "They said it must have been my medications affecting my mind, and yet no one else has ever had the same side effects. The drug has been out for many years. So why should I be the only one made crazy by it?"

Mr. Bender leaned closer. "What do you remember? What was it like?"

"At first—at first I thought my son was a demon. My Jeremy, who I love more than anything in this world. I wanted to attack him, even to kill him. It's almost too horrible to remember." Her voice broke, and despite his irritation, Simon couldn't help feeling sorry for her. No wonder she'd look for an explanation, no matter how strange, if something had made her want to hurt her own child. "Then all the people turned into demons. Not just Jeremy, but everyone. It seemed to me that if I didn't kill them all, they would kill us."

Mr. Bender looked triumphant. "Does that sound like a medication side effect to you, Caldani? Because it sure doesn't to me."

During his former life as a big-firm litigator, Simon had heard more horror stories about pharmaceuticals than he could have retold in an hour. So he cut to the chase. "What else? Seriously. What else do you think could possibly make people see demons?"

"They can see demons if the demons are real," Mr. Bender said.

Mrs. Prasad gasped—more out of shock than fear, Simon thought. Surely she didn't believe anything that crazy. "Demons? Come on." He pointed skyward. "Don't you think if the devil were after us, he'd come up with something scarier than a rain cloud?"

"Some kids nearly drowned last night. Kids the same age as our daughters. If that doesn't scare you, I don't know what will." Mr. Bender met Simon's eyes, and he no longer came across as a blowhard. He was just another father, one who needed an enemy he could see, and fight, to keep his children safe. More quietly, Mr. Bender said, "Need some help with that car?"

"Nope. Got it." Simon managed to smile as Mr. Bender nodded and went on his way.

By now Cole was loudly singing along to the radio, happily kicking up his feet in the backseat, assuming (wrongly) that he was too late for school to have to go at all. Simon finished up for Mrs. Prasad as quickly as he could. "Here. Try it now."

She laughed out loud when the car's engine revved. "You're a miracle worker, Mr. Caldani."

"Simon, please. And no trouble."

"If you're Simon, I'm Archana." Her smile faded. "What Mr. Bender said—do you think there's any truth to it? That the demons and witchcraft I saw might have been real?"

"I'm sure it seemed real. But, come on. There are places experiencing floods all around the world every day. It's just our turn." He gave her a pat on the shoulder, hoping to reassure her.

She nodded, but her expression remained doubtful. "And yet there was also the fire, and the terrible disease. We were under quarantine two weeks ago! I realize it's superstitious to think of . . . other explanations. But you can't help wondering."

Another voice behind him said, "I know I'm wondering. And I'm scared."

Simon turned to see Elizabeth Pike standing near them, still in one of her pretty white dresses. It never occurred to him to wonder whether she ought to be outside without a coat on a rainy December day; he just smiled. Now that Elizabeth seemed to have gotten over her little crush on him, Simon was happy to see her again. Such a nice girl. "There's no need to be scared, Elizabeth."

"Don't tell her that," Mrs. Prasad said. She edged closer to Elizabeth, clearly protective. "You need to watch yourself, young lady. Don't run any unnecessary risks."

"I won't." Elizabeth turned toward Simon, still heartbreakingly lovely. "Just like I know Nadia takes care. She's very cautious, makes sure she won't be seen."

"What do you mean?" Simon asked.

Elizabeth said only, "I'm sure Nadia is careful. But tell her to be safe? I would never want her to do anything dangerous." She turned to Mrs. Prasad then. "We should all be more careful these days. Could I ride with you?"

"Of course, dear," Archana said, giving Elizabeth's shoulder a motherly pat.

Did Mrs. Prasad even say where she was going? But the question didn't linger in Simon's mind. It couldn't. He was simply glad Elizabeth was being looked after.

As he got back in the car, Simon found himself remembering what Elizabeth had said about his daughter. Her words were cryptic, and unsettling, and they stayed with him far longer than any questions about Elizabeth Pike.

❦

Vintage clothes were awesome and everything, but Verlaine was only prepared to sacrifice one beautiful '40s dress to the rain gods. From now on her outfits were going to be a bit more action-ready. So: 1970s high-waisted jeans and peasant blouse, complete with floppy hat for rain cover.

"Bring it," Verlaine muttered as she looked into the mirror and cocked her hat just so.

Technically she could have skipped school. Uncle Dave and Uncle Gary would've let her, since they hadn't stopped freaking out since the firefighters had called them last night. She'd been made to drink hot tea and hotter soup, and she'd awoken to find that Uncle Gary had layered about four blankets on top of her during the night. ("You could have died of hypothermia down there! Freezing cold water can be fatal! Don't you remember *Titanic*?")

But Verlaine had reporting to do.

"Hi! Verlaine Laughton, reporting for the *Lightning Rod*—"

"I know who you are," Mrs. Purdhy said patiently. "You're in my sixth period physics class."

"Right, yes, but we're supposed to do the interviews like we would in the real world." Verlaine angled her phone to show a little more of the rain-spattered windows behind Mrs. Purdhy. "How have you personally been affected by the flooding?"

"Our house is on high ground, thank goodness. So we're all right." But she glanced to the side, clearly ill at ease. "Still, everything that's been going on in this town recently—it makes you wonder whether maybe it's time to move. I hear the Midwest is nice."

Verlaine made a quick note to herself—*potential teacher departure at end of year, prepare good-bye tribute?*—and kept collecting interviews. She spoke to students and teachers alike, rich and poor, from the top of the social ladder to the bottom rung, one of the lunch ladies, two of the janitors . . . but despite the diverse cross section of people, one theme kept coming up over and over again.

"Something spooky is going on here," said sophomore Carlie Cahill. "The haunted house seemed like just an accident, but everything since then? We've made God angry or something."

School secretary Kari Johnston shook her head. "Dark forces are at work. Spirits. You mark my words." Kari clutched her books tightly to her chest, and when Verlaine took a step forward, she skittered back.

You'd think I'd pulled a knife or something. Verlaine sighed. *Some people.*

"Some people say it's witches. I don't know if I believe that or not, but something is definitely, for sure, not right," said track star Sonny Adcock as he zipped his waterproof coat before heading to the gym building. He never once looked her in the eyes.

"It's totally witches," Kendall Bender said blithely as she slid her books into her locker. "Because, like, that disease last month was definitely not normal, plus maybe the haunted house was built on an ancient Indian burial mound—excuse me, Native American burial mound, and also, it turns out Mateo Perez? We all thought he was just a total weirdo? It turns out a witch cursed his family hundreds of years ago and that's why he acts that way. He told me so himself."

"Mateo—told you this?" Verlaine attempted to conceal her shock. What, were they in full-disclosure mode now? Why didn't anybody tell her?

"Yeah. Explains a lot, right?" Kendall shut her locker door and shrugged. "After school I'm going by St. Mary's to get some holy water. Like, we're not Catholic, but Protestants don't have any holy water, which is a serious problem and I think we should look into it. That should be a story."

"I'll bring it up at the next editorial meeting."

Once she'd really thought about it, the town's sudden turn toward the spooky wasn't so astonishing. Maybe they didn't understand the real supernatural forces at work, but too many strange things had happened for people not to realize something was up. (Also, apparently Mateo was going around filling people in on the details, which she needed to learn more about, pronto.)

Yet Verlaine remembered the first time the town's fears had fixated on witchcraft. The crowd at the hospital had turned ugly, which had freaked her out, but it was worse than that.

They had turned on her.

When she got home, she immediately locked the door behind her, and put on the chain, too. Grabbed a snack and the cat, went into her bedroom, and locked that door. Still feeling the need to cocoon, she dug in her closet until she found the leopard-print Slanket her dads had given her as a gag gift a couple of birthdays ago.

Once she was wrapped up in it, Verlaine finally felt a little safer. *A little more ridiculous, too,* she thought as she caught a glimpse of herself in her mirror. *I look like a spotted potato.*

Her phone rang; it was Asa.

"I was going to ask how you are," he said, "but your hello sounded like you were about to start laughing."

"Because I look like an idiot in this Slanket," she said.

"What is a Slanket?"

"Something not even hell could come up with. Don't ask."

"But you're all right?"

She bit her lower lip, cradled the phone against her cheek. "Yeah."

"I couldn't stay—"

"Because EMTs would've figured out something was up. I know that." *I know you wouldn't leave me after something like that, not unless you had to.*

Dangerous and adored. He was both of these things to her, and she couldn't untangle one from the other.

"Asa," she ventured, "how did you become a demon?"

"I traded myself for revenge for my sister's death."

It amazed her to think of him being like just another normal guy, with a house and a family and a life. "How did she die?"

"Murdered, by a Sorceress. I don't think she was a witch;

I think she just—got in someone's way. Or maybe her death was merely convenient, like Jeremy's. I only know how much it hurt to lose her."

"Tell me about her. You must have loved her a lot."

"I must have done." His voice was more ragged now. "But you see, when I made my bargain, I wasn't clear enough. I asked to avenge her. I didn't also say that I wanted to remember her. Being in the demonic realm—it does things to your mind. Warps your memory of who and what you were before. All that's left of my sister is how much I loved her. I can hardly picture her face. I don't even remember her name."

Verlaine's throat tightened. "I'm sorry."

"Me too."

They were quiet together on the phone for a few moments. She wanted to think of some way to comfort him, but she couldn't. Maybe it was enough just to listen. To be there.

When Asa spoke again, his words were brisk. "So. You're warm and safe. And alive. Good job, us."

"Thank you for coming with me," she said. "I don't think I would've made it out of there without you."

"I'm glad I could be there to help you—this time."

It was always between them, the threat of what was to come.

Just as she hung up, though, she thought . . . *to avenge his sister.*

To avenge a sister?

Verlaine climbed out of bed and grabbed Goodwife Hale's

spell book. By now she'd placed bookmarks in most of the demon-heavy sections, so she was able to immediately flip to the part she'd been thinking of. *Of His Demons and Their Purposes.*

When she'd first found this ledger, she'd been pumped. This was a list of demons! Asa's name had to be on there, right? But the list went on for page after page, enumerating dozens of demons, and it was clear that the list was far from comprehensive.

What had puzzled Verlaine were the notations beside each demon's name; they all said things like *For Power* or *To Slake His Lust.* She'd wondered if those were the talents the demons had, the kinds of magic the One Beneath would use them for. But now she realized—these were the things the demons had traded their mortal lives for.

And beside one of those names was written *To Avenge a Sister.*

She whispered, "Asael."

With his true name, she had the final ingredient—the last thing she needed in order to kill him.

She could've put this part off longer. But Verlaine figured she couldn't feel much more scared and awful than she did at the moment; she might as well get it over with.

In the back of Mrs. Walsh's Book of Shadows, on a page that had never been fully filled in, Verlaine wrote the name. Her handwriting was shaky, but she figured it still counted.

Asael.

Once she'd torn that out, she went to her bookshelf and got something a couple of young men in neckties had given her as part of their missionary work, during the summer; Verlaine had taken it just so they'd feel like they'd accomplished something. Since her dads weren't very religious, this Book of Mormon was the only holy book in the house. One more page, and atop the verses she wrote again, *Asael*.

By now her hands were trembling, but Verlaine kept going. The last time they'd gotten papers back in Novels class, Asa hadn't paid much attention to his; Verlaine had been able to swipe it. A paper he wrote counted as something he possessed, didn't it?

Tears filled her eyes as she wrote *Asael* the third and final time.

She'd thought she couldn't feel any worse, but she'd been wrong.

Nadia didn't even go to school that day. She knew she ought to touch base with Verlaine. Maybe she should have wanted to see Mateo, too—even after he'd blown her off last night. He'd gotten in touch this morning, but only because he was freaking out about waking up on Kendall's porch. The mature thing to do, Nadia figured, was to talk it out with him. What she actually wanted to do was bury her head under her covers for the next twenty years or so.

Her screwed-up feelings about Mateo weren't why she stayed away from Rodman, though. The truth was a whole lot worse than that. Even now, Nadia could feel the pull dragging her back toward Elizabeth's, like it was in her very bones. Was it a kind of magnetism? It was that powerful, that primal.

Almost like being in love, Nadia thought, and shuddered.

When she walked in, Elizabeth wasn't sitting in the front room as usual. After a moment, Nadia heard footsteps on the back steps, and then Elizabeth walked in, her chestnut curls damp. Mud was spattered on her hands and bare feet. She smiled. "How fortunate that you're here. We need to cast another spell of falling apart. A stronger one, this time."

"What do you mean, fortunate?" Nadia said.

Elizabeth didn't even seem to notice that she'd spoken. The smile on her face was genuine—almost gleeful.

That was when it hit Nadia: She hadn't been summoned here. Elizabeth and the One Beneath hadn't called her. The inexorable, undeniable pull she'd felt drawing her toward Elizabeth's house—the attraction and the desire—it had all come from inside her.

Panic locked Nadia in its grip, stealing her focus and almost her breath. *It can't be, it's impossible, I know my own mind and I would never, ever choose to come here.*

Except she had.

It felt good to stand in Elizabeth's house, amid her magic. The warmth from the stove was strangely intoxicating, as though it gave off a kind of perfume Nadia had never been able to smell before. "The stove," she said. It was the only thing she could think of to say. "What's in the stove?"

"Everything I ever stole," Elizabeth said offhandedly as

she took her place on the floor. "Join me. You know the ingredients."

As though sleepwalking, Nadia walked to Elizabeth and sat down. Even as her spirit protested, her fingers seemed to move to the agate charm on her bracelet of their own accord. When the time came to summon the ingredients, Nadia dove into it, unable to resist the pull of the spell.

A woman weeping for something lost forever—Sobbing on the bus after leaving her mother's new apartment in Chicago, knowing Mom would never love her again. The memory twisted, introducing anger Nadia hadn't felt, stealing her hard-won forgiveness.

A time when you were cruelly betrayed—Her horrified realization that Mateo had made out with Elizabeth, that he'd kissed her, held her, as tenderly as he'd ever kissed Nadia. But she didn't let herself think of the fact that Elizabeth had deceived him, that Mateo had thought he was with Nadia the entire time.

And a time when you cruelly betrayed another—Now. This moment. When she cast a spell of darkness with all her might and betrayed everyone she had ever loved.

The power surged through her like electricity: jolting her bones, her nerves. Nadia gasped as she felt it, and imagined she could hear cracking and crumbling all around her. In the first instant she wondered whether Elizabeth's derelict house was finally about to collapse, but then she realized the sounds weren't the kind you heard with your ears.

It wasn't Elizabeth's house that was falling apart. It was Captive's Sound itself—no. Her entire world.

❧ ❧

You're sure you haven't seen Nadia? Mateo texted. It wasn't like her to skip. Once again he thought of how she'd taken off last night, and how she'd blown off the text he'd sent her then. This morning, when he'd been freaking out, Nadia had acted normal, and he thought maybe it would all blow over. Maybe last night she'd been so tired she fell asleep right away. Or Cole could've been having his bad dreams again, so maybe Nadia didn't want to leave her little brother. Mateo had told himself it was no big deal.

But she hadn't gone to school. She hadn't texted him to explain—and it was her turn to reach out to him, definitely, so he hadn't texted her either. By now, Nadia was definitely AWOL.

Verlaine sent back: *Positive, and also, you still haven't explained how Kendall Bender of all people figured out witchcraft was real.*

She didn't figure it out on her own. Everyone knows, by now. She flat out asked me, so what was I supposed to do? Lie about it?

Yes. Lying is the game plan. The only plan we have!

Which was depressing. And true.

Mateo had a choice to make. One, spend the night at home. Make some nachos, play Assassin's Creed, and basically chill out for the first time in what felt like a zillion years. After a while he might even do the homework that was still due because his teachers didn't know about the impending apocalypse.

Or two, find Nadia and learn what the hell was going on—even if he didn't like the answer.

He rode his motorcycle straight to Nadia's house.

Mateo knew she might not be there—and that if she wasn't, then he'd probably find her at Elizabeth's. Although he never wanted to set foot in that creepy house, he'd search it top to bottom if he had to. He needed to be with her, to find out what was going on, because otherwise he couldn't take it.

By the time he reached the Caldani house, Mateo had braced himself to head to Elizabeth's, but Nadia opened the door. She smiled when she saw him, but the happiness didn't touch her eyes. "I was wondering where you were."

"Same thing." Mateo found it hard to speak. All he could do was stare at Nadia.

She didn't look like herself. Nadia had never been one of those girls who wore heels to school or did complicated stuff with her hair every day, but she always looked—pulled together. Sleek. Now her hair was loose and unkempt, and her shirt was rumpled, hanging on her crookedly. She looked like . . . like she did after they'd been making out. Even something about her energy reminded Mateo of the way she felt when they'd been kissing, touching, getting to the brink.

Only then did he realize something struck him as odd about the house, something besides the twisted electricity between them. It was the silence. No video games, no cartoons—"Um, where's Cole?"

"Spending the night at a friend's house. Dad's out of town for a mediation meeting, and without the car I can't pick Cole up in this weather, so a friend's mom said he could stay over, even on a school night. Cole thinks he's getting away with something awesome." Her voice—low and sultry—suggested that she and Mateo could get away with a whole lot more if they seized the moment.

On one level, Mateo knew that was a bad idea.

On most levels, he didn't care if it was a bad idea or not. He just had to touch her.

He slung one arm around her neck, pulling her close. Nadia gasped, but when he leaned in for the kiss, she opened her mouth.

They'd never kissed like this before. Like they were starving for each other. He clutched her against him and backed her against the wall. Nadia hooked one leg around his as his hands slid inside her shirt.

Mateo realized this was screwed up. They needed to talk. Like, seriously talk. Instead they were pawing at each other like they wanted to get each other naked this minute. If they didn't stop soon, they'd wind up in bed.

He didn't stop.

She pushed his jacket off his shoulders. Mateo pressed his whole body against hers, making her whimper, a sound that took away almost all the self-control he had left. Then her hands went to his belt buckle, and Mateo felt—

—it wasn't only desire, or need. It was that strange pulse of energy that had coursed through him last night, when Nadia had performed black magic.

That's what I want so much. The darkness.

Mateo felt like a bucket of ice water had just been dumped

over him. He pulled himself out of Nadia's embrace; she stared at him, panting, her shirt undone so that he could see the white lace of her bra. "Mateo?" she said. Her voice shook. "What's wrong?"

"You know what we're doing right now—you sense that it's not us, right?" He didn't know how else to put it. "Something else is affecting us."

After a moment, Nadia nodded. She turned slightly away as she rebuttoned her shirt; Mateo redid his belt and tried to think about baseball statistics for a minute. Nadia walked a few steps from him, then hugged herself as she leaned against the arched doorway into their living room.

"What's going on?" he said. "Tell me."

"Is it so strange, that I'd want you? That I'd want to make the most of some time alone in this house with my boyfriend?" Her smile was crooked. Warped. "Or can't you believe that you want me? Am I so awful to you now that I work with Elizabeth?"

"Yeah, I'm so not attracted to you that I nearly tore your clothes off." Mateo ran his hands through his hair. "Think, okay? Just think. We've hardly been talking to each other. But now—we come together—and it's like something else is taking us over. It's not right. You know it."

After a long moment, she nodded. "Yes. I know."

It felt as though he had to beg the truth from her, tear it out word by word. "Then what is it? Tell me. You can tell me anything."

"Elizabeth's magic is changing me."

"Are you okay? What did she do to you?" Had Elizabeth cursed Nadia, too? Wasn't bringing her under the control of the One Beneath enough? Mateo clenched his jaw.

Nadia shook her head. "Not Elizabeth. At least, not directly. The magic itself is changing me into someone else. Someone I hardly recognize."

The dark magic he'd felt during the flood—that was what had her scared. "I know you've had to do some terrible things, but that's only because Elizabeth made you. It won't always be this bad."

"It's going to get worse before it gets better. If it ever gets better."

"Don't say that. We're going to win this. You're learning about how she's breaking the One Beneath into this world, so we can stop it."

"I'm not learning enough, and even if I do stop her in time to save everybody else, I don't think—it's not going to be in time to save me." Nadia's voice broke. Mateo tried to reach out to her again, but she pulled away. As she paced back and forth, she tugged at her messy hair; her eyes were red with unshed tears.

He kept his voice gentle. "You're not going to die."

"Death isn't what I'm afraid of." She went very still as she turned to him. He sensed that a decision had been made— the wrong decision. Her gaze was distant, as though she'd never been farther away. "I'm afraid of changing forever. I'm afraid of turning into someone I'd never want to be. Already I've turned into someone besides the person you fell in love with. You don't even know who I am. Who I've become."

She was still herself. But now she was someone else, too—the Sorceress she might become. It was Nadia he loved, but it was the Sorceress who had made him want to forget everything else in the world and slam her against the nearest wall.

He wanted her, and he feared her, and he knew nothing except that he shouldn't let her go.

So he stood to face her and chose his words carefully. "I'm your Steadfast. That means I keep you strong, right? And you do the same for me. Not with the magic, anything like that—but you keep me going, every day. Even if you're . . . changing, the most important things remain the same. They have to." Was he getting through? The expression in her dark eyes was like nothing else he'd ever seen in her or in anyone else. "Nadia—I know you. Better than I know myself. I know you."

Mateo stepped closer, trying to break down the wall she was building between them, but Nadia shook her head. "Not anymore."

This can't be happening. She wouldn't do this to us. Not when we love each other this much.

Nadia said the words anyway. "We can't be together anymore. I love you, Mateo. I always will. But it's over. We're over."

7

ELIZABETH STOOD ON THE SEASHORE, BAREFOOT DESPITE the cold, exposed to the rain.

Her body was mortal now, vulnerable to injury and sickness. While her strength was greater than that of most humans, it was possible for her to bleed or fall sick. Yet she stood in the weather anyway. If she became ill, she would still be able to cast her magic; no disease would strike her down in the limited time this world had left.

For this spell, she needed to feel the damage she was wreaking upon Captive's Sound. She needed the chill to creep all the way through to her bones.

Elizabeth's long chestnut hair caught in the wind. She had stripped down to her white camisole and skirt; her sweater lay crumpled on the damp sand, darkening as the raindrops fell. For the moment the rainfall was lighter. Probably the people in town felt relieved, sure the storms were finally ending. They did not know, as Elizabeth did, that the lull was temporary. Even now, weather patterns across the country were changing as vast banks of clouds were drawn toward Captive's Sound. Soon the weather would be altered throughout the world.

"They will know us at last, my beloved lord," Elizabeth whispered. She knew the One Beneath was near, just beneath the surface of the dark, storm-chopped waves. Listening. Waiting. "They will have time to prepare. The wise will kneel to greet you."

She sensed His pleasure at the thought, and turned her face upward, smiling into the rain. The shivers sweeping through her felt more like shudders of pleasure.

Within her she sensed the One Beneath's response to her thoughts—the comforting, total possessiveness He felt at knowing her to be His most perfect servant, and yet something else, too . . .

The One Beneath's attention wandered, fixated on the thought that Nadia's heart was not yet fully His own. Oh, yes, she owed Him her loyalty now; the darkness had its claws in her, and Elizabeth was enjoying watching the girl's slow deterioration. But that fall was not complete until Nadia was at a point of no turning back.

"Do you want her so very much?" Elizabeth whispered.

Yes. He did. He wanted Nadia more hungrily, more passionately, than He had ever wanted anything else.

More, Elizabeth realized, than He had ever wanted her.

She'd been jealous of Nadia before. Jealous of her inherent

fitness for dark magic, which gave her abilities at seventeen that Elizabeth had not acquired until she was nearly a century old. Yet that was nothing compared to the consuming envy Elizabeth felt at knowing how deeply Nadia was desired by the One Beneath.

This girl who disdains Him. This girl who serves Him only because she must. Whereas I have given Him everything, fought for Him, suffered for Him, lived centuries with no thought other than His escape and His glory—

The One Beneath recognized Elizabeth's jealousy, of course. As she had known He would, He delighted in it. Her jealousy was the proof of her love.

He demands proof still. He will demand proof until the end.

Elizabeth held her hands out. "I will give her to you, my lord. I have given you Nadia Caldani's service, but I will also give you her soul."

Then, at last, Elizabeth would be the most loved.

Kneeling upon the sand, she raked one of her hands through the sand to find a seashell, its broken edge sharp as any knife. A thin trickle of blood flowed into the sand in a snaky path, enough for her to travel by. She called upon the bonds that now tethered Nadia's soul to darkness, and so to Elizabeth herself. The blood bore her out of her own body so that her mind could slip into Nadia's as thin, swift, and silent as a switchblade.

What she found was pain—fresh and sharp as the cut on Elizabeth's arm.

The wedge she'd driven between Nadia and Mateo had

worked. Last night they had parted. Without her Steadfast, Nadia would be weaker; without the certainty of her human love, Nadia would be off-balance. More easily confused, and so more easily turned.

Other factors still tied Nadia to the human world, however.

Those would have to go, too.

Elizabeth could not use this spell often—her spell for reaching into the thoughts of another. It was some of the most dangerous magic anyone could perform. As much as she enjoyed contaminating minds, there was always the risk of being contaminated in return.

So she used her spell carefully, slipping into Nadia's mind and cloaking her suggestion as one of Nadia's own thoughts. *I need to be with someone right now. I need a friend.*

Swiftly Elizabeth withdrew. There was no need to watch Nadia further. She knew Nadia would go to the only friend she had left . . . and because Elizabeth knew the demon Asa, and what he was probably doing, she knew the rest would take care of itself.

No matter how many times Verlaine explained to her dads that being cold and wet didn't actually make people catch colds ("Those are viruses."), they would never believe her. So this afternoon, she sat in her room amid the nest of stuff they'd given her just in case: cough medicine, sinus-headache painkiller, a thermometer, an actual honest-to-God hot-water bottle, and the Slanket. As she scrolled through her Tumblr dash, she saw the usual array of pictures—One Direction, artsy hipster sunset, GIFs of Leonardo DiCaprio chasing an elusive Oscar, One Direction again—and then a quote from a poem. The words struck her as so beautiful that she got a lump in her throat; she knew who this reminded her of, though she didn't even want to admit it to herself.

She hit Reblog before she could talk herself out of it, then lay back on her pillows. *You really, really need to start getting over this,* she told herself.

As if on cue, her phone rang with the ringtone she'd assigned to Asa—Nick Cave's "Red Right Hand." *Asael,* she thought, but pushed that knowledge to the back of her mind. Verlaine took a deep breath before she answered. "You're not calling to ask me to be in your group for the big project in Novels class, are you?"

"Given that said project is due in February, i.e. some months after the end of the world as we know it, I'm not overly concerned."

Last night, she'd forced herself to prepare. To think about killing Asa. And yet talking to him—joking with him—felt like the most natural thing in the world. Thinking of hurting him: that was the crazy part.

If she had only a short time left to spend with him, didn't she want to make the most of it?

Asa's tone changed, going from dry to—something that made her go warm all over. "Are you all right? I didn't see you today at school."

"I'm fine. My dads are just overprotective." She hesitated. "And you're okay? I figured you were. You seemed like you were in better shape than me and Mateo, and since you took off on your own . . ." But she'd worried anyway.

"My shins look like I tried to walk through a field of barbed wire, but besides that, yes, I'm fine."

"Oh, my God, I know, right?" Verlaine glanced down at her own legs, which were black and blue with the two dozen worst bruises she'd had in her life. "That metal staircase—it was like being caught in a food processor or something."

His low laughter sent chills along her spine. The good kind of chills. "Are your dads busy pampering you right now?"

"They're both still at work."

"So—if you had a get-well visitor, that wouldn't result in awkward family introductions?"

She hesitated. "You're right outside my house, aren't you?"

"Not in a stalker sort of way. More of an adorable-romantic-comedy way."

Despite the thousand reasons Verlaine knew this was a bad idea, she started to smile. "Come on in out of the rain."

Instantly, the doorbell rang.

She dashed to answer; when she opened the door, Asa was smiling, too—trim black asymmetrical jacket spattered with rain, cell phone still in his hand. "Gotta let you go," he said into the phone. "Just ran into this hot girl I know."

"You don't want to keep her waiting." Verlaine cut her phone off just as he did.

Asa stepped into the hallway, but he didn't fully shut the door behind him. "I shouldn't stay."

"Right," she said. "This is just—checking up on each

other after a life-threatening experience. The most natural thing in the world."

"Of course," Asa murmured as he ran one hand through her hair. Verlaine stepped closer, like the rest of her was a whole lot more sure about this than her brain was. "Now, what in the world do you have on today?"

"1970s housedress." Verlaine had thought the bright pink might cheer her up on a gloomy day. Now she wished she'd worn something sexier, as in, anything besides this comfy sack of a dress.

Asa didn't seem to mind, though. His fingers traced a line up the side of her neck, then along her chin. "How many files did you get out of the *Guardian*?"

"Not enough. But some. Thanks again for coming with me."

"You know I'd never have let you go in there alone."

There it was again, that swoony feeling that made Verlaine forget all the stuff she was supposed to remember, including the pieces of paper upstairs aligned to help her kill the same guy holding her now. "You'd better go."

"I'm going," Asa said.

He didn't move. She didn't either.

"I am." He repeated the words like he was trying to convince himself. "I'm going right now."

Even as he spoke, he leaned toward Verlaine. She parted her lips for the kiss—*how is it this good every time? How?*—and then she was basking in the heat of him, clutching the collar of his jacket in her hands—

"Verlaine?"

She startled, as did Asa. There, standing in the partly open door, was Nadia.

"What are you doing?" Nadia stepped inside to point a finger at Asa. "Have you messed with her head? Is this magic?"

"No! I wouldn't do that." Asa actually looked offended. "This is just an ordinary clandestine affair with the enemy."

"Exactly." Verlaine nodded. "What he said."

But that didn't make it much better, did it? Nadia definitely didn't think so. Her expression shifted from shock to anger; the fact that Nadia seemed angrier with Asa than with her didn't reassure Verlaine. "You, get out." Nadia jabbed her finger into Asa's arm. "Turn around, walk away, and don't come back."

"Hey! This is my house!" Verlaine stepped close to Asa again, to tell him he could stay, but he shook his head.

"Obviously you two need to talk. Just as obviously, I should find an elsewhere to be." He edged past Nadia in the hallway, as if afraid she might blow up on him like a hand grenade. But he glanced back at Verlaine from the doorway. "I'm glad you're all right."

"You too." She couldn't help smiling at Asa—but as soon as he'd shut the door behind him, she was alone with Nadia. Her smile faded. Verlaine began, "So it seems like I have some explaining to do."

"Explaining? What, you're screwing a demon from hell and you think you can explain that?"

"Screwing?" Verlaine might not have been so incredibly pissed off if she'd actually gotten to have sex with the hot guy. "It's not like that!"

"Oh, you're telling me the demon is a perfect gentleman."

"Actually, he is. Where the hell do you get off telling me who I can date?"

Nadia's eyes widened. "When he's a demon! When he serves Elizabeth and the One Beneath! When he was sent here on earth to hurt us any way he can, which he's already done—remember? You remember that, right? Don't you see this is just one more way to hurt you?"

"You're wrong." Verlaine lifted her chin, using every inch of height she had on Nadia. "Asa saved me at the hospital that day. The One Beneath punished him for it, horribly, sending him to the hell within hell—"

"Funny how Elizabeth never mentioned that." Nadia crossed her arms. "How do you know that's true? I mean, the only way you know it is because Asa told you, right?"

"Well—yes—but still. I know this is for real. Just like both of us know Asa doesn't have any choice but to be what he is. He's enslaved. He'd help us if he could."

"Maybe he would," Nadia admitted, but she wasn't any less angry. "But listen to yourself. Asa doesn't have any choice. If he's commanded to hurt us, or kill us, he does it. The end. You used to remember that. Just last week you were asking me how to kill a demon, and now you're dating one?"

"Asa's the one who warned me," Verlaine shot back. "He told me I might have to destroy him someday, and got me to find out how. Like, if I kill him, he accepts that. Do you understand how much you'd have to care about somebody to say, 'I'll die before I hurt you'?"

Nadia's eyes widened, and Verlaine realized her friend was on the verge of tears. "Of course I know," Nadia whispered. "But I also know love only takes you so far."

As infuriated as Verlaine still was, she could tell Nadia had been wound up even before she barged in here. Maybe some of her bitchtastic temper had nothing to do with Asa. "Did something happen with you and Mateo?"

"I broke up with him, because I had to, for his own good. I can't be around any of you for a while." Blinking fast, Nadia rummaged in her backpack. "I just came by to give you one thing before I go."

Verlaine's eyes widened as Nadia handed her the Cabot family dagger.

They still didn't know how the Cabots had come into possession of it in the first place. All they knew was that the hilt bore a magical symbol, and that only a blade like this had the power to kill a demon. This was the weapon she was supposed to use to kill Asa. All the elements for his murder had come together at last.

She didn't forgive Nadia that moment; it was more as though she was too stunned to remember being angry. Instead of taking the dagger, Verlaine held her hands up in surrender. "I—I don't know if I'm ready for that."

"Well, we have to get ready. You can see what's happening to this town already. Before long, nobody's even going to be pretending things are normal. Elizabeth's only going to get more powerful." Nadia hesitated, and for a moment she seemed more like her usual self than she had in a long time. "Listen, I get that you . . . think you care about Asa. I know it's weird. I know it's awful. But we're all going to have to do awful things before this is done."

She kept holding the dagger out, and finally, Verlaine took it. The metal felt cold in her hand.

Nadia's expression became closed, forbidding. "It's only going to get harder if you wait. And Elizabeth's only going to get stronger. If you intend to stop Asa, you'd better do it soon."

With that, Nadia slung her backpack over her shoulder again and walked out into the rain. Verlaine didn't even shut the door. She just stood there, frozen, watching her friend go and feeling the weight of the heavy knife in her hand.

In her memory, Asa's voice whispered, *Kill me if you can.*

"You guys broke up?" Gage said.

"We're not broken up." Mateo's fists were jammed in the pockets of his waterproof parka as he and Gage walked along. Gage had offered him a ride to the restaurant after school; Mateo, sick of riding his motorcycle through unending rain, had agreed. But nobody was allowed to park anywhere near the town square during the flooding, so they still had to go the last few blocks on foot. "Nadia and I just—aren't seeing each other right now."

From beneath the hood of his raincoat, Gage gave Mateo

a look. "To me that sounds like being broken up."

"You don't understand. She's got a lot to deal with. That's all."

"Whatever you say." They trudged on another few moments in silence, during which Mateo stared miserably at the gray, wet world around them. Down the streets he could see wooden barricades painted with yellow reflective tape, weighted down by sandbags in case the water there got higher than two or three inches. Half the businesses were closed again. La Catrina would soon have to follow suit. He knew Dad was careful with money, and saved a lot, but two closings in two months: They'd take a hit.

Worry about money later—after you worry about surviving the end of the world, okay?

Gage cleared his throat. "Listen, I'm just asking this, okay? Don't get offended."

"Uh, I'll try. What?"

"You and Nadia breaking up—does that have anything to do with your feelings toward Elizabeth?"

"No. It has zero to do with that." Mateo tried to keep his voice level. Merely hearing the name Elizabeth now had the power to make him want to put his fist through a wall.

"Not that I don't trust her," Gage said. "But I didn't want you to be—I don't know. Jealous."

Jealous? Jealous of the way this crazy evil witch turns you into her zombie whenever she wants? You're so stupid, Gage, you don't even see—

Then Gage finished, "I'd hate for anything to mess it up

for our friendship, you know?"

Mateo took the anger, reminded himself that it belonged to Elizabeth, and pushed it away from Gage. "Yeah, I know."

They parted ways just before Mateo walked into La Catrina for the dinner shift—which promised to be as dead as virtually every other shift since the rains had begun. He put up his stuff, waved to his dad in the kitchen (who was getting the refried beans started) and headed out front to start setting up the tables. Just as he did, someone rapped on the front door.

"We're—" Mateo called out, but as he looked up, he recognized who stood there, and the final word choked off.

Beyond the glass panels of the door, beneath a turquoise umbrella, stood Faye Walsh. She was one of the only people in town who knew what was really going on, and the only adult, so far as Mateo could tell.

More than that—she was a Steadfast, just like him.

Dad was busy enough that Mateo was able to let her in and sit with her for a while near the bar, talking in a low voice. Given that Faye was faculty at the high school, maybe it should have felt weird to vent to her about what had happened with Nadia. Then again, a guidance counselor ought to have the listening thing down pat.

"So what do you do?" Mateo finally said. "When the witch you're bound to pulls away from you? I'm supposed to be her strength, and right now Nadia needs all the strength she can get."

He didn't mention the darkness within Nadia, and how

powerfully it had drawn him. Mateo liked Faye and every-thing, but there was no way he was going to talk about his sex life with a faculty member.

Faye considered that for a moment before she answered. "Well, you know I was Steadfast to my mom. She pulled away from me only when she realized Alzheimer's was get-ting her. That was when she turned away from witchcraft entirely."

Insert foot in mouth. "I'm sorry. I forgot."

Faye shook her head. "No, it's okay. You made me think. The fact is, Mateo, as important as it is to stand Steadfast to a witch, we can't solve all their problems for them. We can't fight their battles. I did everything in my power to support my mother in the Craft, but ultimately we came up against an enemy neither one of us could defeat."

"I get that, but you were dealing with a disease. This is about dark magic. This is about exactly the kind of thing a Steadfast is supposed to help with, right?"

"You said Nadia feels compromised by the darkness. That she feels like the magic she's casting with Elizabeth is getting to her."

Is it ever. He remembered the heat between them, the way they'd almost made love right there, up against her wall. Mateo ran one hand through his hair, wondering why nobody understood this the way he did. "Yeah. But that's just another reason Nadia and I should be together."

Faye's full lips pursed; she looked a little like his mother had before she'd told him bad news. "As Steadfasts, we make our witches stronger. We enhance their magic. That means you strengthen the darkness in her just as much as the light."

"I can't believe that. I won't." Once again he found himself struggling to hang on to his temper. "Loving people—caring about them—that's just what black magic doesn't allow, right? Or being loved back. If that's true, Nadia needs me to love her more than ever."

"Maybe so," Faye admitted. "I thought Nadia never should have taken this on. I still doubt her judgment."

"She had to," Mateo reminded Faye, though he knew they'd all gotten in over their heads, so Faye wasn't totally wrong.

"Still, this is where we are now. Nadia has to fight that darkness, and for now she feels like she has to fight it alone. If you love her, trust her. Believe what she says. And you have to accept that sometimes—sometimes, a Steadfast can't save their witch. Sometimes it's your job to stand against her. To stop her, if you can."

That was exactly what Nadia would have said. But Mateo shook his head. "It's my job to save her. And I will."

Now he just had to figure out how.

Asa sat at his computer at home, scrolling through Verlaine's Tumblr. For the most part it seemed to be dedicated to coverage of under-reported news stories, K-pop, vintage fashion, and *Doctor Who*. Every post felt like a peek into her thoughts, a way of snooping around in the soul of this girl he had to stay away from, but wanted so much.

And some of the posts were moodier—deeper glimpses than the others. Melancholy black-and-white portraits. A GIFset of a girl from some television show saying, "I try and I try—and I am never the one." And a bit of love poetry from Pablo Neruda:

I love you as certain dark
Things are to be loved,
In secret, between the
Shadow and the soul.

Maybe she just thought they were pretty words. Maybe she hadn't been thinking of him when she posted this.

But maybe she had.

He closed his eyes, thinking of the way she'd kissed him this afternoon. If only Nadia hadn't come in—they could have had hours together in her house, in her room. Oh, for a couple of hours in Verlaine's arms . . .

"Jeremy!" his father called.

He turned, confused. Dad sounded alarmed. Scared?

Asa went down the stairs two at a time, loping to the front door to see his father zipping up his parka. "What's up? Where are you going?" It was almost dinnertime; he could smell his mother's curry simmering.

"I just got a call—the river's overflowing its banks. Every able-bodied man needs to go out and start helping with the sandbags. That includes you, if you'll go."

"Of course I'll go," Asa said. He was offended by the

suggestion that he wouldn't—until he remembered that his parents still judged him by the real Jeremy's actions, sometimes, and Jeremy probably would have refused to so much as get his shoes wet.

"Women are able-bodied, too!" his mother called from the kitchen. "Let me put this up and I'll come with you!"

Asa would have liked to argue. His mother was a tiny woman, barely over five feet. And yet he knew better than either of his parents could just how serious the situation really was. Captive's Sound needed all the help it could get.

They drove together to the forests on the outskirts of town, where a crowd had gathered. Headlights from various cars illuminated the scene: a couple hundred men and a few dozen women, all of them wearing raincoats and boots, forming a sandbag assembly line. Huge dump trucks of sand were parked farther up from the river, where their tires wouldn't sink too deeply into the gooey mud that now covered most of town. People shouted orders, not out of anger, but to be heard over the rumble of truck motors and the omnipresent rain.

"You there!" one of the men yelled at Asa. "We need young knees and backs at the riverbank."

So he ran down to join the others at the rapidly forming wall of sandbags. The intense mood caught Asa so powerfully that he'd worked for several minutes—catching the heavy sandbags tossed to him, bracing them against his chest, then settling them into the wall—before realizing he was working alongside Mateo Perez.

"You're allowed to do this?" Mateo panted.

"My parents are here, too," Asa said. In the distance, he could see Alejandro Perez helping fill bags with sand in one of the big trucks.

"I didn't mean that. I meant—isn't this the One Beneath's work? Are you allowed to undo it?"

Nobody around them was paying any attention. Why not be honest? "This is more indirect. He wants chaos here, generally, but the flooding of this one river? Probably an afterthought. If it's a problem for demons to help sandbag, trust me, I'll know." The burning straps across his chest were barely there, just a hint of something amiss, at the very edges of his consciousness.

For a few minutes they worked together in silence. Asa's demonic strength made the labor easier—but not easy. Pillow-sized bags filled with wet sand turned out to be tremendously heavy. He did not complain nor let himself slack for an instant. If frail humans could keep up this punishing work, no demon would fall behind.

Finally Mateo said, "How did you become a demon, anyway?"

"I traded my soul and my service to the One Beneath for something I wanted very badly."

"What was it? What could be worth serving in hell forever?"

"I wanted revenge."

"Revenge?" Mateo paused for one moment before resuming his work, slapping another heavy sandbag onto the wall.

"Drop it." It had been hard enough to tell Verlaine how foolish he'd been, how much of his sister was lost to him.

He didn't feel like saying it all over again for Mateo. "Let's just say, I understood I was dealing with dark magic. And I knew—I knew the only weapon against dark magic was more dark magic. Fire must be fought with fire. So I called to the One Beneath."

"How?" Mateo was staring now, fitting the sandbags into the wall almost without glancing at his work. It didn't matter; the sodden weight of them settled into the others just the same.

"You were hoping for some pagan ceremony? Fire and nudity and chanting? For that, you'll have to throw a beach party." Asa smirked. "No, if you want to give yourself to the One Beneath, He knows. He always knows."

"Did He keep His word?"

So many of the details were lost. He only knew that it had been late at night, and he had been looking up at the stars— so much brighter than they were now, unfiltered by electric light. What had he been wearing? Had he been alone? All he held on to were the stars, his fear, and his conviction.

But no time in hell, no magic in any realm, had the power to make Asa forget the way the Sorceress had screamed when her own dark power had been turned upon her. If only he could hear Elizabeth scream that way, just once.

"He did," Asa said. "The One Beneath kept His bargain. He always does."

"You mean the devil lives up to His promises?" Mateo asked. He had never stopped hauling sandbags.

"Of course. You don't understand Him yet, do you? He

always keeps His promises. He'll twist them against you if He can—and He usually can; He's talented in that way. But He keeps them. Ironically, the lord of hell is as trustworthy a partner as you'll ever find. In the end, you always learn you damned yourself more completely than He ever could."

Asa knew his sister would never have wanted to be avenged at the cost of the entire world's damnation. Yet here he was, sworn to bring it about, because of his love for her.

When he'd made the bargain, he'd believed . . .

What had he believed? It seemed to Asa there was something important about that bargain he was forgetting. That memory was lost, like so much of his mortal life. How any of it could be more important than being sworn to eternal service to the One Beneath escaped him.

"Was it worth it?" Mateo's face was closed off, unreadable. Maybe he meant to taunt Asa; maybe he genuinely wanted to know.

With a shrug, Asa said, "An act like that—it goes beyond regret or remorse. I'm transformed now. Not the human being I was. It's impossible for me to say what it's worth."

If he had not sworn himself as demon to the One Beneath, he would never have been forced to live in the body of a dead boy and make a mockery of his parents' love. He would never have had to help destroy the world.

He would never have met Verlaine, or fallen in love with her.

Beyond regret, Asa thought.

The river rushed over its own banks, widening and deepening, swallowing mud and trees.

At its edges, the water bubbled and moved. The mud writhed. From it rose the figure of a woman, soaked to the skin.

Elizabeth opened her eyes. She could feel the river rushing around her now—and experience the power she had unleashed in the most primal way. By now the currents were so strong the mud itself flowed; Elizabeth thrust her hands into the muck so that she could feel it oozing between her fingers, moving inexorably forward.

I did this, she thought. *For you, my beloved lord.*

Would He credit Nadia's help? Would He think so much of the strength Nadia added to the spells that He would fail to understand that Elizabeth, His most faithful and devoted servant, was the creator of it all?

Not after tonight.

And tonight, she would take away the last bonds tying Nadia to the mortal world.

With a smile, Elizabeth summoned the ingredients for moving water, and bid the river to run wild.

"Where the heck are they?"

"I don't know, Dad," Nadia said for the fifteenth time in as many minutes. "It's not like 'the far bend in the river' is something we can plug into GPS."

She was driving the car in an attempt to get her dad to the sandbagging line. Verlaine had come over to babysit Cole for the "few minutes" they'd thought the trip would take, but she and her father had been lost for more than half an hour now. Unfortunately, the alert that had gone out had been written by locals, for locals, which meant newcomers who didn't know the exact location were out of luck.

"I knew I should have driven out with Vera's dads," her father grumbled. "Would've been less trouble all around. At least I could have remembered to ask them."

"Verlaine," Nadia corrected him absently. She kept following along the side of the river as best she could. Sooner or later she'd see the sandbagging line. Of course she had no idea what it would look like, but the huge crowd of people would probably be a tip-off.

Then a strange sensation rippled through her—not pleasure, but the memory of it, but twisted somehow. Nadia's eyes widened as she realized Elizabeth had just cast dark magic of intense power—without her, and yet she'd still felt it.

"Jesus Christ," her father swore. "The river."

Nadia gripped the steering wheel as she saw it. The river was rising—no, surging, welling up so deep and so fast that it looked almost like a tidal wave.

In the woods, perched on the wet branches of trees, were countless crows. Elizabeth watched the scene through their eyes.

Now Nadia had an emergency to deal with. The lives of many people she loved were in the balance. This was the exact sort of situation where love could lead to mistakes.

Time for Nadia to make hers.

❧

"Holy shit," Dad said. When her father actually swore in front of her, Nadia knew it was bad. But she could tell that for herself. Her mind raced ahead, realizing what was about to happen.

The sandbag line. It would be completely overrun, flooded with torrents of water so powerful no one could possibly remain standing. They'd be knocked down and washed away. All those people are out there—Verlaine's dads—and probably Mateo, too . . .

"We have to stop the car," she said.

"Stop the car? Like hell. Nadia, we have to get away from this." Dad's face had gone white. "The road ahead gets closer to the river. We could be washed out. Or washed away."

"Not a problem." There was nowhere to pull over; the ditches on both sides of the small country road were feet deep in water. Nobody else was driving anywhere nearby, so to hell with it. Nadia just stopped the car in the middle of the road. "Dad—hang on, okay?"

"Just what do you think you're doing, young lady?"

Young lady meant she was in serious trouble. But she had to get a few feet away from him, right now, because if she didn't cast a spell to quiet the river, at least a little bit, everyone on the sandbagging line might be dead within minutes.

She pushed open the door and ran into the rain. With a leap she cleared the ditch—barely—and felt cold mud spatter all over her pant legs. Although the mud slipped beneath her feet and made her wobble, Nadia kept running despite hearing her father call after her. The river swelled further; she hadn't thought there was this much water outside the ocean.

Quickly, quickly, do it now!

Nadia grabbed the agate charm on her bracelet and cast the spell for moving water—moving it backward, slowing it, stilling it.

Her magic crackled against Elizabeth's; the collision rocked her to her bones. It was as though Nadia could see Elizabeth in front of her for a moment, staring in disbelief and white-hot anger.

Despite that, the waters quieted. Although the river remained storm-swollen, its flow was no longer much greater than it had been a few minutes ago. As the wind whipped her damp hair around her, she wiped the raindrops from her face and tried to think about what might happen next. The surge that had already passed through couldn't be stopped any longer; Nadia prayed what she'd done would be enough.

"Nadia?"

The voice was right behind her. Startled, Nadia jumped around to see Dad standing there, eyes wide.

Every excuse she could have made, every story she would've invented, died unspoken in her throat. There was no getting around this. Nadia had broken another of the First Laws, and this was the one that would tear her life to shreds.

Dad had seen her cast a spell, and he understood what he'd seen.

Dad knew.

8

"JUST TELL ME," SAID NADIA'S FATHER, FOR ABOUT THE six hundredth time since they'd gotten back into the car.

"It's not important," Nadia lied. It felt like the six thousandth time. "Can we just keep going?"

"No, we can't. Because the river—it did something that doesn't happen in the natural world. I saw the laws of physics change. And I'm almost positive my daughter was involved." Her dad's voice was sharp-edged, but he was obviously fighting to remain calm. "It doesn't make any sense. I realize that. But I know what I saw."

You can explain magic away easily, most of the time, Mom had said. She'd kept Dad fooled for almost twenty years, but apparently she was better at this than Nadia was.

Dad kept going, though now his words were halting and unsure. "People in town—they've been saying—it's a lot of superstitious nonsense, or I thought it was—but now—now

I just need to understand what's going on here."

He looked so hurt. So lost.

Screw the First Laws. She'd broken most of them by now anyway. How could the situation get any worse? Once—just once—Nadia wanted to tell the truth.

She took a deep breath. "I'm a witch."

Dad blinked. Whatever answer he'd been expecting, it wasn't that. "What do you—what—is this, I don't know, Wicca or something?"

"No. That's a completely separate religion. This is the Craft, the true Craft, that's been handed down from woman to woman since the beginning of time." It felt . . . so incredibly good to say it. Just to say it. Nadia had heard the phrase *the truth will set you free*, but she hadn't truly understood it until this moment. "With my spells I can do almost anything you can imagine. Do you want to see one? Here."

He didn't say yes, but he looked too astonished to object.

Swiftly Nadia took hold of the pearl charm on her bracelet and did a spell for light:

Sunrise in summer
Moonlight in winter
Fire in darkness

She kept the memories sweet and simple.

Getting up early for a school trip back in Chicago, sniffing the delicious aroma of coffee from the kitchen, as she stood at the balcony and watched the first daylight playing on the river.

The night of Thanksgiving, when the clouds had cleared and the moon shone down on Captive's Sound, the whole town silvered with a thin dusting of snow.

Mateo's house, his fireplace crackling as she looked from the flames to his face and felt her breath catch in her chest.

Dad said, "Son of a bitch."

Nadia opened her eyes to see a soft glow suffusing the interior of the car. It was as though she were holding some sort of candle in her hands, though there was no visible flame; the gentle light emanated from the space between her hands, responding to her magic. Her father stared at it with wide eyes.

She wasn't prepared for what he said next. "Elizabeth tried to warn me."

"Elizabeth? She tried to warn you about *me*?" It seemed like there wasn't one single thing in Nadia's life that Elizabeth wasn't determined to screw up. "She said something bad about me and you listened to her?"

"She was trying to tell me about your witchcraft." Dad kept shaking his head. "I wouldn't believe her. I still can't believe—"

"I turned back the river," Nadia interrupted. She wasn't interested in hearing more about how her father was taking advice from a Sorceress; anger edged every word she spoke. "You're right about that. I also saved Mateo from the fire at the haunted house, which by the way was zero percent natural. That disease that swept through town last month? Dark magic. I'm the one who saved all those people. But right now I'm mixed up in something harder than all the rest. Elizabeth, the one you've been listening to—she's a Sorceress, a dark witch, and I'm trying to stop her from destroying this whole town."

"This whole world" would have been more accurate, but she didn't want to push Dad all the way to the brink.

"Elizabeth? Your friend?" He looked so confused. "But she seems like a sweet girl."

"Sweet? That's the last thing on earth Elizabeth is." Nadia folded her arms across her chest. "She tried to seduce you. I know, because she told me."

Then she wished she hadn't said it, because her father's face—Nadia never, ever had needed to see her father looking so humiliated. Elizabeth was the one she was angry with. Not Dad. Not even now.

Awkwardly, she added, "You were strong to resist her. Most men—that kind of dark magic—they would have given in. So you proved you're not like that."

"Did Elizabeth teach you this?" Dad's expression was shifting from bewilderment to anger that matched her own. "Did she get you involved in witchcraft and whatever the hell else this is?"

"No. I've always been a witch. Mom taught me."

That made it even worse. Her father went so pale she thought he might faint. "Your mother knew?"

"Mom's a powerful witch. She taught me, just like her mom taught her since she was a little girl. And when she— Dad, when she left—" This was the hardest part to say, but the most important. If Dad could understand just one thing, it needed to be what had really happened with Mom. "She didn't go away because she didn't love us anymore. She went because she *couldn't* love us anymore. Mom—she gave up her ability to love. She sacrificed it to protect me from darkness." The weight of what her mother had done for her bore down on Nadia every day. "It was the most heroic thing she could have done. She—basically she tore open her heart and let all the love pour out, just so I'd be safe."

It hadn't worked. That was the worst part. Elizabeth and the One Beneath had designed their traps so well that all Mom's sacrifice had come to nothing.

"Your mother," Dad repeated. "This can't be real. It can't."

Nadia lifted her hands; the glowing, unearthly light between them rose with her, reminding him of what she could do.

Dad's lips parted, and for a moment she thought she saw . . . wonder. Amazement. He knew now, really truly knew that magic was real, that it could be helpful and even beautiful. He understood what she could do, and there was no need to pretend anymore.

Finally, she felt like she might have something to hold on to.

Then Dad said, "You're telling me my whole life has been a lie."

It felt like a slap. Nadia gaped at him, unable to find words.

"My marriage was a sham, because I never—I had no idea who I'd actually married. Twenty-three years and I never

156

even knew her." His voice had started to shake, and he couldn't meet her eyes any longer. "I don't even know you. My own daughter. You've been lying to me your whole life. If I don't know you, I don't know a single person on this whole goddamned planet, and I never have."

Nadia realized she was shivering. The cold and the wet had hardly been able to affect her before, as overwhelmed as she'd been by Dad finding out. Now she was chilled to the marrow, and her own father didn't want her anymore. The light she'd conjured offered no heat.

"I'm going," she said, opening the car door. "Don't worry, I won't come by the house. You and Cole are safe. I promise you'll always be safe."

"Wait. No." Dad forced himself to look at her again, or so it seemed to her. "You can't run off like this. It's late—out here in the dark—"

Nadia raised one of her hands above her head and let the lingering magic of her spell gain strength, until the light blazed above her like a torch. Dad's eyes went wide, and she knew he was beyond being able to speak another word.

"I can take care of myself," she said. Then she turned and walked away from the life she used to know.

By the time the sandbagging was done, the sky was light gray—what passed for sunrise in a town where the sun hadn't been seen in a long time. Mateo ached from his shoulders to his abs to his thighs; the coarse burlap of the bags had worn away the skin of his fingers, though his hands had been too numb from cold to feel it at the time. Even as he stared down at the raw curls of peeling skin, he couldn't make himself care about it much. It felt . . . appropriate.

Worn down to the bone. That's me.

Nobody riding in the truck back to town said much. A few people had taken off earlier in the night, mostly older guys or people who had been injured. Mr. Prasad had thrown out his back, and his wife had driven him home around one a.m., which was why Asa sat next to Mateo in the flatbed of the truck. For the moment, the rain had died down to a sprinkle. Nobody made any effort to shelter themselves from it. They were all soaked, as wet as they could get, and by now no one could care any longer.

Maybe that's how Elizabeth finishes us off, Mateo thought. *She wears us all down until we're too tired to care. She's bringing the battle only after she's sure we won't fight back.*

The truck rumbled toward the town square—and, to Mateo's surprise, pulled to a stop in front of La Catrina, just as his father walked out. "Everybody!" Dad called. "We've got huevos rancheros, toast, and sausage for anyone who wants it."

A low rumble of enthusiasm and some clapping answered this. Mateo realized he was starving; until this moment he'd been too tired to notice, and apparently most of the guys in the trucks had the same reaction.

Gage breathed a sigh of relief. "Your dad is the greatest human being I have ever known."

"Yeah, think I'll hang on to him."

As they began jumping out of the truck, most people

trudged straight toward La Catrina, ready to chow down. However, a few simply waved and headed toward their vehicles or businesses, either too exhausted to eat or too eager to get home and sleep. Among them Mateo saw Asa. Mrs. Prasad had come to pick him up, even now standing beside her car and smiling at the demon she thought was her son.

"Hey," Mateo called to Asa. "Sure you won't stop in?"

Asa gave him a look, like, *Since when are we best friends?* Which was a valid question. But all night—all the weary hours they'd worked—Mateo had thought about Asa's story.

About how the One Beneath kept His word.

"Apparently Dad's already making pancakes," Asa said. "If you think I'm passing up what may be my last chance on earth to eat pancakes, you are sorely mistaken."

Mrs. Prasad laughed. "Teenagers! So melodramatic. 'Last chance on earth.'"

Mateo and Asa looked at each other, and for one second it was so funny that Mateo thought he might lose it. Not that the apocalypse was a laugh riot, but—at the moment, Mateo was so tired he couldn't think straight.

Which was what made it the worst possible moment to see Elizabeth.

To any human untouched by magic, she would have looked bad enough: dripping wet, her once-white dress dingy and torn, hair and skin grimy from the mud. Her ruined shoes sopped through the puddles as though they might come to pieces at any moment.

To Mateo—to a Steadfast, able to see magic—she looked

like something out of hell. Around her radiated a strange sort of energy, like a fever made visible, Mateo thought. Her eyes were as flat and black as those of a snake.

All of that, Mateo could have dealt with. By now he was used to the fact that Elizabeth looked like a walking nightmare only he could see. What he couldn't handle—the thing that drove him completely out of his mind with rage—was that she was also smiling.

Elizabeth was destroying them all, was hurting Nadia, had taken Nadia away from him, and she could stand there and smile.

He didn't make the decision to go after her. It was more like he saw her smiling, and then his body started running of its own accord. By the time he knew he was going to attack her, his hands were already clenched into fists, and he was only a few feet away.

Her head jerked toward him, but after that momentary surprise, Elizabeth's smile only broadened.

I'm going to wipe that smile off her face forever, Mateo thought. *Just once in her entire long evil life, Elizabeth Pike is going to be sorry.*

In the moment before he would have collided with her, an immense weight struck him on the back and took him down. The concrete sidewalk rushed up to meet him as he fell heavily into a puddle. He wanted to swear but couldn't suck the breath into his lungs.

"What the hell are you doing?" Gage yelled. "Dude, calm down."

"She's got you brainwashed." Mateo tried to throw Gage

off—but the breath was still knocked out of him, and Gage was a big guy.

"He's like this," Elizabeth said quietly, though not so quietly that the many people watching nearby couldn't hear. "He was like this when we were together. But I never wanted to say anything. I never wanted anyone to think Mateo was . . . crazy."

A murmur went through the group, and Mateo braced himself for the usual catcalls about how the Cabots all lost their minds. Instead, someone said, "It's more witchcraft. That family's cursed."

Elizabeth raised an eyebrow; apparently she hadn't been expecting that. She didn't seem dismayed, though. Everybody was looking at Mateo, and nobody was looking at her, which was exactly how she wanted it.

"Witchcraft warps men's minds. They're not responsible for their actions," said Asa, who still stood there with Mrs. Prasad. He was smiling, darkly amused, but Mateo knew he'd just been bailed out.

"Whatever you're seeing isn't real, buddy," called a man Mateo hardly knew. "That's just Elizabeth Pike. You two are friends. Remember that. Try to think about what's real." Others nodded and murmured, and the dangerous mood calmed.

Except for Gage.

Gage's voice was low as he said, "You were like this when you were with Elizabeth? You used to hurt her?"

His best friend was looking at him like he was a horrible human being. No, like he was a monster. It was totally unfair. And there wasn't one thing Mateo could do about it.

He said the safest thing possible. "We weren't together. It was one night."

Mateo badly wanted to add, *I never hurt her,* but that wouldn't fly just after Gage had seen him try to attack Elizabeth. And no, he might never have injured Elizabeth, but not for lack of wanting.

"He lies," Elizabeth whispered as she lay one pale, muddy hand on Gage's shoulder. Once again Mateo saw that strange shimmer of red around Gage—the lingering magic that proved Elizabeth had him in her thrall.

He could get used to the idea that she was trying to destroy the world as he knew it, but he just couldn't take her stealing his best friend.

"Gage, come on." Mateo put his hand on Gage's shoulder—where Elizabeth had touched him moments ago—determined to shake him out of it if he had to.

But then he felt it again. The jolt.

Mateo had no name for it. This particular burst of energy or heat or whatever it was—it had come to him a couple of times in the past months. The first time had been when he'd awakened Gage out of the thrall. And sure enough, Gage shook his head, the reddish glow around him disappeared, and his eyes looked normal instead of flat and dead.

I broke it. That was me. I can break the thrall. How? Mateo hardly had time to ask himself this question before he realized that this time was different. Because Gage was turning toward Elizabeth, his expression shifting into horror.

"Oh, my God," Gage said. He took a couple of steps away

from Elizabeth, like she might electrocute him. "What did you do to me?"

Elizabeth glared at Mateo . . . and moved backward.

He'd done something Elizabeth didn't expect and couldn't explain, and it had intimidated her. For the first time, Mateo actually felt like he had Elizabeth on the run.

His triumph was brief. She stalked away before he even had time to gloat, which meant he was now alone with a very, very confused Gage. "What did she do to me?"

Explaining was impossible. Mateo tried distraction. "You're tired. You spaced out, that's all. Come on, let's get something to eat."

Gage shook his head. "That wasn't me being tired. Mateo, she was inside my head. Like she was controlling me. I know it sounds crazy, but I swear to God—something's not right." His eyes widened. "They were talking about witches . . ."

If he hadn't been so astounded, Mateo would have wanted to applaud. Gage Calloway had just done what virtually nobody else in Captive's Sound had ever managed: He'd seen right through Elizabeth, on his own.

That hadn't happened the last time Mateo broke the thrall. Did that mean he'd managed to destroy Elizabeth's hold on Gage for good? It had to.

"We need to talk," Mateo said to Gage. It couldn't be against the First Laws to talk about witchcraft with someone who'd figured it out. Probably.

At that moment, Mateo's dad appeared. "Come on, son," he said, scooping one arm under Mateo's to help him to his feet. "You, too, Gage. You guys have been up all night.

And Mateo, you're not yourself." Under his breath he added, "Did you take your meds?"

"Yeah," Mateo lied. The meds were for the seizures he didn't have.

Back inside the restaurant, while the rest of the sandbag crew helped themselves to the buffet Dad had set up, Mateo and Gage sat in the kitchen away from the rest. This way Mateo could heat his feet by the comfortingly warm stove, and Dad got a chance to fuss over him, while Gage tried to process the fact that the world worked completely differently than he'd ever imagined.

"Witchcraft, real. Elizabeth, bad witch. Nadia, good witch. Jeremy, actually some kind of zombie demon thing called Asa. Verlaine, mixed up in this but nobody really knows how. End of the world, heading our way." Gage counted these points off on his fingers. "Have I got the basics here?"

"Pretty much. Oh, wait. Ms. Walsh, the counselor at school? She knows about this, too. Okay, that covers it."

"Then I want to hear more about this end of the world . . ." Gage's voice trailed off as Dad returned. "Uh, about this new band, The End of the World. Just dropped a new album?"

Mateo stifled a smile; Gage didn't need to come up with a lie, because his father was far too worried to pay attention to their conversation. "It's too much strain for you, Mateo," Dad said as he poured them both some more Aztec hot chocolate. "I understand wanting to help out when there's trouble, but you can't pull all-nighters like this. Not while you're on medication for seizures."

Cautiously, Mateo ventured, "You heard what those guys said about a curse. About witchcraft." Maybe he could bring his father into the fold, too.

"*Madre de Dios*. They're being ridiculous. They all are in this town!" Dad retied his apron around his waist. "I should have insisted your mother and I move back to Guadalajara. Maybe when things calm down a bit, we should."

"I don't want to move to Guadalajara."

Dad's hand rested briefly on Mateo's arm. "Something's got to change, son. You deserve that much."

Then he was off, acting like nothing in the world was wrong as he laughed and talked with the group out front. Gage leaned forward and put his head in his hands as he muttered, "Too much new information. Crazy information. My brain is full."

Best to leave him for a few moments to deal. Mateo took a sip of the hot chocolate and tried to think.

Something did need to change. Something radical. Nadia's plan for taking Elizabeth out seemed like it was destined to fail, because Elizabeth's hooks were in her so deeply that it was like . . . like Nadia's thoughts and emotions weren't even totally her own anymore.

He had to do this. He had to find a way out, for Nadia— and through her, for everyone else.

Once again he found himself remembering what Asa had said.

The One Beneath keeps His bargains.

Asa went home, ate pancakes, and waited for the very brief period of time it took his parents to fall asleep.

Then, as duty commanded, he went to Elizabeth's.

The human body he wore was tired, but demonic endurance went beyond that. He took the rickety steps up to Elizabeth's door two at a time and strolled in—then stopped. "What are you doing here?"

Nadia smiled at him wanly. "I guess I live here now."

She looked like hell. Her hair was tangled, her clothes inadequate to the chill: by now Nadia Caldani looked less like a part of the human race than Elizabeth did. Worst of all was the way she'd made herself a pallet on one of the few corners of the floor where no broken glass lay. It was as though she thought she didn't deserve any better.

"A hammock, at least," he said. "Floors are dangerous. But why on earth are you here? I'm assuming you're not charmed by the ambiance."

"My dad saw me cast a spell." Nadia's voice was small. "He said his whole life was a lie. That he didn't even know me. I can't go home anymore. I can't stay with Mateo or Verlaine, because I poison them. So I'm stuck here. This is the only place I have left."

Asa knew how it felt, and how much harder it had to be for her to bear. He at least could always say this was better than hell.

So he went on one knee, low enough to bring his face near hers and slide one hand behind her neck. "I'm sorry," he whispered. "I really am."

Nadia nodded, closing her eyes as tears began to well. He

leaned his forehead against hers for a few moments. Although he knew she could not win—it was impossible—he wanted her to go down fighting. To scare Elizabeth and the One Beneath, even if only once. They deserved a scare at least.

And surely Nadia deserved some small victory.

Quickly he kissed her forehead, then stepped away before Elizabeth entered the room.

"Our new resident," she said, nodding toward the place where Nadia sat. Elizabeth's smile seemed more strained than usual. Why wasn't she glad to have Nadia under her wing? Or was there something else troubling her? "Two servants for the One Beneath."

"You mean, for you." Asa leaned against the cracked plaster wall. "As you never cease to remind me."

"You are a demon," Elizabeth snapped. "During your mortal life you swore yourself to serve the One Beneath so long as He reigned in hell, if only He would grant you one wish. You received what you wanted. Now you owe Him service. Why do I have to remind you of this? Have centuries in hell been insufficient to teach you who and what you are?"

Asa held his hands up in mock surrender. Something was bothering Elizabeth. Someone had gotten the better of her. Obviously not Nadia, who stared at the two of them as though she were too stunned to fully comprehend what was going on. Who could it have been?

Again calm, Elizabeth said, "We can begin our work in earnest now."

"The town is half-submerged in water," Asa said. "And you tell us we haven't even begun?"

Elizabeth's eyes glinted dangerously. "This world still stands, doesn't it?"

"What do we do next?" Nadia didn't budge from her place on the floor. To Asa she looked like a broken doll, an abandoned thing.

"The town's destruction weakens the mortal world just at the point where the One Beneath will break through." Elizabeth's tiny feet wove a twisting pattern through the broken glass on the floor as she walked toward her stove, which glowed with all the stolen glory, love, and beauty Elizabeth had amassed during her long and larcenous existence. Asa stared into its orange light until his eyes burned and he had to turn away. "Every proof of witchcraft we give will incite the town's hatred, as will every person we wound through our magic. That hatred will arm Him with the final weapons He needs to shatter the barrier, and come through to rule at last."

Nadia's face jerked up toward Elizabeth's. Although she otherwise didn't budge, Asa could sense the difference in her. She no longer looked like someone dead; life had returned to her eyes. "First you used shock," she said to Elizabeth. "Then sorrow. And finally hate. The shock of the fire, the sorrow of the illness, and hatred because of—of everything that's happening now. Each time you took human emotion and twisted it into exactly what you needed."

"Witchcraft relies on our memories. Harnessing the power of group emotion is the next logical step toward greater power. Finally you see it." Elizabeth's smile was no longer taunting; her admiration was sincere, and so the scariest thing Asa had ever seen. "You're finally becoming one with darkness."

Asa tried to study Nadia's expression without being noticed doing it. Did she understand that Elizabeth finally trusted her—and was giving her the information she needed?

Or was she becoming lost in the darkness alongside Elizabeth?

She has nothing left, Asa thought. Nadia was no longer even as tied to this world as he was.

He was bound to it by what he felt for Verlaine.

This world could not fall. It could not. It had to endure forever, because Verlaine lived here, and she deserved to be happy. To grow up. To go on.

Everything else Elizabeth said about their tasks that morning was empty for Asa. He took note of it, remembered it, but didn't care. From that moment on, he had his own agenda. A new resolution burned in him—bright, hot, and deadly.

Maybe he could finish his part in this sooner than Elizabeth expected. Even today.

⟋ ⟍

Classes Canceled Until Further Notice
Rising Floodwaters Endanger Rodman High, Other
*   Municipal Buildings and Homes*
Meteorologists Stumped

Verlaine hit Post, then grabbed her backpack and headed out of the *Lightning Rod* office. By now she was the only student still on campus; the handful of other students who had shown up today had all been sent home at morning break.

Nobody else remained at Rodman High except a handful of teachers hauling their stuff from their classrooms, and one janitor who was valiantly battling the water in the principal's office with a Shop-Vac.

Today's outfit: '50s-style capri pants (good for high-water situations) and a clingy, soft, pearl-gray sweater. She'd knotted a black-and-white polka-dotted scarf around her hair for a sort of retro headband, which also helped keep it dry. But as Verlaine walked out toward the muddy school parking lot, she could take little pride in her latest vintage outfit. The whole thing was hidden under her hooded black raincoat, and anyway, with the apocalypse drawing nigh, fashion was starting to feel less fun. More trivial. More stupid.

And then she heard a strange rustle, and was overcome by the unmistakable sensation that she was being watched.

Verlaine clutched the straps of her backpack as she turned around, but she saw no one anywhere near. No buildings stood especially close to the lot, and hers was among only a handful of cars parked there. She could hear nothing but the patter of rain on her raincoat.

It's nothing, she told herself.

Once she was in her car, she figured, she would feel better. More secure. The land yacht was basically the same as an army tank, if tanks came in maroon. Instead, though, Verlaine felt even more insecure—like she didn't have any idea where she was going.

Home. I'm going home. But even her way back to her house

had changed. She bit her lower lip as she steered the car around yet another washed-out street. It was like she had to map Captive's Sound all over again—through alleys, on unfamiliar paths.

The entire way, Verlaine couldn't shake the sensation that she was being watched.

As she passed one of her neighbors' houses, she noticed that their front yard looked like they'd put in a swimming pool—which, of course, they hadn't. The Meades' yard had caved in from one of the sinkholes that had carved gashes throughout town in October; now the floodwaters had filled the hole completely.

She would take a picture. She'd report. Once she started doing her job again, Verlaine figured she'd stop being so paranoid.

Okay, they're not home, she thought as she slid the hood of her raincoat back over her head and grabbed her messenger bag. *I'll ask their permission to run the photo later.*

Made sense. But now she was all alone, in the dark.

Just take the picture and stop being a wuss. Verlaine lifted her phone, careful to keep the lens dry—

A hand clamped over her shoulder.

She gasped and dropped her phone. *It's wet*, she thought, in the strange numbness of panic, before she was spun around to face Asa.

"Wandering around Captive's Sound as night falls." His smile was not kind. "I would've thought you'd know better by now."

So she should have felt relieved. It was Asa. Her defender, her friend, her not-quite-boyfriend. But she didn't.

Slowly, Verlaine said, "You've been following me since school, haven't you?"

"You felt it? All the more reason you should have been more careful."

How could Asa have followed her when he was on foot? Maybe his demonic speed allowed him to keep up—or he'd just stopped time to catch her wherever he liked. It didn't matter. Verlaine could only stare at Asa and realize that somewhere along the line, she'd stopped thinking of him as a demon.

She shouldn't have.

He tilted his head—black coat hanging perfectly from his angular frame, cheekbones highlighting his large, dark eyes—his sensual handsomeness only stronger now that he'd gone back to being scary as hell. "You said you know how to kill me," he murmured. "Tell me."

"Don't you know?" That was stupid. Of course he knew. But why did Asa want her to say it? He stood there, staring, waiting. Almost as though he wanted her to say the wrong thing—

Too bad, because she wouldn't. "Blade consecrated to white magic? Check. Anointed with the 'blood of the sea,' because nobody in ye olden days could just say 'seawater,' check. And all three pieces of paper: word of god and word of witch and word of you. So I'm set." Verlaine lifted her chin. "Satisfied?"

"Almost." Asa's voice had become nearly a purr—but not like an ordinary cat. Like a leopard or a panther. Something stronger and more dangerous. "I presume you keep these items on you at all times. Doing anything else would be highly unsafe."

Verlaine did keep them with her. She thought of it less as arming herself against Asa, more as keeping her dads from finding the knife and freaking out. Or, at least, she used to think of it that way. Now she didn't know what to believe. Instead of answering him out loud, she clutched her waterproof backpack closer

Asa's grin was brilliant in the constant twilight of rain. "Good girl."

Her mood was shifting from freaked out to pissed off. "Why the pop quiz? Why the stalker act? What's going on?"

"I'm about to try to kill you."

Had she heard that right? She couldn't have.

Asa took a step toward her, and Verlaine skittered backward; the mud sloshed around her boots. "No, you're not."

"Oh, yes, I am. You see, I'm making it easier for you." His entire body had tensed, and she found herself thinking of a panther again, one closing in on prey. "I realize you're not a natural killer. The farthest thing from it, really. But anyone can kill to defend their own life."

"Wait. Hang on—wait!" Verlaine held up her free hand, but he was coming closer, and while his eyes remained beautiful, they no longer looked entirely human. The heat of him was close enough to sear the damp air. "Why now?"

"Do you think there will be a good time? That will never come. So today. Now, Verlaine. Now."

He pounced.

Verlaine screamed as he slammed into her, his weight taking them both down. They fell into the mud, and Asa's hands pinned her shoulders down. Desperately she twisted to the side, rolling him off her.

Get the knife get the knife get the frickin' knife—Verlaine managed to reach inside her backpack. Her hand closed around the hilt just as Asa tackled her again.

Their bodies tangled together. The last time they'd been this close they'd been making out in her car, and she'd thought that had to be what love felt like. Whatever love was, it didn't feel like this—cold and wet, her body shaking, her eyes hot with tears even as her voice shrieked in rage.

Verlaine wedged her feet against Asa's chest and kicked him back so hard he fell into the deep pool of water, almost going under. That gave her time. Only a few seconds, but that was enough.

She slammed the crumpled three papers on the ground, then stabbed the knife through them. There. Now all she had to do was stab Asa, and he'd be dead. Gone forever.

Asa leaped from the pool, his movements inhumanly graceful and swift. Within an instant he was crouched over her. "And now she has a knife," he singsonged. "Too bad she doesn't know how to use it. Maybe I'll demonstrate."

He means it. Asa means it. He's going to kill me if I don't kill him first.

And yet she also realized, in a flash of terrible insight, that he wanted her to win.

He was ready to die for her.

So she had to be ready to kill.

Verlaine shoved herself up fast enough to body-slam him, the top of her head making contact with his jaw. Her reward was a muffled cry of pain. She seized her momentary advantage, pushing Asa onto the ground and collapsing atop him. The knife was heavy in her fist, but she could angle it, bring it around—

—and she stopped, right there, with the blade just in front of his chest.

"Hesitation. I'm disappointed in you." Asa's eyes met hers evenly. "Did you want to say good-bye? Waste of time."

Maybe she'd meant to say good-bye, that and no more before she sent Asa back to hell. But when Verlaine looked at him like that—knowing he'd attacked her only to give her the chance to finish him off, that he was at this moment trying to sacrifice his own life for hers—she knew there was no way she could ever kill him. No matter what the stakes were, even her own life, she couldn't kill the guy she—the guy she loved.

"No." She straightened her fingers until the dagger slid from her hand into the mud. "I won't."

Asa's face contorted into a terrible grimace. "You little fool."

He's going to kill me after all. Verlaine knew he meant to do it. She could sense it in an almost animal way, her hair

175

prickling upright on her scalp, adrenaline coursing through her veins. Still she didn't grab the knife.

Lightning-fast, he rolled her over. His weight thudded on top of her, so that he held her down. Asa growled, "Then I have to—I have to—"

Verlaine closed her eyes.

Less than three seconds passed. They felt like years.

When she opened her eyes again, she saw Asa looking down at her. He was shaking. "I'm a fool, too."

She didn't know what to say, what to think. She didn't care. "Shut up and kiss me."

He did. Verlaine wound her hands in his hair, reveling in the taste of Asa's mouth as they opened their lips. The kiss was desperate, each of them clutching the other close, not caring about the chill in the air or the mud covering their bodies. Raindrops beat down on Verlaine's face, wetted Asa's hair as she wove her fingers through it, and none of it mattered. She only wanted to stay close to him. It had felt like this when they'd tried to save each other from drowning only to find they were trapped.

But as Verlaine tried to pull him even closer, Asa pulled away. "I should go."

"Don't."

"When I'm with you, I want to—I want to talk to you. Make you laugh. Protect you, kiss you, love you—"

Verlaine knew that was bad news, but when she heard him say it, all she could feel was a wild, leaping joy.

"—and none of it does either of us any good."

"Maybe we should stop worrying about what happens in the end." She stroked his cheek with one hand. When her fingers touched his skin, he closed his eyes. "Maybe we should stop thinking about anything besides right now."

He slowly, slowly turned his head and kissed her wet fingertips. Lightning flashed, illuminating them for one brilliant instant—blue-white amid the dark.

Then he stood up, leaving her sitting in the mud. "Sounds nice," he said. He sounded like his usual sardonic self again. "Forgetting everything else in the world but each other. But I can't do that."

"Why not?"

Asa smiled grimly. "Because I know what happens in the end."

In an instant he was gone. Verlaine wondered if he had stopped time—and if he had remained there a long time, watching her, before he left. She wanted him to have done that, even though she knew it was a stupid thing to want.

Probably she should get up from the mud, but she was trembling so violently that she wasn't sure she could even stand yet. Instead Verlaine crawled to the place in the mud where her phone had fallen. She lifted it from the muck to see the light of its screen.

"It still works," she said, like that was important, and for some reason that was the moment when she started to cry.

Nadia had taken Asa's advice about the hammock, mostly because she figured the spiders were still around someplace.

(Weirdly, they seemed to leave Elizabeth alone. Spiders were more perceptive than Nadia had thought.)

Maybe she should have been deeply depressed as she lay there in her hammock amid the dilapidated ruin that Elizabeth called home. Instead Nadia felt numb. Happiness seemed like nothing but a memory, and probably she'd never again get to spend any meaningful time with any of the people she most loved. The one that hurt most was Cole— her baby brother couldn't possibly understand what was going on, and she hadn't even gotten to say good-bye . . .

Nadia shut her eyes. She had to stay focused on the one thing that was keeping her going.

Finally she understood what Elizabeth was up to. *The ultimate weapon is forged from hate.* Elizabeth was forging a weapon now, from the anger and suspicion of people affected by the flood.

What a Sorceress couldn't understand was that adversity brought people together, too. According to Asa, the men in town had worked side by side all night, each one trying to help the others.

Now that Nadia understood Elizabeth's plan and its weaknesses, she would finally have a chance to strike back.

Striking back, however, would involve sinking herself more deeply into dark magic than she ever had before . . . beyond the point of no return. Still, if you gave yourself to darkness forever, sometimes you could get something in return. Bargains could be struck. Deals could be made.

If she failed to stop Elizabeth, and the One Beneath

ascended into this world—the aftermath would be horrible, but some people would survive. They would live in a more frightening and dangerous world than they'd ever imagined. Still—while there was life, there was hope.

Over the past couple of months she'd already laid as many protective charms and spells on her house and her family as she could. Everything Nadia could do to protect Dad and Cole, she'd done. Maybe they would never even know her magic was the reason they'd survived, but she didn't care about getting credit. She just wanted to give them a chance. Even in the hellscape to come, they'd have a chance.

Mateo, though . . .

She had to find a way to protect Mateo.

The curse bound him so powerfully to Elizabeth, and to dark magic itself. When Nadia had made him a Steadfast, she had only made him more avidly hunted by the powers of darkness. If she failed in her battle against the One Beneath, she would also have to face the horrible knowledge that she had damned Mateo to death, and to hell.

She had to break the curse. She had to make sure Mateo would be safe. And there was no way Nadia could do that.

Unless she made a bargain.

Nadia knew what the price would be, and it was the worst price she could ever imagine paying.

If that was what it took to save Mateo . . .

Nadia took a deep breath and whispered, "Okay."

9

THE PHONE RANG, WAKING MATEO UP. HE GRABBED FOR his cell phone, only to groggily realize the call was on their landline, the one that was in the phone book but that no one except telemarketers and political robocalls ever used. And nobody ever called before seven a.m.

Except in an emergency.

He dashed into the living room, hoping the phone hadn't yet woken up his dad. The only other sound was the constant drumming of rain on the windows. "Hello?"

"This is Simon Caldani. Nadia's father." He sounded terrible, like he was sick.

Fear seemed to circle Mateo's heart, and squeeze tightly. "Is Nadia okay?"

"She's not with you?" Mr. Caldani's voice cracked. "I was just sure . . . I'd been counting on her being at your place."

When the father of a teenage girl actually hoped she'd

slept over at her boyfriend's, things were seriously bad. "Is she missing?"

A long pause followed. "Nadia and I—the other night—she told me some things that I—I didn't react well." What could he possibly mean?

Then Mateo knew.

He said, "She told you what's really going on, didn't she?"

"Mateo, I—I'm not sure what you mean."

"You know now. You know the truth."

Footsteps just outside the kitchen made Mateo look up to see his dad in his rumpled pajamas, shuffling toward the coffeemaker. Dad mouthed, *What truth?* Mateo waved his hand, like, *I'll tell you later,* which actually meant he'd come up with the best lie he could on the spot.

Mr. Caldani said, very evenly, "I'm not sure we're talking about the same thing. But—if we are—then you understand why I was unnerved. I . . . reacted badly. But I never meant to hurt Nadia, or scare her away. She took off, and she hasn't come back home, and I'm worried sick."

"That makes two of us."

Nadia was more than able to take care of herself, at least against any mortal danger. Mateo knew that. But she was up against dangers infinitely worse than any mugger or kidnapper could ever be. Now she was facing them alone.

For her to have told her father about her witchcraft—to have broken the First Law against freely revealing the Craft to a man—Nadia had to have been completely desperate.

Hold on, Mateo thought, resolve hardening within him.

I'm going to get you out of this. I'll save you, Nadia.

If it's the last thing I do.

Even a Sorceress had to sleep.

Nadia stared at Elizabeth as she dozed in her hammock, long chestnut curls trailing down almost to the floor. Some people looked innocent or vulnerable when they slept; Elizabeth did not. She looked more like an Egyptian from a sarcophagus lid: hard, unmovable, just waiting to rise again, stronger than before.

Still, Elizabeth had cast no special enchantments before going to sleep. Nadia knew she would be protected—but probably the protections were for Elizabeth's personal safety. She wouldn't have cast protective spells around her things.

She rose from the floor, walking just like normal so that if Elizabeth woke up, she wouldn't become suspicious.

Nadia glanced over her shoulder. Elizabeth remained sound asleep.

For a moment she considered going through the old cabinet at the far end of the room, the creaking one where Elizabeth kept the bones of the Cabots. Whatever Elizabeth wanted them for . . . it couldn't be good.

But Nadia didn't know what they were for. She'd reviewed everything she ever knew about curses; the bones of Mateo's ancestors wouldn't allow her to break the curse on him. If they had, she would have stolen them in an instant, and risked Elizabeth's wrath. Otherwise . . .

If you don't know what they do, leave them. You can't use them to help Mateo, so stealing them isn't worth the risk of tipping Eliza-beth off. Instead she went into the back room where Elizabeth kept her Book of Shadows.

She couldn't steal it today; Nadia knew that much. Moving against the Book of Shadows would be dangerous enough at any time—but with Elizabeth just in the next room, able to spring instantly to the book's defense, it was suicide. What she needed to do was consult the spell book. Learn from it. Accept some of the darkness it had to share.

Nadia walked into the back room, trying not to think of the last time she'd been there, and all the spiders. What little light filtered through the filthy window illuminated a nearly bare room. The Book of Shadows lay almost in the center of the floor. In a few places, the ceiling had begun to leak—raindrops pattered down onto the wood below—but no water had fallen on the spell book. It kept itself safe.

She sat down on the floor, crisscross, opposite the book. Her eyes flicked toward the corners, half-expecting to see spiders begin to scurry forth. Nothing like that happened. Yet she was aware that somehow, the book was . . . listening.

Nadia laid one of her hands on the cover of the Book of Shadows. Was she imagining it, or was it slightly colder than the rest of the room? "Demons," she whispered. "I want to learn more about demons."

When she went to open the book, it let her. The pages were so old and brittle, yellowed with age; in many places, the ink had faded almost to invisibility. Spells were layered on top of spells, drawings on top of drawings, until the pages looked almost scarred. Still, Nadia could make out enough. While the pages didn't magically flip to the information she needed, she found herself searching in the right area—and that hadn't been a lucky guess.

The Book of Shadows wanted her to know what a demon was. How one was made. Why the One Beneath needed demons, ever and always.

Nadia's eyes scanned over the words without pausing. As quickly as she read, she absorbed every word, understood every connection. Her mother's training—her own discipline—and the strange, vital darkness she'd sensed bubbling within her ever since she swore herself to the One Beneath: All of them worked together to help her understand.

Magic had never come this easily before.

Once she had finished reading, Nadia closed the Book of Shadows, then once again lay her hand on the icy cover—thanking it, in a way. Then she walked out of the house without pausing, only glancing back once at Elizabeth, who remained as still and silent as before.

Now I finally know what to do. I can keep Mateo alive. That way, even if I lose, and the One Beneath enters this world, Mateo will at least have a chance.

Nadia was ready to give up what little she had left, just to give him that chance.

Both the *Lightning Rod* and the *Guardian* were effectively shut down—but in Verlaine's opinion, that didn't mean the town of Captive's Sound should be without news.

(Besides Weather TV. They had hourly reports on Captive's Sound by now, with a little special logo, "Rhode Island Rain Rampage." But that was mostly a chipper meteorologist wearing hip waders and a smile as he kept pointing at a flooded street behind him. The people who lived here already knew about the washed-out roads.)

Verlaine dressed for the occasion, thinking of all the tough-talking 1940s movie stars who had played intrepid "girl reporters." Wide-legged, high-waisted tweed slacks and a cream-colored blouse complete with a bow at the neck: one hundred percent Katharine Hepburn. Well, except for the galoshes. Still, Verlaine thought the overall effect worked.

"You look amazing, sweetheart," Uncle Gary said as she gave him and Uncle Dave a ride to La Catrina; the Perez family restaurant was turning into a sort of makeshift headquarters for the town's relief efforts. "Most people would let themselves go at a time of crisis, but not you. You just keep bringing the fabulous."

"That's aimed at me, isn't it?" Uncle Dave said, between sips of coffee from his thermos.

Uncle Gary pursed his lips, a look of disapproval exaggerated to be funny. "I didn't say one word about that god-awful plaid shirt. Not one."

It felt so good to smile again. Since the last time she'd seen Asa—that terrible fight, and their even more desperate kisses—Verlaine didn't think she'd spent one happy moment. Right now, okay, they were headed into an emergency flood situation, but this was about as close to happy as she was

185

going to get for a while. She'd take it.

Verlaine pulled the land yacht into the La Catrina parking lot. As her dads headed toward where the men were gathering to figure out who needed what done, she put on her trench coat, wished for her fedora, settled for a scarf over her hair and decided to get to work.

But that was more easily said than done.

"Excuse me, sir," Verlaine said as she walked up to one man. "I'm putting something together for the *Guardian*'s online edition. I was wondering if you'd share a little bit about how the flooding has personally affected you."

He stared at her for a moment that went on too long. Rain pattered down around them, and their shelter under La Catrina's awning felt flimsy. Finally he said, "It's made me wonder, is what."

"Wonder what specifically?" Verlaine angled her phone to get this as a voice memo, and gave him her best smile.

The man remained unmoved. "What's causing this. Or I should say, who."

"Who?" For one moment, Verlaine felt hopeful. Were people beginning to doubt Elizabeth? Would they turn on her in some crazy torch-wielding mob straight out of an old monster movie?

Then she remembered who was always suspected of witchcraft first. Women who were outcasts. Burdens. Unliked and unloved.

People like her.

Her interviewee stared at her, as though daring her to ask

186

more; Verlaine thought it might be wisest to move on.

"Excuse me, Mr. Bender?" Riley's dad—she knew him. No, she didn't like him, but right now, familiarity was welcome. "I'm putting together a story for the *Guardian*—"

"Does it help you? Getting our voices on tape?"

Verlaine stared down at her phone in her hand. The voice recorder's needle wobbled with her words as she said, "Well, it makes it easier to transcribe later on."

"I mean, do you need our voices for something?" Mr. Bender took a step toward her—just a step—but it took some courage not to skitter back from him. "They say some people think photographs steal their souls. Maybe someone could do that by recording voices, if they knew how."

I've been accused of soul theft, and it's not even lunchtime. "You're tired," she said, keeping a smile on her face though she knew by now it had to look plastic. "I'm sorry to have bothered you."

"She's giving you trouble?" some other man said from behind her. He walked up to Verlaine, but he spoke to Mr. Bender . . . and every other man around, which was a few dozen by then. Verlaine looked around wildly for her dads; they were talking to the guys in the Red Cross van, still unaware of any fuss.

Verlaine dropped her phone in the pocket of her trench coat—but left the audio recording on, just in case. In case of what? She hardly knew. "Thanks for your time," she said to Mr. Bender, and the others who were listening. "I have to run."

But someone stepped between her and her car. It was old Mr. Thurman, who ran the hardware store where they bought lightbulbs and snow shovels. His gaze was flat when he looked at Verlaine, like he'd never seen her at all. "She's always around," he said hoarsely. "Whenever something goes wrong. You ever noticed that? The first flood downtown. That fever that nearly killed so many people—"

"Including my own dad," Verlaine shot back.

That didn't help. Instead Mr. Bender laughed, a harsh sound. "See? She'll do it to anyone? Even the folks who raised her."

"Do what, exactly?" She stood up straight, using all of her five feet eleven inches in her best effort at being intimidating. Sometimes that worked.

Today it didn't. Mr. Thurman took a step closer to her and said, "Witchcraft."

Nobody laughed. Nobody looked embarrassed for him. All these men staring at her, surrounding her—they believed in witchcraft now. They knew the truth.

But they were blaming the wrong person.

It's not me, Verlaine wanted to shout. *It's Elizabeth Pike. She's been ruining all your lives for longer than you can imagine. She's the one you need to go after, not me!* Yet if she sicced the group on Elizabeth, right now that was as good as setting them on Nadia, too.

And Asa . . .

She looked around wildly, wishing he would appear in that sudden way he had. If Asa were here, he could clap his hands together, stop time, step between the raindrops and take her away from all this. However, Asa was nowhere to be seen.

Her dads finally seemed to realize something was up—they were hurrying toward her now—but there were only two of them, versus, what, twenty-five others? Thirty?

At least they can't burn you at the stake, Verlaine thought wildly, her brain making jokes to try and distract her from the terror. *Not in this rain.*

Witches weren't always burned. They could be drowned. Or stoned. Hanged.

"You're wrong about me," she said as calmly as she could manage. "I have to go." Then she began walking toward her car, determined to keep her head high and acknowledge nothing.

Someone stepped in front of her. She jerked to a stop. Verlaine tried to walk around him, but a hand closed around her elbow, and that was it. From the first moment one of them touched her, a line had been crossed and now anything could happen.

"Stop it!" Verlaine cried out, but the hand spun her around, so hard that she staggered and caught herself against the wall of La Catrina. Hands fumbled at her coat pockets, and in her first fear she thought they were going to rip it off her—but no, they wanted the phone, thinking maybe that it was actually some instrument of dark magic hidden in an iPhone case. No way in hell were they getting her phone. "Stop it!"

As she slapped at the hands around her, she heard Uncle Dave yelling, "What the hell is going on? Let go of her!" Verlaine knew her dads were fighting to get to her, but could they make it through all these guys?

A hand fisted in her hair, and she yelped in pain. Roughly someone yelled, "My brother was in the basement of his office the night the square flooded. You could have killed him!"

"I was trapped, too! I nearly drowned, too!"

Nobody was listening to Verlaine any longer.

Her world blurred and fractured, turning into a kaleidoscope of images each more horrifying than the last: angry faces, hands tearing at her hair and skin, fingernails actually digging into the flesh of her wrist, and above her only the gray sky and the relentless rain.

"Stop!"

Some of the men around Verlaine fell, tackled to the ground—by Mateo.

Verlaine could have wept for joy as Mateo wrestled his way through them to stand in front of her like a human shield. "This is our restaurant!" he yelled. "You're trespassing on private property. Get out of here!"

Some of the men pulled back—not shamed, but unsure what to do. A guy in the back grumbled, "You're the one who's cursed. You should be with us, not against us."

"You leave my friend alone." Mateo's hands were balled into fists. He was ready to fight for her, even when the odds were twenty-to-one. Verlaine thought that if she weren't in love with Asa and Mateo weren't in love with Nadia, she might have fallen for him in that instant.

"She's no one's friend," Mr. Bender said, and his broad meaty hand thudded against Mateo's chest, trying to push him away.

Mateo slugged him.

Not hit. Not slapped. Slugged. His full fist, powered by the weight of his whole body, smashed straight into Mr. Bender's nose. Droplets of blood sprayed into the air.

That seemed to get through to most people—they began backing off—but some other guy turned on Mateo then, and Verlaine had never seen a fight like this. Mateo lost it. He struck at anyone who came near, with all his strength, and he was so much angrier than anyone else that none of his attackers could match him. Every punch, every blow, seemed meant to kill. Verlaine began shaking, even though he was on her side.

"Verlaine!" Uncle Gary finally pushed through the crowd, too. She launched herself into his arms. When he hugged her close, she was safe and that should have been the end of it.

But Mateo didn't stop.

It's not just about me, Verlaine thought in a daze. *Not anymore. He's been so angry for so long that he can't hold it back another second.*

Mateo never stopped, not even when the police car drove up with its sirens wailing. Not when the cops shouted for him to "desist." Not until the moment they grabbed Mateo, blood on his knuckles and face, and slapped the handcuffs around his wrists.

❧ ❧

So, this was what jail looked like.

Mateo was the only guy in lockup—hardly surprising in Captive's Sound, but he was still grateful. This way he could sit quietly on the long bench in this gray, cinder-block room and tell himself he didn't mind being arrested.

He did.

The worst part had been his father. Hearing Dad plead with the cops, the one brush of his hand as he tried to draw Mateo nearer to him instead of letting the police put him in the back of their car: That had been awful. His father could be kind of oblivious when it came to what was really going on, but he'd always stood up for Mateo. Getting arrested felt like letting him down.

None of it had been good, though. Not seeing those jerks, in a frenzy of fear, going after Verlaine—Mateo knew he'd never forget that, the sight of people going crazy, or of one of his friends screaming and pleading for her life. Not the way Verlaine had cried when the cops cuffed him; she'd tried to explain to the police, but nobody was listening to her anymore (not that they ever had). Besides, her dads wanted to get her the hell out of there, which was definitely the smart move. Were they back at home? He hoped not. Mateo could easily imagine a mob forming there later on tonight.

Today. Whatever time it was—he'd lost track. The sky was always dark, and the rain was always falling. Day versus night didn't seem to matter much any longer.

Mateo got to his feet; his entire body was aching and sore. He'd thrown more punches in that fight than he'd taken, but he'd taken a few. A couple streaks of blood had dried on his shirt and jeans. He wondered what his face looked like. He walked to the bars and tapped on them, surprised at how thick and heavy they were—though he shouldn't have been.

Maybe I should have gotten myself arrested earlier, he thought. *It won't matter if I have one of my visions when I go to sleep; no getting out of here.*

Not much of a bright side.

"Perez!" A policeman came hurrying toward his cell, cloudy-clear vinyl raincoat over his uniform, and a plastic Baggie over his hat. "You've been bailed out."

"Bailed out?" Mateo's heart sank. His dad only had so much cash on hand right now—the closings of the restaurant were hurting them badly—and now he'd just had to lay out a lot of it to free his son.

"What are you so glum about? She's got the money, so you don't have to do the time. Besides, don't know if you kids noticed, but we've got bigger problems right now than some juvenile delinquent case."

There were so many things wrong with that, Mateo couldn't even start listing them all. But he didn't want to argue. *She* had bailed him out? Could that mean Nadia?

Heart full, he hurried to the door, walked out into the waiting area, and saw his grandmother.

Grandma virtually never set foot out of her enormous, gloomy mansion on the Hill. Mateo had never seen her anywhere else. She wore a long black coat that only emphasized the pallor of her skin, with the hood drawn up. Around her head was wound a dark blue scarf, draped just so, intended to hide the terrible scars that warped one side of her face.

The scarf didn't hide them completely, though. Nothing could. In his final insanity, Mateo's grandfather had set a fire that had damaged their mansion—and very nearly killed Grandma. Left behind were the red, twisted creases disfiguring her face; they were burn marks but looked more like gashes left by the claws of some great beast. One of her eyes was forever milked over, though that couldn't diminish the intensity of her disapproving stare.

"I see it's come to this," she said. "Your curse."

Mateo glanced over at the cop, but he was paying no attention, already speaking into his walkie-talkie about yet another washed-out road. "What happened today had nothing to do with that. People were freaking out about witchcraft, and going after one of my friends instead of the actual evil witch in town."

Grandma cocked her head, clearly interested despite herself. She had believed in some element of the supernatural all along—and knew that Mateo and Nadia understood the real goings on in Captive's Sound, the ones hidden just beneath the surface. "The flooding—this is dark magic, too?"

When did Grandma become one of the few people I could talk to about this? Mateo forced himself to focus. "Yeah. This is . . . the end, I guess. Either we stop the people behind this, or they'll win." Calling Elizabeth and the One Beneath "people" was stretching the definition a bit, but never mind. "We don't want to see what it looks like if they win."

"That girlfriend of yours, Miss Caldani—"

Mateo smiled even though his throat was closing up. "She's on it," he said. "She's our best chance."

Nadia was the only thing that mattered. Her safety—her ability to go on—that had to come first. When he put it like that, his path became very clear.

Grandma put one wrinkled hand in the purse she carried, then drew out a single key. She offered it to him, and after a moment Mateo took it. The old-fashioned brass was heavy in his palm. Was this the key to some secret chamber, some ancient treasure of the Cabots that might turn the tide?

Instead she said, "That opens the front and back doors. There is also a security system, which I have shut off. You may phone the security company to reset the codes if you so desire, although I doubt the occasion will ever arise."

"Grandma?"

"The house is yours." Her tone was brisk. "It always would have been, upon my death. I have no other living descendants, thank God, and I cannot imagine what any charity would want with the place. I always thought I'd live out my life there. I have had no use for life these many years . . . but I find I'm not ready to die either."

Was she talking about committing suicide? Mateo flashed back to his mother's death, the way she'd set out in a rowboat to surrender her life to the sea. His chest tightened. As weird and creepy a relationship as he'd always had with his grandma, there was no way in hell he was going to lose someone else like that. "You don't have to . . . leave," he said.

"Whatever it is you're planning, it's going to be okay."

"Okay?" She parroted him, then gave a short, harsh laugh. "The darkness that has tortured your family for generations is about to burst forth and unleash itself upon the whole world. How is that okay?"

"Nadia can stop them. I know she can." He knew he had a way to make sure of it. Once he'd done what he had to do, nothing else would hold Nadia back.

"I wish your Miss Caldani good luck. But if a battle is coming, and this is the battleground, I prefer not to wait upon it. I am leaving Captive's Sound, and I do not expect to return. Therefore I give you your inheritance now. Make what use of it you can in the time you have."

Mateo could only stare at her. Where would Grandma go? Presumably that antiquated butler of hers was traveling along. But if they ran to the far edges of the earth, and the One Beneath succeeded, she still wouldn't have run far enough. Her escape was futile, but she'd always been driven by fear. That was the only emotion left in her, really. No hope, no curiosity, no love.

This is the last time I'll ever see her, Mateo thought. She was his grandmother, his only living relative aside from Dad, and he should have felt sad, or worried—something like that. Instead he only felt numb.

"Thanks for the house," he said.

Grandma simply wrapped her coat more tightly around her. "The papers are signed over to you, in the desk of the upstairs library, should anyone ever get around to asking."

She didn't hug him, didn't even say good-bye. Mateo's grandmother simply turned away and took her tiny, wobbling steps toward the door. The butler waiting there opened the door and held a large black umbrella over her head as they set out in the rain. Mateo stood there, watching her dark shape until it vanished into the gray.

What had she been like as a young mother? What had Mom been like as a little girl? Had Grandma been able to love and cherish her, or had Mom turned out great despite being raised by a woman made of pain and ice? He'd never know.

"Gonna hang around here all day?" the policeman said, between squawks from his walkie-talkie. "Most people are kinda in a hurry to get out of jail once they're free to go."

Mateo realized he should find his father right away; Dad was probably worried sick, trying to get the bank to open up so he could bail out his son. (Grandma would never have called Dad to explain what was going on.) But he had another errand, even more important.

He'll probably be at home, Mateo reasoned as he set out through the rain, his only protection a cheap plastic poncho the policeman had grudgingly lent him. *Or at Elizabeth's, but I can't go to him there. If I do that, she might realize what I'm planning.* He didn't intend to let Elizabeth stand in his way.

When Mrs. Prasad opened the door, she smiled and welcomed him into the kitchen and even gave him a snickerdoodle. "Jeremy! One of your school friends is here!"

Asa thumped down the stairs and looked into the kitchen

in bewilderment. When he saw Mateo sitting there, he raised an eyebrow. "Mateo! Hey. Uh—want to play video games in my room?"

Which sounded like something out of the cheesiest commercial in the world, but Mateo stifled a laugh. "Sure."

Once they were alone, Asa muttered, "What are you doing here?"

"I need you to help me do something. Or—I guess, really, you only have to explain the details. After that, I won't need any more help."

Asa closed the door to his bedroom, to be sure Jeremy's mother wouldn't hear. "Help with what?"

"I have to free Nadia from her deal with the One Beneath. I can't do that without giving the One Beneath another soul in return." Mateo took a deep breath. "So I'm going to give him mine."

10

AS ASA LOOKED AT MATEO, HE WONDERED WHETHER reasoning would ever get through to him, or whether a punch to the face would be required. "You're a fool."

"This is what has to happen," Mateo insisted. "My life for hers."

"This isn't as easy as self-sacrifice, you know."

"*Easy?* Self-sacrifice. That's your idea of easy?"

Asa took a step closer to Mateo, lest his "mother" overhear. "As heroic as it may be, the mere act of laying down your life for the one you love? Yes, it's easy. The quicker it is, the easier it is. Virtually anyone would throw themselves in front of a train for their child or lover; many people would do it for a stranger. That impulse—that breathtaking leap out of yourself for someone else—it's easier than we ever dare imagine. I think if humans truly understood they were capable of that, they couldn't handle it. They'd never stop wondering why they act like such moronic asses the rest of the time."

Mateo looked confused. "This isn't about jumping in front of a train."

"No. As I said, that would be easy. Only a flash of pain, certainly messy, but also very, very quick. You make the decision. You leap. You die. Sacrifice made. But that's not the bargain you propose to strike, Mateo. You're planning something very, very slow. Certainly messy. And more painful than you can possibly imagine." Asa pushed up the sleeve of his sweater, revealing the jagged scar left from one of Elizabeth's spells last month. She had needed to cause someone immense agony to do her work, so she'd sliced him to the bone, and all his demonic powers had not yet erased the damage left behind.

Although Mateo blanched when he saw the scar, he didn't waver. "You know Nadia is our only chance against Elizabeth's plan."

"I'm technically Team Evil. You remember that, right?"

Mateo ignored this. "Nadia's not doing well. She's cut off from her family, and she cut herself off from me and Verlaine. Being alone like that, with only Elizabeth to turn to, that can't be good. It's like . . . her soul is drowning. You've seen her, haven't you?"

Asa could not bring himself to describe Nadia's state of despair. He simply nodded.

"She has to be freed from that darkness, at least for a little while. That's the only way she's going to win. The only way for me to free her from that darkness is by trading something valuable to the One Beneath. I don't have anything else He wants. Only my soul."

Why did his noble idiocy have to make so much sense? "The One Beneath—He keeps His deals, but He twists them. He always finds a way."

"How much worse can He make it for me? Once I'm a demon, that's as low as it gets. No offense."

"None taken. But you're talking about the powers and dimensions of hell. You don't know just how low it can be. First of all, you'd still have to bear your curse, but now you'd have to endure it for eternity. Now add to that torments for the slightest disobedience, the guilt and the shame of it, having to plot against the girl you love—"

He'd said too much, Asa realized. But there was no taking it back.

"The girl you love?" Mateo stared at him in disbelief, then anger. "Are you telling me you've fallen in love with Nadia, too?"

Asa laughed out loud. "No, Romeo, lovely as your Juliet is, she has no hold over me."

"Then you have to mean—who, Verlaine? Seriously?"

"You say it like that because Elizabeth's magic keeps you from truly seeing her, or connecting with her," Asa said quietly. "Which you know. That magic doesn't affect demons. I see the true Verlaine—the only one that matters—and she is more beautiful than you can possibly imagine. And she is mine, or she would be, if I had the right to love her. I don't. I never will again. Because I'm a demon. Do you see now what you're about to do?"

Mateo paused, obviously torn. The first thing he said was, "You need to leave Verlaine alone."

"I know, and I try. By the way, I heard about your valiant defense of her this morning. Thank you."

It killed Asa to think about Verlaine persecuted—endangered—while he was powerless to help. This was as bad as anything hell had to offer. Surely Mateo had to see that.

He didn't. Instead he said something Asa would never have expected. "Nadia's mother gave up her ability to love, to try and keep Nadia safe."

". . . Yes, she did."

"I love Nadia that much, too. I'm willing to give up just as much. If sacrificing my ability to be with Nadia is part of the price I pay for her freedom, then that's how it is."

Asa tried one last time. "Do you remember how that deal worked out for Nadia's mom?"

Mateo insisted, "Tell me how this is done. Explain. Help me make the best deal I can make—and you can do that, right? Because it's all about delivering another demon to the One Beneath."

Sadness settled over Asa, heavy and hopeless. "As you wish."

Elizabeth stopped midstep, then jerked her face up toward the sky.

Rain fell on her open eyes, but she didn't blink. Absolute stillness would allow the message to take shape more clearly within her mind.

She stood at the foot of the Hill, in the center of the road. Although the Hill was of course the highest ground in town, nobody was driving there either—mostly because there was nowhere in town for them to go. The thick mud surrounding them all steadied Elizabeth; she imagined it as concrete settling, turning hard as stone. By now she had given up all pretense of normality. Without the need to maintain some presence at the high school, Elizabeth was free to let her body degenerate. Her dress was no more than rags now, her flesh mortified with cuts and bruises she had not bothered to tend. What bliss it would be if she died at the very moment of the One Beneath's return, so that her mortal self perished along with the mortal world.

Still, those who should serve her defied her.

Nadia plotted against her? Yes, that was it. Earlier, Elizabeth had cast a sophisticated variant on Betrayer's Snare, knowing that at any moment Nadia might turn on her. And it was Betrayer's Snare twitching now, alerting Elizabeth to the possibility that her student—the beloved of the One Beneath—remained disloyal, even after losing all her ties to the regular world.

How disappointing, and yet how gratifying, too. Elizabeth's chagrin at failing to fully convert Nadia was outweighed only by her pleasure that Nadia was not so perfect a student as the One Beneath had wanted her to be.

"I will give her to you, beloved lord," she whispered up into the rain.

Yet there was more danger—more trouble, more disloyalty.

Her eyes darkened. Elizabeth walked out of the street, into a small patch of trees preserved in a copse halfway up the Hill, perhaps to make the fine houses upon it look even grander. Once she was surrounded by the trees, by life, she raised a hand to the sky and summoned one of her crows.

It flew to her without hesitation, perching in her hand even as she clutched it around the throat. "Transform," she whispered.

The crow vanished. (Dead? Transported elsewhere? It was irrelevant to the spell and Elizabeth did not care.) In its place appeared Asa, wearing only a T-shirt and jeans, stumbling back in surprise—but she tightened her hand around his neck.

He went very still, and said nothing.

"You are not stupid," she said. "You know you have been disloyal to me, yet you have not been returned to hell, so you have not been disloyal to the One Beneath. Therefore this is mine to learn and punish."

The magic she wielded—raw and primitive—lashed out of her hand into his chest. He cried out as it closed around his heart, squeezing it so that it could hardly beat. Elizabeth smiled.

"You think you can hide things from me," she whispered. "You think your soul is not mine to claim. Learn, beast. Learn what I am."

And she reached inside his chest to tear out the truth.

Asa screamed. Her fingers plunged through skin and muscles; her hand embedded in the core of him so that she felt his caged heartbeat against her knuckles, his panting lungs swelling against her fingers, the slip of his bloody liver upon her palm. His torn flesh gaped and puckered around her wrist. Elizabeth cocked her head, studying his face in its rictus of pain.

The truth was no tangible thing for her to pull forth, like one of his bones. Instead she felt it like the liquid run of blood within Asa's body, somehow flowing into her to blossom red and certain within her thoughts.

"Mateo Perez," she whispered. Then she pulled back her hand.

The demon fell to the ground, landing with a wet splat in the mud. He gasped feebly for breath. With amusement Elizabeth recalled that she had punctured his diaphragm, which made it impossible for him to breathe. She could have stood there and watched him suffocate within minutes.

Yet he was still a tool, and while work remained to be done . . .

Absently she cast a spell of healing, while meditating upon what she had learned. So Mateo wanted to trade himself as a demon in order to free Nadia? An interesting gambit— given Nadia's own plans, an ironic one—and it might have worked, against a lesser opponent. Instead this, too, was a tool for her to use.

"Beast. Get up."

"I don't think I can yet." Asa sat in the mud, one hand to his perfectly healed chest. His T-shirt gaped open, the tears in the cloth still bloody. He shook, either from shock or cold, possibly both, and the raindrops on his face looked like tears.

"Your weakness does not interest me. Your service does."

Asa looked up at her. "Let him make the trade. Let him do it. Then you'll have two servants instead of one, and you can do the One Beneath's work on your own. He doesn't need Nadia Caldani, not really. He doesn't need anyone but you."

The flattery pleased her—as he had no doubt known it would, but that did not change the fact that Asa was correct. "Finally you pay me proper respect. In return, I'll let you keep it."

He sat there in the mud for a long moment before he asked, "Keep what?"

"Your love for the girl. Verlaine, the gray-haired thing. I was considering tearing it out of you, just like I tore out the truth. Then I could hold it in front of you so you could watch it die. Every feeling you had for her would crumble like ash."

Merely telling him, and seeing his horror, was nearly as much fun as doing it would have been. He said, "Anything but that."

Bold words, from a demon who knew precisely what "anything" could mean, from her. Elizabeth's smile widened. "Or I could give it back to you just after I made you kill her. Maybe in time to watch her dying in your arms, betrayed by you, afraid of you—"

Asa prostrated himself in front of her. Kneeling in the mud, like the low, worthless slave he was: At last he was learning. "Do you want me to beg you? I will. I'll do anything you ask, if you spare her that."

"I already said I would not steal your pathetic love . . . at least, not as of now. But your service to me must be worthy."

"Name my task."

"Mateo Perez just left your house after telling you he wants to become a demon." Elizabeth leaned against the nearest tree; the leaves were so thick she was almost sheltered from the rain. "Help him. Make him swear it. Bring him over to our side. But do this at the hour I ask. The minute. The moment. Do you understand?"

Although Asa looked wary, he was too beaten down to fight—too desperate to protect his silly mortal love. He nodded, and Elizabeth's plan was nearly complete.

Nadia didn't know where Elizabeth was at the moment, and she didn't care. More time alone in this house gave her more time to prepare for what she had to do next.

It wasn't that she needed anything physical, not at this point. Nadia was as prepared for the task ahead as she was ever going to get.

But this required resolve. It required . . . giving up on her life completely, and that was a hard thing to do.

I walked away from Mateo. I told Verlaine good-bye. I left my family. There's nothing else left.

Lies, and she knew it. Nadia still loved her dad and her brother so much that she felt hollow without them. Still worried about whether or not Verlaine would be able to stand up

to Asa, or would fall prey to him in the end. And Mateo—
she hadn't known you could hurt for someone, ache because
of his absence, every single moment.

If I could only see him one more time . . .

No. If she saw Mateo again, it would just make her want
her life back, so that she could spend it with him. That could
never happen. Her old life was just one more thing she had
to lay down in order to get the job done.

Nadia slipped on her raincoat. Water still beaded along
its plastic surface; it felt like nothing ever got dry now. She
shivered as she put it on and looked outside the window.
Twilight, maybe? Hours and times of day made no sense
to her any longer now that she had no schedule and the sun
never shone.

On one wall hung the broken remnants of a mirror, its
remaining glass in the oval frame spotted with age. Nadia
stepped in front of it and looked at herself.

Could this—this wreck of a person—be her?

Her fingers ran through her tangled hair as she stared at
her pale, disheveled reflection. She looked younger somehow. Like Cole after one of his nightmares, or like a little
lost kid. Quickly Nadia combed through her hair with her
fingers; it didn't make much difference, but she didn't want
to go to her doom looking like total crap.

Now I know how Elizabeth ended up like this, she thought.
*How she became so disconnected from normal life, and human emo-
tions.*

Nadia's only consolation was that she wouldn't forget her

love for Mateo, her family or her friends. She would remember them for eternity—the eternity she spent in hell.

She would break the curse on Mateo as she offered herself to the One Beneath. Because Nadia had already sworn her loyalty to Him, all she had left to offer was her service as a demon.

Elizabeth's Book of Shadows had made it clear that the more innate magical power someone had, the more powerful a demon that person could become. Nadia didn't think the One Beneath had ever had a Sorceress demon before. Such a person would gain magic and abilities almost as vast and as dark as those of the One Beneath Himself, yet would be completely bound to Him, unable to serve any other, until the end of time.

Nadia could imagine no worse fate for herself. But if she could save Mateo—make the One Beneath spare his life as the price of her demonhood—then it was what she had to do. She had nothing else left to give.

From a distance, Elizabeth watched Nadia leave her house. So determined, so sure. Elizabeth smiled, then walked inside.

First she stepped to the back room, simply to look at her Book of Shadows. It had known just what to show Nadia Caldani; once again, it had served as an extension of her will. "I think you could almost live without me," she murmured as she bent to stroke along the book's spine with two fingers, the same way one might touch a pet.

Then she went to her battered chest of drawers. The only sounds were the creaking and scraping of the old drawer as she opened it, and the endless pattering of rain through cracks, onto the floor or into one of the small bowls Nadia had set around to catch leaks. *Imagine, worrying about something as trivial as puddles of rain.*

Elizabeth's hand closed over the bones of the Cabots. They were dusty with age, feather light. She curled her fingers into a fist, crushingly tight, and felt the bones crack into powder.

Holding her fist over one of the bowls on the floor, she opened her fingers; the bone dust fell into it, turning the water yellow-gray. Then Elizabeth took the bowl in both hands, lifted it to her lips, and drank. The bitter grit scratched her throat all the way down.

There. Elizabeth rose, re-energized. She pulled her power around her like a cloak, swirling and dark—and instantly the world around her shifted. Now she stood on the edge of the main highway that led to Captive's Sound. The storm rumbled above her as she laughed.

Nadia was coming to this exact place. Elizabeth had been right behind her, and ahead of her, all along.

It took all Mateo's willpower not to go see his dad.

Swearing himself over as a demon wouldn't kill him instantly, or even soon; Asa had explained that much. At first, he'd carry on much as he had before. He wouldn't join the One Beneath in the demonic realm until he died.

(Which, granted, could be really soon. But he didn't let himself think about that too long.) He'd have to say good-bye to Dad sometime soon. But not yet.

As they'd arranged, Asa came to his house to pick him up. When Mateo opened the door, he frowned. "You look terrible."

Asa's skin seemed ashen; his dark eyes were dull. He hunched slightly as he stood on Mateo's stoop, like he had stomach cramps. But his smile was as bright as ever. "We've all had better days, haven't we? Well. I assume I have. Can't precisely recall."

You won't even remember being happy. You'll forget Dad, and Mom—and Nadia . . .

If forgetting her was the price of saving her, then he had to pay it. Mateo zipped up his coat. "Come on. Let's go."

The late Jeremy Prasad's sports car was exponentially nicer than any other vehicle Mateo had ever ridden in. Something about the comfort of it—the incline of the soft leather seats, the perfect clarity of the stereo sound—well, it seemed slightly surreal, and more unnerving than luxurious. Like he was in the first-class suite of that plane in *Inception* and Leonardo DiCaprio was about to screw with his head. "Where are we going?"

"You tell me, at this point." Asa kept staring resolutely ahead at the road, like he was afraid he'd lose his way. "We need to go to the place where you first met Nadia."

"Why there? It's just a stretch of road on the outskirts of town."

"You're doing this to free Nadia. Your vow takes its strength from your love for her. So the vow will be strongest at a place that's significant to you both. Where better than the place you first met?"

He could think of a couple of other possibilities, but their first meeting was a good choice. He'd never been able to drive along that section of road again without flashing back to that first moment, the way he'd held his hand out for hers. Besides, out there they'd be far away from any potential witnesses or interruptions.

Nothing would stop him. Nothing would stand in the way.

He settled back in the seat. "Head north."

Nadia walked north.

The vow would be strongest where she'd met Mateo. That, or at his house, where they'd spent so many hours curled together in each other's arms—but going there was impossible. So, back to the place on the roadside where they'd first met.

This was where her family had first driven into Captive's Sound, and where they had collided with the magical barrier Elizabeth had erected around the town. When Nadia's Book of Shadows had passed through that barrier, Elizabeth had been warned of the presence of a new witch—and their car had gone off the road into a ditch.

Rain beat down on the hood of her coat as Nadia trudged on. That night, she'd been so terrified, both of the darkness ahead and for her family. Dad had bruised his ribs, and poor little Cole had screamed and screamed. Although her father had managed to fish Cole out of their overturned car, Nadia had been knee-deep in water before she looked up and saw Mateo.

His visions had brought him to her side; he'd known her before they ever met. Mateo's first act had been to save her life.

She remembered the warmth of his hand closing over hers.

I'm going to return the favor, Mateo, Nadia swore as she headed down the road, ignoring the wet legs of her jeans and the shivers racking her body. *You saved me for a little while, at least. Now I have to be the one who saves you.*

Elizabeth had already cast her spell of opacity, which would hide Mateo and Nadia from each other's sight. Such spells only worked for a few minutes, particularly when the two people knew and loved one another as they did. A few minutes would be sufficient.

She could shape the external circumstances to time Nadia's vow. Asa would be able to do the same for Mateo.

Do you see how I serve you, beloved lord? Elizabeth knelt in the mud, feeling the cold muck ooze around her knees. She longed to sink into it, to be one with the world the One Beneath would shatter, if only to feel His power so completely. *I am giving you everything you ever wanted. Everything I am.*

❧ ☙

The magical barrier around town—Nadia had told Mateo about it before, but even with his Steadfast power he could barely see it. It was hardly more than a faint greenish glow, flickering in and out within the rain.

Asa's demonic ability must have allowed him to see it, too, because he pulled the car right up to it without any guidance from Mateo; they were parked just short of the line. "Here we go."

Mateo hesitated. "What else do we have to do?"

"I told you there was no elaborate ceremony." Asa acted as though he were bored, though obviously he wasn't; he still looked weird, no matter how lazily he spoke. "Chant if you feel like it. Make up some words, use the lyrics from 'Single Ladies,' whatever. Knock yourself out. But there's no ritual here. Just stand at the place where you met her, call in your soul to the One Beneath, and tell Him you're giving Him your service as a demon in return for Nadia's freedom. That's all."

One deep breath—and Mateo stepped out of the car.

On the night of the crash, the first night Nadia had met Mateo, the ditches on either side of this road had been partly filled with water. Now, however, they were full almost to the brim, on the verge of overflowing and flooding the road.

It wasn't necessary to jump back in. Just to stand here, and remember.

Her eyes filled with tears. She stood there on the road where they'd met and thought of how she'd first seen him that night—illuminated by lightning, so beautiful she'd hardly been able to believe he was real. It seemed impossible to Nadia that someone so perfect had ever been hers.

Asa had never hated himself as much as he did at this instant.

He was betraying people he had come to care about—against his will, and yet . . . He was helping Elizabeth do something for the One Beneath, a deed both dark and cruel. And he had begun to realize that his sister, the long-ago girl he'd nearly forgotten, would never have wanted him to become something like this. Not for the sake of vengeance.

Hadn't it been for something else, too? Asa could no longer recall. But he knew he would never have made this bargain if he'd known then what he knew now: that he would become a slave, and be denied even the memory of his sister's face.

Mateo braced his shoulders, about to speak. Nadia wasn't quite ready yet. "Now," Elizabeth whispered.

He brought his hands together, stopping time for Mateo—but not for Nadia. In this swift instant, she wouldn't even perceive the momentary lapse in the rain.

Neither Mateo or Nadia was capable of seeing each other, thanks to Elizabeth's spell. They were now prepared to vow at almost the exact same instant.

Before he brought his hands back together, Asa muttered to Elizabeth, "Aren't you ashamed of yourself? Even a little?"

Elizabeth smiled. "Shame is useless. Best left behind."

Mateo's hands curled into fists in his coat pockets. Into the rain, staring into the dark, he said, "You need more demons. You could use one here and now. If you will allow Nadia her freedom—her ability to walk away from your service—then you can have my service instead. I'll bear the curse and do your will forever."

Nadia's tears mingled with the rain as she whispered, "I'll be more than your Sorceress. I'll be your demon. Spare Mateo's life, and every power of darkness I'll possess will be yours. I'll belong to you."

At the same moment, they whispered the words, "I swear."

Lightning split the sky. Nadia screamed—the bolt had come so close she could smell the ozone. Its light seemed to linger longer than the strike itself—or the night wasn't as dark as she'd thought it was—and suddenly she could fully see her surroundings. The car parked in the middle of the road, motor running, headlights shining brightly though she'd never glimpsed them before. Sitting across from her, on the other side of the ditch, was Elizabeth, who wore a wicked grin. Asa stood at Elizabeth's side; he looked terrible.

Next to Nadia was Mateo.

"What are you doing here?" he said. "Did—did I bring you here?"

That wasn't even possible, unless . . .

Nadia turned back to Elizabeth. "What did you do?"

Elizabeth shrugged. "Nothing you didn't want to do on your own. You both chose freely. We only influenced the timing."

The timing? But then it sank in to Nadia. Mateo had made some kind of vow on his own. What? "Mateo's safe," she said desperately. "He has to be. My vow did that much."

Mateo didn't look grateful or happy. He looked stunned. "Oh, no," he whispered.

"You're one step ahead, Mateo," Asa said. "For once."

"I swore myself to the One Beneath for you," Mateo said. "As a demon. So you'd be free."

"I swore myself to Him as a demon! So you'd survive!" The horror of it splintered within Nadia like shattering glass, shredding her from the inside out. "And you'd just set me free, but I swore myself to Him again—"

Elizabeth had used their love for each other against them. Now they were both enslaved. Both lost. They had given up everything for each other, and yet for nothing. The very lives they'd tried to protect for each other—they'd given away.

"The One Beneath will have His own purposes for you," Elizabeth said to Nadia. "But you, Mateo—I've taken you for my own. At first I was collecting the bones of your ancestors in case I needed to intensify your curse, but your foresight hasn't been that much help to Nadia, has it? So I still had the bones. I consumed them. They are part of my body now, which means you will serve me as my demon, chained to me in whatever realm I walk, for all eternity."

This couldn't be happening. It couldn't. And yet Nadia knew this was all real.

Mateo's voice had begun to shake. "You lied to us."

"This is the truth," Elizabeth replied, smiling.

In a rage, Mateo leaped over the ditch and tackled Asa against a tree. "You tricked me!" he shouted. "You used me!"

"I didn't have any choice!" Asa yelled back. His expression was set. "I serve the One Beneath. I can't help it. As you're both about to discover."

We're lost, Nadia thought, looking helplessly toward Mateo. *They've already won.*

11

AT LEAST THERE WAS NO MORE REASON FOR THEM TO BE apart.

Nadia lay curled in Mateo's embrace as they lay in front of the fireplace in his house. Mr. Perez was out helping with relief efforts, so they could be alone together in their mutual desolation.

"What did it matter, what happened to me?" Mateo whispered, his breath warm against the back of her neck. He spooned her, both of them lying in near-fetal positions, numbed with shock.

"I wanted to give you a chance."

He kissed her shoulder again. "I just mean—didn't you know I'd want to be the one to sacrifice for you? To give up everything so you'd be safe?"

As her eyes welled, her view of the fire blurred, orange and yellow swimming and streaking, as hot as her tears.

"Didn't you know I'd feel the same way about you?"

They weren't arguing; they had no anger left for that. Nadia remained in both horror and awe. Mateo had sworn himself as a demon, just as she had. He had given himself to the forces of hell forever, knowing what that really meant— and yet he had done it because he thought it might help her.

She shuddered. Mateo hugged her more closely, and she closed her eyes. If she concentrated hard, maybe she could forget the rest of the world. Maybe she could feel nothing but his arm around her, anchoring her against his body. Maybe nothing farther away than Mateo even existed, except for the fire.

I was scared he wanted the darkness in me, she thought. *Or that the darkness in me wanted him.* That seemed so stupid now. Of course Mateo had loved her darkness, because he loved all of her, all her shades and shadows. He accepted her completely, just as she accepted him. Why hadn't she understood that?

Mateo whispered, "It's just so unfair—"

"You can't think about that." Nadia turned over to face Mateo, took his face in one hand. "If we start thinking about how they've cheated us, it's going to . . . block out everything else. I feel like, if I think about it, really think about it, I'll start screaming and I'll never stop."

Just when the anger might have taken her over anyway, Mateo pressed his lips to her forehead. Some of the tension in her limbs relaxed, and once again she breathed in the scent of him and tried to forget the rest of the world.

His hands wound through her rain-damp hair. They

kissed, softly, but Nadia felt the heat of it in every inch of her body.

"At least—" The cold comfort was difficult to force from her lips. "At least if we both have to go to hell, we'll be together there. Forever."

"Stop it." Mateo rolled her over onto her back, suddenly forceful. "Stop talking like it's all over, because it's not. It can't be over. Maybe He's going to drag me down to the demonic realm, because I can't get out of that. But you can. You're going to survive, Nadia. You're going to win. If you have to cast the same spells Elizabeth cast to stay around for hundreds of years, then you do it, do you hear me? He can't turn you into a demon if you're still alive, so figure out how to live forever. You do whatever it takes." His voice shook with emotion. "You will win. Someday, it's going to happen. I don't know if it's a week from now or a thousand years, but *you will win*."

Nadia knew how long the odds were, even more than Mateo did or could. But when she saw the intensity of the conviction in his eyes, she believed. She had to believe.

He gives me back my faith, she thought. *He gives me back myself.*

Mateo looked down at her, his arms framing either side of her body, as he whispered, "Let them drag me down to hell. I'll fight for you even there. So you can't give up. You can never give up."

Giving up felt—like a luxury. Like it would be so easy, such a relief, to just let it all go and give in. But as she framed

Mateo's face with her hands, she knew she would never surrender. "Never give up," she whispered, and then she kissed him.

They'd made out before. Done more than that. But Nadia had always stopped them just short of making love. It wasn't that she didn't love Mateo, or that she didn't want him. She'd wanted him almost since the moment she'd seen him. Still, she had wanted to wait for a time when they weren't in danger. Not fighting for their lives and souls. She'd wanted a time when they were free. Then all the worry and fear would be gone. Then she and Mateo could come together in total joy.

Now Nadia knew that day would never come.

With shaking fingers, she peeled his T-shirt up his lean torso; Mateo helped her, shrugging the shirt away so that his tan, muscular chest was laid bare to her. Then she got rid of her shirt, too.

Mateo pulled her against him, and the warmth of skin against skin made her gasp. "Are you sure?" he whispered between kisses.

Nadia pulled him closer, winding her arms and legs around him to keep him close. "Very, very sure."

The eighteenth harassment call of the night drove Uncle Dave over the edge. "First off, our little girl is not a witch!" he shouted into the phone receiver, as Verlaine curled into a ball on the couch and Uncle Gary embraced her protectively. "Second, calling people late at night and just making weird noises isn't doing anything to help the people of Captive's Sound. Finally, did you forget that such a thing as caller ID exists, *Nancy McGinley*?" He paused, then gave Verlaine and Uncle Gary a small, tight smile. "She hung up. Big shock there, huh?"

"I'm so sorry," Verlaine repeated. "I don't know why everyone focused on me all of a sudden."

She did know, of course—but it wasn't like she could explain the reason to her dads.

"They're not only focused on you," Uncle Gary said, surprising her. "Yesterday morning, several people were whispering about Lorraine Calloway, and someone was even talking crazy about Faye Walsh, your guidance counselor. I was going to set them straight about gossiping when that fracas broke out around you."

Uncle Dave shook his head as he paced the floor, neatly stepping over Smuckers, who napped unconcerned in the middle of their living room. "It's like people have gone insane. Not that the sanity level in Captive's Sound was ever sky high. But seriously? Witchcraft? People believe in witchcraft now?"

Verlaine was trying to think of something suitably innocuous to say when Uncle Gary cleared his throat. "I don't think that's impossible."

She turned to stare at him; so did Uncle Dave, who said, "Gary, what are you talking about?"

Uncle Gary held up his hands, as though in surrender. "You know I know Verlaine's not mixed up in any of this crazy stuff. But let's be realistic, okay? What's been happening in town these past few months . . . it's not right."

It's not just superstition and fear talking, Verlaine realized. *It's also common sense. I mean, anyone would have to know by now, wouldn't they?*

Uncle Dave remained deep in denial. "I'm the first to admit that Captive's Sound has had a stretch of bad luck. You don't want to see what's happened to our property values. Still, we're talking about rain." He gestured at the television set, currently tuned to Weather TV; onscreen was the once-chipper meteorologist, wearing hip waders as he gave his report from the raging river that had been Clark Boulevard. The wind buffeted the weather guy so hard that he had to hang onto a street sign to stay upright. Apparently Uncle Dave felt this proved his point. "See, rain isn't magic. It's just rain."

"It's more than rain," Uncle Gary said. His voice was quieter. "Have you forgotten the sinkholes? What happened to Verlaine, when she wound up in the hospital? Or the weird fever that put me in the hospital? When I was unconscious— mostly I was just, you know, out of it, but every once in a while I felt like I was watching something . . . dark and terrible. Like movement behind a curtain, and if I pulled that curtain aside I'd see something I never wanted to see."

The One Beneath, Verlaine realized. He had nearly revealed Himself to Uncle Gary while he lay unconscious and helpless. He'd come that close to devouring her dad's soul and his life. Why did she have to keep this secret? Why did she have to keep lying to the only people who really loved her?

You know, it's not like the First Laws of the Craft actually apply to me. I'm not a witch!

"It's true," Verlaine said. "There is such a thing as witch-craft."

Uncle Dave frowned like he thought Verlaine had lost her mind. Uncle Gary took her hands. "Oh, sweetheart. Were you dabbling? You can tell us. We won't be angry."

"No! No dabbling. I mean, I don't even have the power in the first place. But Nadia does."

"Nadia Caldani?" Uncle Dave said. "You think your best friend is a witch?"

"I know she is. We more or less met when she levitated the land yacht out of a ditch."

"Levitation?" Uncle Gary whispered, looking deeply freaked out. Verlaine squeezed his hands right back.

"She can do tons of stuff. Forecast the future, at least a little bit, and cast protective spells, and change the currents of the water—" Except the last time Nadia had done that, Verlaine had very nearly gotten killed. Which had been a total accident! Still, maybe she shouldn't have mentioned it. She plowed on. "Nadia's not the reason any of this is happening. She's a good witch."

Uncle Gary didn't look one bit reassured. "Like Glinda?"

"Fewer poufy pink ball gowns, more designer jeans, but same basic idea," Verlaine said. "The Wicked Witch of the West is Elizabeth Pike."

"Oh, come on." Uncle Dave started to laugh. "You've

always liked her! Everyone does."

"Elizabeth's a peach," Uncle Gary agreed.

Verlaine shook her head, laughing even though she wanted to scream. "That's just one of Elizabeth's tricks, making people think they like her. You don't have any idea what she really is."

Uncle Gary's arm went around her shoulders, an embrace meant to soothe. "Sweetheart, we believe you about the witchcraft—"

"I never said that," Uncle Dave interjected.

"—but we can't fall into the trap," Uncle Gary continued as though Uncle Dave hadn't even spoken. "Times like these scare people. We're dealing with something beyond anything we've ever seen before, you know? So we suspect our friends and neighbors. We turn on one another instead of coming together. That's why you're thinking these strange thoughts about Elizabeth, and why other people are thinking strange thoughts about you."

"No, I know the truth about Elizabeth. You have to believe me." Verlaine stood up from the sofa. She wanted to shake them—just to make them see—but she didn't want to shake them because she loved them. How was she supposed to get through to them? Maybe Nadia could come over and do a demo, like levitate the cat or something. No, that wouldn't work, not with Nadia cutting herself off from everyone, plus it would freak Smuckers out. Would they believe Faye Walsh, maybe? Or Mateo?

Not Mateo—they'll think he's just gone crazy from the Cabot Curse . . .

As she thought this, however, the images on the television set, which had been only blurs to her before, suddenly demanded her attention. Verlaine gaped as she saw Weather TV's view of the town square . . . with the columns collapsing under the portico of the town hall.

"Oh, my God." Uncle Dave grabbed the remote and turned up the volume.

Now they could hear the meteorologist say, "—apparently a meeting was being held inside—can't confirm that at this time—but buildings are beginning to be washed away by the flooding here in tiny Captive's Sound, Rhode Island. We repeat, this is coming to you live—"

Uncle Gary was already on his feet. "We have to get down there. Try to help out."

"Half the people in town who run relief efforts would've been in that meeting." Uncle Dave ran for his raincoat, or car keys—probably both, Verlaine realized. "Let's move."

She had already grabbed her smartphone, thinking *Live footage first, interviews later,* when she remembered what had happened the last time she tried to cover a story. All those angry faces, the shouts, the hands grabbing at her, pushing her down . . .

Uncle Gary took her hand. "Sweetheart, maybe you should stay put. Just until people calm down."

"No. I won't hide. If I do, then it's—it's like I'm admitting I'm guilty." Verlaine squared her shoulders. She had no intention of hiding while the actual guilty party, aka one Miss Elizabeth Pike, got to run around town doing whatever she wanted. "We're wasting time. Come on. Let's go."

The roads had turned into rivers.

Verlaine stood on the roof of her dads' car. They'd parked on one of the slopes leading down toward the square, a couple of blocks away from the worst of the flooding. She intended to stay back—at least, until her dads were too involved in the relief efforts to notice her. But even from here, the view was terrifying.

As rain lashed her trench coat (combined with a fedora for a vaguely Carmen Sandiego effect), Verlaine used two fingers on her touch screen to zoom in. Now the video fully showed the square more than two feet deep in water, churned by a current strong enough to whip white foam around every sign or tree it met. Although her field of vision was narrow, Verlaine could make out part of the line of oversize vehicles—garbage trucks, fire trucks, and even a school bus—that stretched from the road by the coffee shop to what remained of the town hall.

By now three of the five front columns had fallen. The remnants of the portico roof hung on by a few rafters; the large beams of wood swayed like slender tree branches in the wind. Water flowed through the front doors, which had either been opened or torn away by the flood. Atop the heavy vehicles stood a human chain of people—her dads among them—who were helping the shaken escapees climb down from an open second-floor window. From there, each person was passed along the chain, hanging on to hands to steady them; that steadying was necessary, because the current was strong enough to rock even the fire truck. If the waters rose much higher, the trucks could be washed out of the line or even overturned.

They're so scared, she thought, watching one woman stand there trembling, unwilling to take the long step or short jump that would get her to the next vehicle in line. *They're right to be scared.*

Verlaine couldn't take it anymore. Surely there was some way she could help. Even if that meant just getting better footage, so people could see what was really going on here, she needed to do it.

So she hurried down the hill until her boots splashed into the water. Only ankle-deep, though—any farther in than that, and she'd be in danger, too. Her place right next to the final fire truck allowed her to hear the shouting.

"Hang on!"

"Keep moving!"

"One more!"

Every available person, except for her, was up on the trucks. Verlaine positioned herself near the end of the line, where a few huddled escapees sat on benches or leaned against the wall. The two paramedics on hand were doing all they could—but that wasn't nearly enough. "I can help," she said. "I could maybe put those foil blankets around people, or—or I could serve some hot soup or coffee if you have that. Just tell me what to do."

One of the women on the bench lifted her head, staring with such venom that Verlaine took a step backward. "You can get out of here," the woman snarled. "Witch."

The memory flashed in front of her again—all those shouts, all those men striking at her—but even though she shook, Verlaine stood her ground. "I'm not a witch. I want you to try to be rational, okay? If I'd cast a spell to put people in danger, would I be here trying to help save them? How does that make sense to you?"

Nobody answered her, but they didn't look convinced, either. The weight of their stares felt leaden. Verlaine decided to just do what she could on her own. As far as she could see, the best help she could offer would be assisting people when they climbed off the final fire truck. The guy coming now was wobbly, clearly almost in shock, so she boosted herself on the back bumper and took his arm to steady him.

He let her do it, though he stared at her. The same stare met her when she got the next woman down, and the one after that. In Verlaine's opinion, this wasn't really appropriate behavior toward someone who was helping maybe save your life . . . but she wasn't doing this for thanks. She was doing it because it needed to be done.

Wait—Verlaine glanced down at her boots. Water was now lapping at the top, starting to splash inside, cold and wet. *The water's rising faster and faster. This is getting more dangerous.*

At that moment, the school bus rocked violently in the current. Everyone atop it cried out, and most of them dropped down to their knees or on their bellies, so they could hang on better. But one man toppled over and fell into the water.

He's going to drown! Verlaine thought—then told herself

that was stupid. The water wasn't even three feet deep. Who could drown in water so shallow?

Then she saw him try to stand, only to be knocked down by the current. He tried again, and fell again, this time going completely under the water. Only then did Verlaine realize the current was the danger, the thing that could kill.

Helpless, she turned around, looking for someone who could go get him, but every rescuer was atop one of the vehicles. Instead she saw the fire hose.

Verlaine grabbed the nozzle and started unspooling the hose—wow, it was a lot heavier than she'd thought—until it fell in loops completely free from the truck. Then she tied the nozzle end around her waist as firmly as she could. Which was maybe not that firm, but the loose circle around her would have to do. With that she waded into the current.

She'd known the current was strong from observation alone; being in it was a whole lot scarier. The water pounded against her legs, like a hundred blows falling so close together that there was no telling them apart. Verlaine was able to stay upright—but barely. Instead of walking, she had to slide her feet forward, keeping her rain boots against the ground at every moment. Shuffling forward, she called to the struggling man, "Hang on! I'm coming!"

The wind snatched the fedora from her head, tossing it into the dark water. Despite the danger, she felt a quick pang—a beautiful fedora, destroyed—but it was only a brief flicker in her mind. Verlaine remained focused on getting to this guy if she could. Already he'd been knocked several feet away from the school bus. Would the hose be long enough to reach?

Verlaine took another few steps, and the knot at her waist tightened. The fire hose stretched taut between her and the truck, and she was still just short of the drowning man. She held her hand out to him, and he tried to grab for it, but couldn't reach. Instead he was knocked down again, dunked beneath the water.

You can do this. Verlaine braced herself, then untied the knot around her waist.

"Verlaine Iris Laughton! What do you think you're doing?" Uncle Gary yelled. She didn't dare turn around to see his face. "You put that fire hose back on this instant!"

One more deep breath. Then she clamped her hand around the very tip of the hose and stretched her arm out again. "Come on! You can make it!"

The drowning man clutched her hand, and she had him.

With all her strength, she pulled him against the current until he was next to her, when she towed him to his feet. He leaned against her as she started following the fire hose back in. The water level lowered until finally they could both walk normally. As they staggered into the rescue area, Verlaine finally let herself smile. "Got him."

The woman from the bench hurried to them, took the gasping, exhausted man in her arms—then spat in Verlaine's face.

She was too shocked to react. The spit was hot against her cheek for the instant it took to be washed away by the cold rain.

"Witch," the woman said again, before she pulled the man away.

For an instant, Verlaine thought she might cry. When a hand touched her shoulder, terror seized her. Were they going to attack her again? But when she whirled around, she saw Gage Calloway, the only one who had a smile for her.

"Don't let 'em get to you," he said. "You did good out there."

Now she really was going to cry. The only words that came out of her choked throat were, "I'm not a witch."

"I know that, all right? You're okay." Gage hugged her.

So few people outside her family had ever hugged her. Verlaine had held herself together despite the cruelty, but his kindness undid her completely. She leaned her head against his chest and sobbed.

"I know," Gage repeated. "I know."

Asa lay in his bed, the exact same place and position he'd maintained ever since he'd gotten home. He hadn't budged since he'd been forced to betray Mateo and Nadia. His chest ached from the place Elizabeth had ripped open in his torso; while the physical wound had healed through the power of dark magic, it seemed as though he could still feel her fingers grasping and clawing inside him, slithering between his organs. But the pain wasn't what kept him under the covers, in his sloppiest sweats, refusing to acknowledge the world outside. It was the shame.

Mateo's eyes when he looked at Asa—the hollowed-out horror there, knowing himself damned to demonhood— Asa couldn't stop seeing that. When he did manage to banish Mateo's face from his memory, it was replaced with the image of Nadia shivering in the rain, or crumpled on Elizabeth's floor. She'd been so hopeless, so lost. So unlike the vibrant, defiant girl she'd been such a short time ago.

All thanks to you, he told himself.

Well. Not all thanks. Elizabeth deserved her enormous share of the blame. None of this had been Asa's idea.

But he'd had to do it anyway. That was what being a demon meant.

He scrunched further under his covers, hoping to hide from reality completely, but that was when his mother rapped on the door and walked in, without waiting for an answer. "Jeremy, darling. I brought you some of those Cool Ranch Doritos you like, and the last of the snickerdoodles. And just a little of the curry. Won't you eat just a little?"

"I love your curry," Asa said, which was true. Even telling a small truth like this reminded him how much of his existence was a lie. The woman beaming down at him with love was the same one who had reacted with entirely justified disgust and horror when she'd seen him for one instant as his true demonic self. She loved her son—but her son was dead and gone.

"Good. Then you eat up." She put the heaping plate on his nightstand—three-fourths junk food, one-fourth actual nutritious meal.

He ate the curry first. The spices worked their magic, waking him up despite himself. Asa decided he could at least watch some TV. That was about as much of the real world as he could handle.

One touch of the remote, and Jeremy's ultra-big-screen TV jolted into light. He'd last been watching Weather TV— it was hilarious when the meteorologists had to hang on to trees in strong winds. But any chance of laughter faded as he realized he was looking at Captive's Sound, specifically the town square. Specifically, he was looking at a rescue.

And the rescuer wandering out into the waters—

It can't be, Asa told himself, but then the fedora blew off her head, revealing that long shock of silver hair. He sat up, then scrambled closer to the television as though it could bring him nearer Verlaine.

While she struggled in the current, his stomach clenched. Asa imagined he could feel the cold water rushing around him, battering him. When Verlaine untied the fire hose around her waist, his hand went to his mouth, and he bit down on his thumb, hard. It was the only way to keep from crying out.

He wanted to jump up, run out of his house, and dash straight to the square. The floodwater wouldn't stop him. He'd wade into it, daring the current to take him down, and make sure Verlaine was safe—or no, he'd stop time, stop the water exactly where it was and lift her out. He would take Verlaine from the cold water, save that person she seemed so worried about, get her to safety and wrap her in his embrace, where his heat would comfort her. In that moment it seemed worth it, to be a demon, if only he could keep Verlaine warm.

Even as he raised his hands, Verlaine grabbed the man in the water and started back.

Asa breathed out, slumping back onto the bed. A smile spread across his face. *You underestimate her. As much as you worship her, you still don't understand exactly how much she's worth.*

The Weather TV anchors chattered happily about the "death-defying rescue" as Asa watched Verlaine make her way out of the water. Her silver hair was soaked now, sleek against the curves of her head and shoulders, as someone took the weakened man from her—and spat in her face.

First he felt the shock—cold and hot and cold again, as though it had happened to him instead of her. Then came the rage. *How dare they? How DARE they? Do you want to know what a demon can do? You don't. Trust me, you don't. But you're going to find out—*

Then Asa stopped himself.

He could not help Verlaine, precisely because he was a demon. Even if he went to her now, even if he avenged this outrageous insult, Verlaine would remain isolated, despised and alone. Even if somehow Elizabeth's plan failed—and by now Asa saw no way for that to happen—Verlaine's situation wouldn't change.

Unless . . .

Asa had always known how he could save her. How he could change everything for her. But to do this would mean instant damnation, to be sent to the hell within hell, a place of infinite torment and torture. There he would remain forever. He'd gone to this place once for helping her, but only for a few days. Even that brief time had felt like centuries of anguish. To know that he would be there forever without any hope of escape, ever . . .

He looked again at the television screen. The announcers didn't seem to have noticed what had happened to Verlaine. Gage Calloway hurried to her side and folded her in an embrace; the sight of another guy's arms around her shoulders awakened the demonic side of his nature, the desire to slash and hurt. Yet Gage was helping Verlaine more than Asa himself ever could.

Unless.

Asa got up, put on some decent clothes, and headed downstairs. His mother brightened to see him. "You're up! I was starting to worry."

His father sat on the sofa, too; he'd thrown out his back sandbagging, which was the only reason he hadn't been at that town hall meeting tonight. "Can you believe this?" he said, pointing at the screen.

"Nope. It's unbelievable," Asa agreed. He looked at his parents—Jeremy's parents—as though seeing them for the first time. They'd spoiled their son, spoiled him truly rotten, but they'd done it because they loved him so much. It was humbling to be loved like that. Shameful to steal that love.

His mother noticed the coat he wore. "Are you going out in this? And it's awfully late."

"My friend Mateo called." Lies came readily to him. "They're patching their roof. It's a mess—this isn't exactly when you want a leak, right? I thought I'd help out. Stay over there for a couple of days and work on the repairs with them. Don't worry. His house isn't in one of the flood areas."

They beamed. "You're a good friend," Mr. Prasad said.

"Don't forget—you know, cell phone service is getting weird. Because of the storms. I might not be in touch for a while." Asa wanted them not to worry. He couldn't protect them from the pain they would soon feel, but he could give them a couple more days of ignorant bliss.

"But be careful out there."

"I will." The lie was even easier this time.

He drove to Elizabeth's house, knowing she was out. Lately she hardly did more than slither in the muck like a serpent, glorying in the disintegration of the earth around them. Only her Book of Shadows stood watch, and it would not recognize a demon as an enemy until too late.

Asa walked across the broken glass, feeling slivers of it slice into his rain boots, even into his feet. It didn't matter. Nothing mattered but that stove glowing in the corner, the one that radiated such unearthly light and heat. The fuel inside looked like coals flickering with fire, lit up orange and blue within the ash. They would be hotter than coal could ever be.

Inside its light was everything Elizabeth had ever stolen— all the love she had taken from others in her unnatural lifetime.

He dropped to his knees and opened the stove. Its iron door burned his hand. Skin still red and smoking, he reached inside.

Although he'd tried to prepare himself for the pain, he still screamed.

Hell within hell is like this. It will always be like this. You will feel this forever.

Asa kept going even as his flesh blackened. Even as the pain made him dizzy and weak. Over and over again, he reclaimed everything Elizabeth had ever taken, clutching it in his burned claw of a hand.

Then he would press it against his chest, letting it burn its way in.

A demon was a vessel for dark magic. So much evil he had carried; so much wrong. He could carry this.

Even though it would destroy him.

12

VERLAINE SAT IN THE BACKSEAT OF THE CAR, WRINGING water out of her heavy, damp hair. Every muscle in her body ached, as though she'd been trying out for the Olympic weightlifting team instead of standing in rushing water. She felt so exhausted she thought she might have fallen asleep right then and there, if sheer astonishment hadn't kept her awake.

Her dads had stayed behind to keep helping with the rescue effort, though only after frantically demanding to know if she was okay; they finally believed her about the eightieth time she told them so. Besides, she had a lift home, and company. Apparently Team Not Evil had a couple of new members.

"So when I texted Mateo earlier, he said he was with Nadia," Gage explained from the seat next to her. "I figured, hey, Nadia's dad probably needs to know she's okay. I knew

I couldn't tell him what was going on, like, in a witchcraft sense, but then he already knew."

"Not that I'm having an easy time believing any of this." Mr. Caldani never turned around, but Verlaine could see his eyes in the rearview mirror. He looked shaken, like he didn't believe where he was. Verlaine couldn't blame him. Everything about this seemed surreal: talking with everyone about witchcraft like it was no big deal, the '80s station playing Prince on the car radio, water inside her boots sloshing with every turn of the car. "Of course Nadia told me the truth. She's my daughter; I believe in her. I just—I don't think the world I've been living in is the world I thought I lived in. At all."

"I know how that feels. Basically, we live in Night Vale."

Mr. Caldani frowned. "Where?"

"Forget it." Verlaine wanted to explain more, about both black magic and podcasts, but knew she couldn't. She wasn't even going to be able to remain conscious long enough to get through it all. Instead she took up her phone—somehow, miraculously, still working perfectly. Quickly tapping out a text with her thumbs, she said, "Let's swing by Dublin Street, okay?"

"What for?" Mr. Caldani said, even as he made the left turn to take them there.

"We're going to pick up someone who can clarify a few things for you." At least Verlaine hoped so, since her text hadn't yet been answered.

Sure enough, just as they pulled in front of Faye Walsh's

house, Faye hurried out, turquoise umbrella held over her head.

"You?" Mr. Caldani looked equal parts surprised and betrayed as Faye slid into the shotgun seat. "The school guidance counselor knows about all this?"

"You told them?" Faye gave Verlaine a look. "You know what the First Laws say about men."

Verlaine was too tired to deal with this. "Gage figured it out himself when Mateo broke the thrall. Nadia told her dad. So don't try to push this off on me."

"Mateo broke the thrall?" Faye turned around to stare at Gage. "He's a man. That's impossible."

Gage held up his hands as if in surrender. "All I know is the thrall is broken, and thank God, because Elizabeth's house—I remember glass, and spiders, and all kinds of scary crap, and we were in the middle of it . . . uh, spending quality time together."

Mr. Caldani didn't seem to care about Gage having "quality time" with Elizabeth. His attention remained on Faye. "You're an adult who knows about—about all of this, and you let Nadia put herself in danger?"

"Listen to me." Faye turned to him. Her voice was quiet, but the command in it made Verlaine sit up straighter. "Simon, I know you're upset and scared. You should be. But Nadia's a witch in her own right. I'm not. I couldn't have stopped her from taking on Elizabeth if I'd tried, and I didn't try. You know why? Because as young as Nadia is, she's the best chance we've got."

Silence followed, leavened only by the *slap-slap* of windshield wipers and the radio quietly playing "I Would Die 4 U." Then Mr. Caldani finally looked Faye in the eyes. "Will you help me understand this?"

Faye rested her hand briefly on his shoulder. "Of course."

Verlaine slumped back in her seat. Maybe she ought to have some kind of reaction to all of this, but she couldn't. "Faye can do the explaining. You guys sort it out, okay? I'm going to bed."

Once they'd dropped her off at her house, Verlaine was able to answer the dozen furious/worried/proud/furious-again text messages her dads had sent to make sure she really, really, really was okay. Able to dry her hair, and change into her favorite jammies, the pink-and-black satin ones that looked so 1950s to her. Then she curled into bed, into a ball, and tried not to think about the contempt in that woman's face in the moment before she'd spit.

They hate me. They'll always hate me. If I leave the house again, I'll be spit on again. Hit again.

How long before someone tries to kill me?

How long before they actually do it?

She pulled the pillow over her head, wishing she could hide in bed forever. At least she'd be asleep soon, safe from everything but nightmares.

And then . . . something changed.

Verlaine went very still, then peeked out from under the pillow. "Asa?"

He stood in the center of her room, shaking and wet. The

heat that always radiated from him was stronger now, so powerful that she felt it against her skin as though she were standing in front of an open oven.

"Did you stop time to get in here?" Of course he had. That was the weird shift she'd felt, the pause he'd used to get inside. He was almost hidden in the shadows of her darkened room, but not so much that she couldn't see the intensity in his eyes, or the way his entire body trembled. "Asa, are you all right?"

It occurred to her that he might have come here to try to kill her again, and yet still she was afraid for him, not herself.

"Do you trust me?" he whispered.

Verlaine knew she shouldn't. Knew she was a fool to admit it. But she told the truth. "Yes."

"Come here."

Is this a sex thing? I think this might be a sex thing.

I'm okay with that.

Slowly she pushed back the covers and rose to her feet. Her heart beat faster as she crossed her bedroom to stand in front of him. Asa's dark eyes searched hers, with a desperation like that of the drowning man she'd saved earlier that night. Then she was close enough to see the blackened, ragged state of his clothing, and—"Oh, my God, Asa, your hand. Are you okay?"

He silenced her with a kiss.

They had kissed passionately before. This went beyond all that. He pulled her close, raked his hands along her body and through her hair, opened his mouth to devour her. Verlaine hadn't known she could be kissed like this, heat and need taking her over.

But this was more than a kiss—this was something else—something fusing her together with Asa in perfect completion—

"Asa, what's happening?"

"Shhh." He framed his face with her hands. She could feel the rain still damp against his skin. By now he was glowing slightly, like he was melting. She was melting, too. "Trust me. Believe."

Her entire body trembling, Verlaine nodded. "I do."

"I love you," Asa said, and kissed her again before she could answer. This kiss went on and on, until they seemed to be one body instead of two, and the joy of it—of no longer being locked in herself, no longer being lonely, being less alone and more loved than she had thought it was possible to be—welled up inside Verlaine until it blacked out everything else.

All of it gone: Sight. Sound. Taste. Touch.

I love you, too, she thought, knowing he would understand her now. Even her mind was his. Then thought disappeared, leaving nothing.

The best part, Mateo thought, was being tangled up with her.

Nadia slept next to and on top of him. Her head on his shoulder, her hand under his pillow, their legs linked. His left arm was starting to fall asleep. He didn't care. Every part of it was new—the scent of their skin, not masked with perfume or aftershave. Or the tiny sound she made as she breathed, not a snore, but a soft little *mmm*. Every exhalation was warm against his collarbone.

Last night had been . . . okay, not quite as smooth as he always imagined. He had never thought having sex could involve so much talking. Starting and stopping as they figured each other out. And laughing. How come sex scenes never showed people laughing? Yet somehow it was all so much hotter than those sleek images from movies and porn, because it was real. Because he hadn't had sex with "a girl"—he'd made love with Nadia, all of her, every quirk and freckle and sigh that made her herself and no one else.

Mateo kissed her forehead, and she stirred. "Mmmm." Nadia opened one eye to peer at him. "Hey there."

"Hey," he said softly. They kissed again, and he put his hand to her cheek—

—then froze as he heard the front door open, and Dad called, "Mateo?"

Nadia stared at him, open-mouthed. Mateo wanted to tell her what to do, but the only words in his mind at the moment were *oh shit oh shit oh shit.*

Dad's footsteps came down the hallway. Nadia rolled out of his bed before Mateo could tell her to stay, and he heard her scoot under it. Which was crazy—he'd rather have had his father freak out than make Nadia hide under the bed— but he didn't even have time to whisper that to her before Dad opened the door. "You okay? Didn't return my texts last night."

"I, uh, sorry." *Did I throw away the condom wrapper? I don't think I did. It's on the nightstand! Don't look at the nightstand. Don't even glance at it.* "I was really tired. I fell asleep early."

"A teenager went to bed early," Dad said. "Will wonders never cease. Listen, I camped out at La Catrina last night. Could use your help there today if you're feeling up to it."

Dad still believed Mateo's arrest for assault was due to the "seizures," or maybe the seizure medication. "I can work. Definitely." At that moment he would have agreed to stand outside La Catrina in a chicken costume—*anything*—if it would just get his father to leave. It seemed to him like he could feel Nadia under the bed, holding her breath.

But his father's head was drooping, and his eyes were bloodshot. "I'm gonna catch a couple hours of sleep before heading back to the restaurant."

Mateo had thought of himself and Nadia as the people fighting hardest to protect Captive's Sound—but Dad fought, too, in his own way, feeding the people who were working hard. "Go ahead. I'll get in as soon as I can, so no rush. Sleep all you want. Is the restaurant still high and dry?" La Catrina was on a small hill, which he'd hated when his only concern was how heavy the trash bins were.

"For now." Dad plodded out, and after a moment he heard the door to his father's bedroom open and shut.

He leaned over the bed just in time to see Nadia stick her head out and look up at him. The urge to laugh seized him, and she bit her lip, and he had to bury his face against the mattress to keep from cracking up. She was still shaking with laughter when she climbed back into the bed with him.

"Oh, my God," she whispered between giggles. Mateo put his arms around her from behind and rolled them both over so they could laugh into the pillow.

When he could breathe again, he looked over at Nadia, who was wiping tears of laughter from her eyes. Even then, her smile was becoming sadder. "I didn't think I'd ever laugh like that again."

"I know," Mateo murmured.

They were both still bound to the One Beneath. Both still doomed. But for now, they were alive, and together, and happy. Maybe this was their last moment to be with each other like this, without anything else in the way. All the more reason to hold on to it.

He folded her against his chest, and she sighed, as though letting go of a great burden.

They'd worry about sneaking her out of the house later. For now, Mateo intended to lie there with her and pretend they had all the time in the world.

Verlaine opened her eyes. She lay across her bed—head perpendicular to the pillow—in her pajamas, totally alone.

She sat bolt upright, hair falling around her face, as she tried to remember exactly what had happened. *Asa was here—we kissed—oh, my God, did we kiss—and then—what?*

Maybe this was what it was like when you got roofied. But Asa hadn't done that to her. What had he done?

Her hands trailed through her hair, along her body. She didn't feel any different, and yet she did . . . it was impossible to find words for it. When Asa had kissed her—oh, that was no ordinary kiss.

What do demon kisses do? Nadia and I never went over demon kisses! What if I have amnesia? What have I forgotten?

If I forgot losing my virginity, that is the most pathetic thing ever.

No, that couldn't be right. Her pajamas were still on, underwear, too, and she sensed that whatever had happened with her and Asa last night, physically it had been no more than a kiss. When she remembered that kiss, though—when pleasure rippled inside her almost as powerfully as it had last night—Verlaine wondered if maybe it should count as sex.

Yeah. It should. Maybe that's just how demons do it.

Why had Asa left, though? Even if he had to sneak back home, and avoid interrogation by her dads (which, now that she thought of it, was a good idea), he should have woken her to say good-bye. Were demons bad at morning-after etiquette?

Then Verlaine recalled the state Asa had been in when he came to her. His body shaking, the desperation in his eyes, the terrible burns on his hand . . .

Fear clamped around her heart, like cold metal. Asa's in trouble. Last night he came here to—

The next words should have been *say good-bye.* But Verlaine wouldn't let herself go there, even in her mind.

She ran to the closet, grabbed the first thing she laid her hand on (1960s blue-and-white shift, plus black leggings for not freezing), tucked her silver hair back into a sloppy bun, scrawled a near-illegible note to her dads, and ran out the door. The land yacht was still parked back near the town square, which meant she'd have to go on foot. Although Verlaine pulled up the hood of her raincoat for protection against the lightly falling rain, she knew people would still recognize her. Okay, so, the next person who saw her would at the least look at her like she was dirt; maybe they'd be violent like the mob at La Catrina. Maybe she'd get spit on again—which somehow seemed even worse.

Verlaine didn't care how much they hated her. If they wanted to fight? Fine, she'd fight. *I'm taller than half the men in town. About time they remembered it!* Her hands balled into fists at her sides as she walked faster, then faster, then finally ran, her rain boots splashing in the deep puddles that had almost swallowed every sidewalk.

As she ran, snatches of memory from the night before came back to her—the warmth of Asa's embrace, and the whisper of his voice inside her own mind. *You should always have had this, Verlaine. You should always have had love.*

Finally she got to the Prasads' house. Panting, she climbed the steps. Maybe Asa had simply wanted to let her sleep last night; maybe he was here at home, hanging out, and he'd open the door to see her and take her into his arms. Maybe, just once, it could be that simple.

When she rang the bell, it was Mrs. Prasad who answered. Before she could say anything, Verlaine blurted out, "Is Jeremy home?"

"No, dear. He went to help his friend Mateo last night and stayed over." Mrs. Prasad's face lit up with the most beautiful smile. "Your name is Verlaine, isn't it? I've always thought that was a lovely name."

"Uh, thank you." Nobody had ever said that before.

To Verlaine's astonishment, Mrs. Prasad's smile only widened. "Would you like to come in and wait for Jeremy? Or maybe you'd just like to get warm and dry. I'm about to bake a fresh batch of Christmas cookies. You could have some straight out of the oven!"

Verlaine's stomach grumbled, hoping for cookies; she'd run out of the house without eating any breakfast. What struck her was how kind Mrs. Prasad was being. How . . . normal. Nobody ever casually invited her in, or offered her cookies. It was as though Mrs. Prasad could see her, really see her, in the way only Asa ever had before.

Asa must have told them about her. Won them over. Her heart contracted, tight with love and fear for him all over again.

"That sounds great," Verlaine said, "but I can't. Not today. Sorry."

"Some other time, then." Mrs. Prasad just kept beaming at her.

As Verlaine hurried back down the stairs, she heard another voice—Mr. Prasad's—ask, "Who was it?"

"That beautiful Laughton girl," Mrs. Prasad said, and then, just before Verlaine passed out of earshot, "She must have all the boys after her!"

Just the one, Verlaine thought. *One is enough, if I can just find him again. Asa, where are you?*

Mrs. Prasad had said that Asa went over to Mateo's. Verlaine had figured that was a lie Asa had told to cover up his night at her house, because A) he had been at her house, and B) Asa and Mateo weren't exactly BFFs. What if it wasn't a lie? Maybe he'd gone to see Mateo afterward. If Asa were plotting against Elizabeth again, he could have turned to Mateo, or he might have been delivering a message from Nadia.

Verlaine couldn't tell whether those possibilities were actually plausible, or whether she was desperately trying to convince herself that they were. Either way, she had to find Mateo next.

Will he be at home or at La Catrina? She kept running through the rain, ignoring the painful stitch cramping her side. *La Catrina's closer. I'll go there first.*

As she ran, more and more of the night before came back to her. Some flashes of memory made her flush with astonishment and desire—the intensity of Asa's kiss, or the way she'd melted into his arms. But those weren't the ones that made her push herself harder, start running faster. The flashes of memory that haunted her were Asa's words inside her head.

Take it back. Take it all back. This is the last thing I can give you. The only thing worth giving.

What did he mean, *the last thing*?

As Verlaine rounded the corner of the town square—the one corner of it still not blocked off by orange traffic cones—a fireman caught sight of her. She braced herself for an order to pull back, or worse; instead, the man grinned and waved. "Morning, beautiful!"

What was that about? Verlaine kept going, but as she did so, more and more people saw her. Every single one lit up with a smile.

"Hi, Verlaine!"

"Good morning, sunshine!"

"Have a wonderful day!"

Not every person shouted happy greetings at her. More of them stared and smiled, practically glowing with admiration.

Take it back.

Verlaine gasped and stopped in her tracks. Another memory bloomed hot and bright within her mind—the searing pain/pleasure of Asa's hands on her, the sense that her heart was filling with something far more tangible than emotion, a weight she'd been lacking for too long . . .

Her ability to be loved. That was what Elizabeth had stolen from Verlaine so long ago—and that was what Asa had returned to her.

For a few seconds, Verlaine simply stood there as she tried to take it in. She'd spent her entire life sealed off from being appreciated, loved, or even really seen by anyone besides her dads. Every single day, she'd braced herself to endure insults or the constant, dull misery of being ignored. Could it be over? Was that possible?

Everyone was smiling at her. Absolutely everyone. Even if Asa gave Verlaine back all her ability to be loved, that wouldn't make every single person she met instantly adore her.

Verlaine's eyes widened as she finally glimpsed the truth. Asa had given her back her ability to be loved, the ability Elizabeth had stolen. Yet Verlaine wasn't the only one Elizabeth had stolen from. According to Asa, Elizabeth had done this over and over through the centuries, collecting so much . . . lovability that nobody could help cherishing her.

Asa had given Verlaine *everything* Elizabeth had stolen. All the mislaid love and adoration of the past four hundred years now lived and glowed inside Verlaine, shining on everyone who crossed her path.

Slowly Verlaine started walking again, heading toward La Catrina. A policeman fell into step beside her, an umbrella in his hand. "Wouldn't want you to get any wetter," he said, presenting it to her.

"Thanks." Her voice sounded faint even to her own ears. Everybody was staring. Grinning like she was chocolate and Christmas rolled into one. This was weird. Vaguely awesome, but definitely weird.

La Catrina seemed like a beacon of normality, with its brilliant yellow-and-lime-green sign still bright against the dark, rainy sky. Verlaine hurried through the door, folding the black umbrella back in on itself with a small shower of water droplets. "Is Mateo here?"

The rescue workers who had been shoveling food into their mouths all stopped, and virtually every one of them smiled and answered her by pointing or calling, "Over there!" One man called, "Hey, Mateo! The prettiest girl in town's come to see you."

A moment later the kitchen door swung open as Mateo came through, black apron tied around his waist. "Nadia?" he said, before catching sight of Verlaine.

It was like Mateo turned into a statue, or like somebody had hit "pause" on reality. He just stood there, staring at Verlaine, until she waved her hand in front of his face. "Mateo?"

"Sorry," he said, shaking his head. "It's just—you're very—wow. Just wow. I mean, you know I love Nadia, but I can still mention that you're totally gorgeous, can't I? For a compliment. Because you're—amazing."

This was flattering but extremely inconvenient. Verlaine snapped her fingers in front of him. "Pull yourself together!"

He shook his head and tried to focus on her anew. "Okay. Sorry. Whoa."

"Where is Asa? Have you seen him?"

"No. Not since early last night." Mateo's dazed grin faded as darker memories crowded into his mind. "He trapped me into a bad bargain. Me and Nadia both. I know he couldn't help it—that's what demons have to do—but still."

What happened? Verlaine wanted to ask, but now she was putting it all together. Asa had been forced to do something unspecified yet wicked to Nadia and Mateo. He'd been upset by that. Guilty. Burdened. Reminded that he wasn't free. So he'd decided to take action. He'd stolen back Verlaine's ability to be loved, and all the other stolen love of Elizabeth's past four centuries, and given them to Verlaine forever.

That meant Asa had gone against the One Beneath. He had betrayed his master. The penalty for what he'd done . . .

Hell beyond hell, Asa had said. Eternal torment. Eternal suffering.

No chance of ever coming back to the mortal realm again.

Last night hadn't been only about giving something back to her, Verlaine realized. Asa had also come to her to say good-bye, forever.

Elizabeth stood knee-deep in brackish water, watching the clouds in the distance.

Once again, the rain over Captive's Sound had nearly ceased because she had wrung out every cloud in the sky. And once again, new rain-fat clouds were being blown toward town to begin the floods anew.

Only another day or two, my beloved lord, she thought. *Our work is nearly done. Soon our rule will dawn bright and glorious on a world broken into pieces at your feet.*

She began walking back toward her house, aware that she should sleep. By now Elizabeth's exhaustion went deeper than any few hours of rest could remedy. For so many years, her body had been all but immortal, preserved by dark magic she had used to keep herself in the service of the One Beneath. That immortality had shattered the night of Halloween, and since then, the toll on her body had been fierce. She was out of practice at eating regularly, sleeping eight hours, or even bandaging small cuts; she owned no coats and few shoes. By now bruises shadowed her freckled skin in deep purple and sickly green. A ragged cough seized her chest at odd moments, and Elizabeth suspected part of the warmth she felt was not the result of her magic, but of an ordinary fever.

This body would collapse soon—but that did not matter. Elizabeth only needed its service a short time longer.

As she walked back toward town, she saw a van emblazoned with the bright yellow words WEATHER TV. Near it stood a young blond man in some sort of waterproof anorak, talking into a camera and microphone held by two women. He was saying, "Meteorologists are saying that the weather system battering the Rhode Island coast is unprecedented, a so-called 'perfect storm' that is in effect stealing rain and moisture from the rest of the country—in fact, the rest of the western hemisphere. All that moisture is coming down right here. We'll keep coming to you live from Captive's Sound."

The people of this world still thought they could understand what was coming. Elizabeth would have found it pathetic were it not so amusing.

Then the young man wearing the anorak lowered his microphone, work apparently done, and stared at Elizabeth. "Hey, are you okay?"

Elizabeth should not have merited their notice, not with her stolen glamours around her. No matter. She simply smiled at the Weather TV crew to put them at their ease.

But her smile did not work. The camera crew only looked more worried for her, and the reporter took a step backward, as though unnerved. One woman said, "What happened to you?"

What could they mean? To them, Elizabeth should have appeared as any other beautiful young woman; dazzled by the magic surrounding her, they should have accepted anything she did, anything she said. They shouldn't even have questioned her decision to stroll through town in the middle of dangerous flooding. Instead, they gaped at her as though the mere sight of her were unnerving.

Elizabeth looked down at herself—at her bare, bloodied feet, the bruises along her legs, the wretched state of her dress. Nobody else should have been able to see it, but they could. They did.

That could only mean her protective shields of beauty and lovability, the glamours that had protected her these many centuries—they were gone.

"Should we call an ambulance?" the reporter whispered to his colleagues. "I think she's in shock."

Although Elizabeth's first instinct was to ignore this, she realized she could not. From now on, she realized with dismay, she would have to grapple with mortal concerns. It didn't matter much, because it wouldn't be for long, yet the distraction alone angered her. *How dare they take away what she had owned for so long? How dare they inconvenience her at the most important stage of her work?* But she would not acknowledge this vulnerability. Would not even admit it could be a problem. She put on her best smile. "I fell down. I'm fine. Walking back to my automobile."

The Weather TV team didn't look convinced, but when Elizabeth turned her back and walked away, they did not follow. Yet they might call the police and report her as injured or dazed. If the police came to her house and saw it for what it was—what would happen?

She walked faster, then ran, until she was all the way back home. The splinters in her rotting front steps jabbed into the soles of her feet as she staggered inside, looking for her woodstove.

For so many years it had burned, consuming the fuel of a hundred people's goodness and love, allowing that heat to radiate from her and dazzle any who came into her presence. Now the stove was black and cold. Empty. Useless.

The demon had done this. Her rage flared brighter and hotter than all the stolen love ever had—but then she felt the consolation of the One Beneath, as He showed her a sliver of Asa's anguish in the realms of hell. The demon's pain was of such intensity that her own nerves quivered in a kind of sympathy that did not touch her heart. Asa was being punished for his betrayal, and his punishment would last into infinity.

Tear into him, she prayed. *Rip him apart again and again, so that I can listen to him howl even here.*

For one moment, it seemed to Elizabeth that she could hear the screams, and she smiled.

"Thanks for letting me stay here," Nadia said, then confessed, "I wasn't even sure you'd let me through the door."

"One month ago, after you made that deal with Elizabeth, I might not have," said Faye Walsh. She stood in the middle of her living room, which was as intimidatingly chic as her wardrobe. Nadia felt like she shouldn't be standing on this Persian rug; shouldn't it be in a museum or something? The furniture was all upholstered in pale ivory, like Faye lived in some alternate universe where nobody ever ate Cheetos. For the moment, however, Nadia lived here. Faye held bed linens in her hands (white with actual lace), because she was preparing to turn one of the sofas into a guest bed.

"Why did you change your mind?" Nadia said, "I'm still sworn to the One Beneath."

"I'd be lying if I said I were at peace with that." Faye began smoothing one of the sheets atop her sofa. "But I've watched this town come apart over the past couple of weeks. I know how close we are to the final crisis. Maybe what you've done can't help us—but maybe it can, and by now I realize you're the only chance we've got."

"It's not just me." Nadia managed to smile. Since spending the night with Mateo, she'd found her smiles came easier than they had in a long time. "Mateo's in this, too. And Verlaine. And your mom, too. I mean, we learned a lot from her Book of Shadows. She's still helping us, even if she can't know it anymore."

Faye's answering smile was strange—sort of bent—which puzzled Nadia until she realized Faye was trying to hold back tears. Embarrassed, Nadia started pushing the spare pillow into its lacy case.

When Faye could speak again, she said, "You know I spoke with your father last night."

"I don't care about the First Laws." Nadia didn't think Faye actually meant to lecture her about telling a man the truth about witchcraft. She thought Faye was going to tell her what Dad was thinking—how angry he was at the daughter he'd never even knew—and Nadia couldn't stand to hear that right now.

At that moment, the doorbell chimed. The interruption was a relief.

When Faye opened the door, she gasped, and Nadia turned around in alarm . . . and gasped just as loudly. "Verlaine?"

Her friend walked toward her, Mateo at her side. But even loving Mateo as she did, Nadia could hardly look at him. Her eyes didn't want to leave Verlaine for an instant. Had she always been this beautiful? Her silver hair shone like silk, and her long, thin face had never appeared so graceful or elegant. Yet Verlaine's overwhelming physical beauty wasn't what struck Nadia the most. Instead it was every memory she had of Verlaine—from the first day they'd met to the day Nadia had told Verlaine good-bye. Every single one of those memories came back to her now, but instead of the veiled, incomplete Verlaine she'd seen before, Nadia saw her for real. All her loyalty. All her humor. All her courage. This was the true Verlaine, her friend, the one she needed so much more than she'd ever been able to realize before.

"Oh, my God." Nadia flung her arms around Verlaine, who hugged her back. "The magic is broken. But how?"

"Asa." Verlaine's voice was husky with unshed tears. "He

stole that love back for me. Gave me all the other love Elizabeth ever stole, too, which is nice, but kind of inconvenient, because on our way here two firemen proposed to me."

"Also Ms. Tseng at the 7-Eleven," Mateo prompted her. "It's legal here now."

"I know. Uncle Dave and Uncle Gary are planning a ceremony this summer, and I have to get a bridesmaid's dress." Verlaine made a sound that was half-sob, half-laugh as she pulled back from Nadia's embrace. Her expression became grave. "Listen. I have to know something."

"Name it," Nadia answered.

"Tell me how to get to hell."

For a moment, nobody spoke. Nadia could tell that Mateo and Faye were as puzzled as she was. Finally Nadia said, "What?"

"Tell me how to get to hell," Verlaine repeated. Now her eyes blazed, and she looked like something out of mythology class, some avenging spirit set loose on the world. "The One Beneath dragged my boyfriend down to hell, and I'm going to bring him back."

By her "boyfriend" she meant Asa, who had helped betray them all. Nadia glanced at Mateo, who said, "Listen—I know he cares about you, but the guy's a demon."

Verlaine turned on Mateo. "I'm not here to ask for your approval! Asa loves me. He loved me enough to take on eternal torment just so I'd have the chance to feel like I mattered. Even though he thought I'd only get to feel it for a few days before the end. Asa did that for me. I don't care if he's a demon. I love him, and I'm going to get him, no matter what it takes."

Faye shot Nadia a look, like, *You have to be the one to talk her down from this.* Mateo had folded his arms across his chest, equally skeptical.

Nadia understood exactly how they felt, but the more she thought about what Verlaine had said, the brighter an idea burned within her mind. "Okay," she said.

Everyone stared, and Mateo said, "Okay what?"

With a smile, Nadia took Verlaine's hands. "Let's go to hell."

13

MINUTES FROM LATEST MEETING OF "TEAM NOT EVIL"
Team leader Nadia Caldani called the meeting. In
attendance: Mateo Perez (Steadfast, catering), Faye Walsh
(Steadfast, temporary landlady), Gage Calloway (formerly
in thrall to Elizabeth), and Verlaine Laughton (sidekick,
chronicler of heroic deeds).

Gage leaned over Verlaine's shoulder to read her notes,
then whispered, "How come we're not 'Team Good'?"

"Nadia's sworn to the One Beneath, and both she and
Mateo are sworn to become demons, so I think maybe technically we can't be considered 'good' at present." Verlaine
kept writing as fast as she could. "But it's the thought that
counts, right? Our intention. That's what's going to get us
straight to hell."

"That doesn't sound as encouraging as you think it does,"
Gage said.

They were sitting around Faye Walsh's dinner table, set apart from the rest of the house in a dining room with mist-green walls and an honest-to-God crystal chandelier hanging from the ceiling. Instead of fine dining, they were having a meeting about how best to keep the world from ending very soon, like possibly tomorrow.

Verlaine had already figured out that they might not all survive. She figured her own chance for survival was probably lower than most, given that she was going to the demonic realm—which definitely counted as a bad idea. But if that was what it took to save Asa from eternal torture, then that was what she had to do. And Verlaine intended to leave a record behind.

If we do die saving the world, she thought, *at least they'll know who to thank*.

"Okay," Nadia said. "Here's what we know so far. All Elizabeth's darkest magic is built on emotions. She created the bridge to this world from sorrow and grief; now she's creating the doorway for the One Beneath from fear and hate." Her face seemed to have changed these past few weeks, Verlaine thought; Nadia seemed older now, but more beautiful in a stark way. It was as though a sculptor had carved her true features from the person she'd been just a few months ago. "From the time I started working with Elizabeth, she told me the ultimate weapon was forged from hate. It's true in more ways than I ever realized before now."

"I thought love was supposed to be stronger than hate," Faye said.

Nadia smiled grimly. "Not in hell."

Gage raised a hand, as though they were still in school. "I just have to say, I'm not one hundred percent comfortable with how often 'hell' is coming up in this conversation."

"Too bad," Verlaine said, still scribbling. "Because that's where we're headed."

"Not all of us," Nadia said. "Just me and Verlaine."

Mateo leaned forward, his elbows were braced against the table. "I don't understand. If the One Beneath has to move heaven and earth—literally—to get into our world, how are we supposed to get to hell like it's, I don't know, a stop on the bus?"

"Not you," Nadia replied, her voice soft. "I need you here. Verlaine needs to find Asa, so she's coming with me to shield me while I destroy the One Beneath's bridge into this world."

Everyone looked around the table at one another. Verlaine's hand stilled, blue pen against notebook paper, as she took that in.

Up until now, she'd thought this was going to be more of a snatch-and-grab rescue mission: Find Asa, grab onto him as tight as she could, and let Nadia bring them back ASAP, preferably before the One Beneath even noticed they were there. Nadia was talking about something much more involved . . . *and wait a second.* "Did you say I'm going to be the one shielding you?" What, did they think she had Kevlar vests for them or something?

"Love is the only defense," Nadia said. "Right now, you're the most beloved person on earth. I mean, literally."

Gage smiled. "I'll say." Faye reached over to pat Verlaine on the shoulder, and both Mateo and Nadia looked at her like kids looked at presents on Christmas morning. It was simultaneously creepy and flattering.

Nadia continued, "You've seen that, for the One Beneath, emotions are real. They're tangible, palpable. That's the material He uses to build everything He creates. So in hell, the love that surrounds you is going to be like—like a suit of armor. It can protect you for a long time. While you're near me, you'll protect me, too."

"So I'm in charge of protecting you from the lord of hell," Verlaine said. Nadia nodded yes. "Ohhhhhkay."

"How can you destroy the bridge?" Mateo said. "Elizabeth built it. She made that happen. After that, I thought we were screwed."

"There was no way we could destroy that bridge while we were in the mortal world." Nadia met his gaze steadily; a small smile even played on her lips. "In hell, as long as Verlaine's defending me, if I have the right weapon—I could destroy it, I think. The door into the mortal world will slam shut again. All Elizabeth's work will have been for nothing."

Gage raised his hand once more. "What's going to stop her from starting all over again?"

Nadia shrugged, and for the first time her tiredness showed; Verlaine wondered how long it had been since she'd slept. "Nothing. But this time we'll know what she's doing from the start. We can shut her down faster, and harder."

Mateo's expression was grim. "So we keep fighting like this forever."

"Fine," Verlaine said, forcing a smile onto her face. "Dandy. Bring it on. Because fighting forever beats the pants off dying any second now."

"I second that." Gage nodded.

Faye had been listening quietly, her hands steepled together. When she spoke, she'd clearly considered her words carefully. "I know it's possible for a mortal to enter the demonic realm while they're still alive. Momma told me that much. But if you're going to destroy His path into the mortal world—that's going to require serious ammunition. Magically speaking, I mean. You're an excellent witch, Nadia, but . . . I just don't know whether you've got that much power on your side."

Nadia only smiled. "Elizabeth taught me about the ultimate weapon. I know what to do. And . . . I'm going to have help."

Quickly Verlaine added, "I just want to emphasize how much help I might not be in hell."

"I didn't mean you." Nadia's expression had become more thoughtful. "I'm going to have to call in serious reinforcements."

What is that supposed to mean? Verlaine wanted to ask, but something about Nadia's quiet intensity kept her from saying anything. The entire group fell silent, taking it all in.

I'm going to hell. She'd jokingly said that before, when she ate the last of the ice cream without checking with her dads, or when she'd reblogged that naked picture of Michael Fass-bender. It wasn't a joke anymore. The place she was going would be so dark and so horrible that it would make Captive's Sound look like the Magic Kingdom. What if Nadia was wrong about this stolen love shielding them? Was she actually going to do this?

Mateo's hand closed over Nadia's, possessive and yet loving. Verlaine found herself remembering the way Asa had cradled her face—the warm touch of his fingers against her skin—and for a moment she missed him so much it hurt, so much she couldn't see or hear anything around her. Nothing seemed closer, or realer, than Asa—even though he wasn't with her.

Yes. She was going to do this. Asa had gone to hell for her; she would do the same for him.

Once Verlaine could focus again, she heard Mateo arguing, "I ought to come with you. I'm sworn to be a demon now, so that probably gives me the power to be there. Whatever the One Beneath throws at me, I can take—or I have to take, I don't know. I could protect you."

"You can't protect me now," Nadia said, caressing his hand. "I need you here—there's work to be done on this side, and you're probably the only one who can do it. Verlaine's the only one who can protect me. She's . . . surrounded by love. She draws it to her. No one in the whole world is as lovable, as adored—"

Verlaine whacked against the table with her palm. "Snap out of it! That's just the magic thing making you think that!

Come on, guys. Try to focus."

Nadia shook her head, and though she didn't stop grinning at Verlaine, she was able to get back to the subject. "Verlaine and I descend into hell. Once we get down there, Verlaine, you'll rescue Asa."

"Right. Yes." This was the most important part. "How do I do that, exactly?"

"You summon him with his real name. Demonic names have even more power in the underworld than they do here. Call to him, and he'll have to come to you." Nadia's expression clouded. "He—he might not look like himself at first. Just know that and be ready, okay?"

"Okay," Verlaine said, though she would have felt better about this if she'd known what Asa would look like, if not himself. Then again, it was a visit to hell, not a beauty pageant. Whatever she saw down there, she'd deal with.

"At some point we'll have to separate, so you can get Asa while I attack," Nadia added. "But we won't be far apart, even if you can't see me."

Gage raised his hand again. "Why wouldn't she be able to see you?"

"I don't know," Nadia said. "I don't know what hell's like any more than you do. We can't afford to assume anything."

Not just descending into hell. Descending into a vast unknown darkness with realms of hell nobody on earth understood. No reason to panic. None at all. Verlaine took slow, deep breaths, like she had that time she nearly fainted at choir practice.

"There's one thing I know for sure, though," Nadia said to Verlaine. "No matter what, don't say one single word to Asa besides his real name. Not one. If you do, the power his name gives you will be—diluted. Maybe even destroyed. Just his name, nothing more."

Verlaine nodded. "Got it."

"How can I help?" Faye said.

Nadia said, "You and Gage will have to keep back the people here who might interfere. That means Mateo has to take on Elizabeth." Her eyes finally went back to him. "You'll be alone."

Mateo shook his head no. "I'll still be with you. Even if I'm not there. You know that."

Verlaine jotted in her notebook, *The meeting came to a standstill for a romantic interlude.*

She used the quiet moment to mentally flip through her wardrobe to pick out the absolute perfect dress to wear to hell.

Faye and Gage bickered a little over who would get the privilege of driving Verlaine home. In the end, they both went along for the ride, which gave Nadia and Mateo a while in Faye's house alone.

Nadia made an important phone call, then walked into the living room, where Mateo waited for her. She sank gratefully onto the couch-turned-bed, into Mateo's arms.

"Who did you call?" he whispered, between kisses to her forehead and her hair.

"I'd better not say." Nadia looked into his eyes, willing him to understand. "The fewer people who know, the less evidence there is beforehand, the less chance Elizabeth or the One Beneath will sense what's happening in advance. If they know beforehand, that gives them a chance to prepare. I'd rather have the advantage of surprise." It was one of the very few advantages they'd get.

Mateo's dark brown eyes were worried. "You know I wouldn't tell."

"Not with words. But you might look at me at the wrong moment. React to the wrong thing Elizabeth said. Consciously you'd never, ever do anything to betray me—I know that. Unconsciously, we can all slip up."

"Okay." Mateo stroked his fingers through her hair; the touch soothed her, so that she shut her eyes and leaned against his chest.

Outside, the falling rain almost sounded peaceful. It was an illusion, but she could indulge that illusion for a few moments longer. Right now Nadia just wanted to pretend that she and Mateo never had to leave this room, that Faye wasn't coming back in a few minutes, that they could hold each other until the very moment she had to go into battle.

"When you defeat the One Beneath," Mateo said, "what happens to us?"

When, he'd said. Not *if*. He believed in her; that belief felt like the only thing holding her up. "Nothing much, at least not right away. We start over again, but smarter this time. Ready."

"That's not what I meant."

Which Nadia had known, really. She hadn't wanted to face it. But this was no time to start acting like a coward. So she lifted her face to Mateo's, so she could look him in the eye. "It doesn't break the deal. We're still sworn as demons. As for my being His Sorceress—that level of betrayal—it might break the bond between me and the One Beneath. Emphasis on *might*. So maybe at least I wouldn't have to serve Him until . . . until I died."

What she didn't add was that breaking that bond might be the thing that killed her. Going back on your word with the One Beneath wasn't as simple as crossing your fingers, or saying, *Sorry, never mind.* There were penalties to be paid.

She didn't hide this from Mateo out of fear. She hid it for his own good. Mateo would need all his strength to go up against Elizabeth. He didn't need distractions. He didn't need to be more afraid for Nadia than he already was. She would bear that knowledge alone.

Mateo sensed her mood, though he didn't seem to guess the reasons for it. "Are you afraid?"

"Well, duh."

He laughed softly. "I meant, right now. This moment."

"Not with you." Nadia slid her arms around his neck and breathed in the scent of his skin. Every memory of their night together flickered through her mind, making her want him all over again.

"Good," Mateo said. "You and me—we belong to each other. Only to each other. Not to the One Beneath, or

273

Elizabeth, or any of her curses. You're mine. I'm yours. No magic is powerful enough to change that."

Nadia kissed him. When his mouth opened against hers, her entire body seemed to go weak, like she didn't have the strength for anything but kissing him back. She fell back onto the couch, towing Mateo down with her, until he lay on top of her and they could twine themselves together.

Mateo pressed down against her, and the pressure made her moan softly. He kissed her harder, with more intensity, and Nadia slid her hands up under his shirt, along the muscles of his back —

—and then she broke the kiss. Panting, she said, "We're on Faye's couch."

"Right. Right." Mateo was breathing hard, too. He leaned his forehead against hers, and she could feel all his yearning. "Sure you don't want to stay the night at my place? If we were really quiet, Dad probably wouldn't know anything."

"I wish I could, but I . . . I can't . . ."

Nadia couldn't concentrate anymore. Even the desire heating her whole body from within seemed further away. Nothing else compared with what she was sensing deep within Mateo at this moment. Now, when they were so close, she realized that there was a kind of energy inside him that hadn't been there before—No. It had been, but less strong, less clear. She knew it now.

"Magic," she said.

Mateo looked down at her. "Magic won't let you stay at my house? Seems like it would help. Couldn't you just, you know, enchant Dad into not hearing us?"

"That's not what I meant." Nadia scooted out from under him, just enough to prop up on her elbows and study Mateo more closely. How had she not sensed this before? But already she understood the answer. Mateo's role as her Steadfast, and his bonds to all the magic that had been done in Captive's Sound during the past few months—those had touched upon a dormant power within him. Awakened it. "You have the potential to do magic. Mateo, you could have been a witch."

"Guys can't be witches," Mateo said, but then he caught himself. "We can't be Steadfasts either, though, and I am one. You mean, the way I was conceived—it makes it possible for me to be a witch?"

Mateo had been conceived via in vitro fertilization. Nadia had already realized that this twist of technology was what had made him exempt from the ancient law of magic that said *No man conceived of woman shall possess the powers of witchcraft.*

Why hadn't she realized that Mateo had the capacity for other forms of magic as well? He didn't seem to have been born into a witching bloodline, but it was possible his father's family was in the Craft and Mr. Perez just didn't know it. Or maybe the Cabots had long had the potential, but it had gone untaught during the centuries of the family curse.

"I think so," Nadia said. "I think you could have learned witchcraft. You broke the thrall over Gage, didn't you? That power is in you."

"Could I learn even now? I mean, I know there wouldn't

be time for me to learn a whole lot before you go up against Elizabeth, but if I could do anything—"

"It's too late now. You would have had to have been trained in childhood . . . at least, I think so." Nadia had always been taught that you had to begin learning witchcraft very early in life, or else you had no chance of ever mastering magic. But had that been true, or just another arbitrary, antiquated rule? "I guess we could try."

"Like today?" Mateo lit up. "I could learn some spells before we go up against Elizabeth?"

This was a definite no. As she shook her head, Nadia said, "Even if you do have the potential to learn magic, there's no way I could teach you anything useful that fast. If we had a few months—maybe even six weeks or so, for something basic—but we don't."

"So this magic inside me helps us exactly zero?" Mateo asked. Nadia shook her head no. He sighed. "Figures."

But he wasn't thinking of the greater implications. Nadia had already realized that other babies would be born to witches through technologies such as IVF. Thousands and thousands of children were born that way every year. Right now, an entire generation of male witches was out there, not knowing their own power.

Was it possible one of them did know? Surely some mom, somewhere, had realized what her little boy could do. Some male witch had been trained since childhood in absolute secret, kept from the rest of the Craft. At least one—but maybe more than one. Who knew who else might be out there?

If this world survives, Nadia realized, *the Craft won't be the same. It will have to change. The old rules, the First Laws—they won't apply anymore.*

We'll have to find our own way.

The thought should have intimidated her; instead, it gave her hope. Maybe there was a free future, filled with infinite possibility, just ahead.

All she had to do was win.

Mateo had already put the possibility aside for now. "Are you sure you won't come home with me? I know you want to."

"I do. But there's something else more important waiting for me."

"What is it?"

"I might be staying here, but that doesn't mean I get to hide. Before we go against the One Beneath, I need to set things right." Nadia took a deep breath. In her mind she could only see the image of her father's face when they'd parted—the betrayal there, and the horror.

Maybe her father still feared her. Maybe he'd learned to hate her. But whatever he was feeling didn't change what was in Nadia's own heart.

"I need to see Dad, and Cole," she said. "I need to go home."

*DON'T BE STUPID. JUST WALK IN. MAYBE THEY DON'T
hate you.*

Nadia stood in front of her house, umbrella overhead shaking under the constant fall of rain, unable to make herself go the next few feet that would take her to her door.

Maybe they do hate me.

So what if they do? This is your home as much as it is theirs.

Except for the part where Dad pays the mortgage and the deed is in his name and everything.

Cole is in there. No matter what Dad thinks, you know Cole still loves you. All these storms must have scared him so much. You need to go in there and hug Cole. The rest is irrelevant.

She couldn't do it for herself, but for Cole, she could. Nadia walked to the door, put her hand on the knob—then decided to knock.

Dad might've changed the locks.

The sound of footsteps coming closer made her gut tense, but Nadia simply dropped the umbrella on the porch and waited. Finally the knob turned, and the door opened—a sliver of warmth and light in the cold, wet darkness—and then her father stood there, staring.

"Hi," Nadia said. Then she felt stupid. It seemed like she should have had something better to say than that, something that might make her dad respond or at least do something besides just *stand there*—

Then Dad pulled her into a hug so tight she could barely breathe. His arms were locked around her, as though she were on the edge of a cliff and he was trying to pull her back to safety.

"Nadia. Sweetheart." Dad's voice cracked on her name, which just made her start crying. "Thank God you're all right. We've been worried sick."

"I'm sorry," she managed to say against his shoulder. "I didn't know if you hated me."

"There is nothing, nothing on this earth that could make me hate you. Ever. Don't you know that?" Dad let go of her to take her face in his hands, and Nadia thought she might be able to get it together until she realized he had tears in his eyes, too. "I should have made sure you always knew that. I'm sorry, sweetheart."

"It's not your fault. It's not." Nadia tried to smile, but the sobs inside her kept welling up, twisting her mouth and making her sniffle.

Then she heard Cole yelling, "Nadia!"

She let go of her father to drop to her knees just in time to scoop Cole into her arms. His baby blue sweater didn't match his red cords at all, and his hair was a mess, plus he smelled like Cap'n Crunch, which meant Dad wasn't doing well at fixing dinner on his own. After so many weeks of knowing the fate of the whole world rested on her shoulders, it was almost comforting to remember that she was needed here, too—to dress her little brother, or make spaghetti, or just be here with them.

Cole wore the biggest smile she'd ever seen. "Nadia, is it true? Dad says you can do magic!"

He told Cole? After the first moment of shock, Nadia found herself smiling, too. If Dad had told Cole, that meant he was able to face it. Her family knew her for who she was, and loved her just the same.

"It's true," Nadia said, hugging Cole again. "It's all absolutely true."

She used the spell for light again. Nadia didn't bother using this one often; the glow was fairly dim, which meant a flashlight was usually just as good if not better.

But to little kids, the sphere was the coolest thing ever.

"Wow," Cole whispered as he sat beside her on the living room floor, staring up at the light overhead. The surface of the sphere rippled slightly, reminding Nadia of NASA films she'd seen of the molten surfaces of stars. "Can you make fireworks?"

Nadia laughed. "I don't know. I never tried."

"Try now!" Cole bounced up and down; the sugar rush was in full force.

"Not now. We're inside, and fireworks wouldn't be any fun inside the house. Plus nobody wants to be outside while it's raining." When Cole looked disappointed, she put her hands on his shoulders. "Hey. Have you been coloring in your Santa coloring book? You know you have to have it all done by Christmas Day if you want your stocking filled."

"I have! Do you want to see? I'll go get it." He dashed for the stairs, leaving Nadia alone with her father for a few moments.

Dad sat in his recliner, leaning on one elbow. Now that Nadia had had a chance to look at him, she could see how exhausted he looked. Normally Dad took better care of himself than most middle-aged guys. Tonight he had at least a day's worth of stubble, and his shirt was rumpled. She thought he might not have slept since he'd learned the truth.

Nadia said, "Did you tell Cole about Mom?"

"No. I didn't know what to say."

"Her not telling you—neither of us telling you—it didn't have anything to do with not loving you. You know that, right? It's one of the First Laws of the Craft. We're never, ever supposed to tell a man, any man, about what we can do." Nadia chewed on her bottom lip.

"Okay." Dad weighed that for a few seconds before he added, "I don't blame you, Nadia. I want you to understand that. Apparently you were doing what you felt like you had to do. That doesn't make it easier for me to deal with the fact that I never knew the woman I married. Not really. In some ways, I'm only starting to get to know you, and you're one of the two people I love most in the world."

"Hey, at least Cole's an open book." That made Dad smile a little, but the joke sounded fake to her. She forced herself to keep going. "You know Mom loved you a lot. She gave that love away to save me. Nothing else could have made her do it."

Her father nodded, though she could tell it hadn't really sunk in yet. His whole world had been turned inside out; Nadia figured it was like one of those optical illusions in books, where you think you're looking at a vase until suddenly you see it's two faces—except this was the past twenty years of his life he was looking at, only now seeing the truth that had been hidden in the shadows.

He said only, "You're back home for good, right? Or until college. Culinary school. Whatever. Where have you been staying?"

"I stayed at Mateo's one night. Right now I'm staying with Faye Walsh—the guidance counselor from school? Her mom was a witch, so she knows what's going on."

She'd been concentrating on not telling him that she'd been driven to go to Elizabeth's; her father could never know how she'd felt there, abandoned and cast out, forced to sleep on the floor and surrounded by broken glass. But after the words came out, Nadia realized that she'd just told her father she'd spent the night with Mateo. *Oh, crap.*

Mercifully, Dad didn't seem to have caught it. "You said the flooding, the rain—that they were part of what Elizabeth was doing to this town. That they were, uh, black magic." He had to clear his throat after getting those words out. "And it's still happening."

"She's still at work. This isn't over until I face Elizabeth one more time. The rain is just the symptom, Dad. If she isn't stopped—the flooding, the collapses, everything else that's happened in Captive's Sound over the past few months—that will seem like nothing, compared to what she's going to do."

"You're the only one who can stop her? There's no one else who can . . . help, or support you, or anything like that? Where are the other witches?"

"I don't know," Nadia said, again condemning the ancient secrecy that had once protected the Craft but now crippled it. "But I'm not alone, Dad. Mateo and Verlaine know the truth, and they're both helping out every way they can."

She couldn't tell him the plan. No way she'd calm him down by saying, *All I have to do is literally descend into hell.*

"What about me?" Dad reached out from where he sat to clasp her hand. "What can I do? Name it, Nadia. Name it and I'm there."

Tears pricked at her eyes again. "It's okay, Dad. You don't have to try to save the world."

"Forget the damn world. You're my baby girl. I want to save you."

Nadia reached up to hug him tightly. "You already have."

"Nadia said we needed a base of operations," Mateo explained. "Someplace where nobody would bother us, and nobody would interfere."

Gage was driving his truck along the few roads in town not closed for flooding—a winding, circuitous path, now, that took forever to reach anyplace. At least nobody else was on the road this early in the morning. Nadia had said they wouldn't make their move until later in the day, but Mateo thought they ought to get ready.

Gage said, "Okay, but isn't the idea that she and Verlaine are going to go to hell, as in actual, you-could-put-it-on-a-map hell? So don't we need to be close to wherever it is that this portal is going to open up?"

"It's going to open in the sound. Underwater. And there's another crack just below the chemistry lab at Rodman. But no, we don't have to be there." The only way this could be worse, Mateo figured, was if they had to row out into the ocean during this final storm—or go to chemistry. "Basically, Nadia says that once the portal's breaking open, every single place on earth will be equally close to hell."

"As in, way too close."

"You got it. So we just need someplace safe, someplace private, and someplace on high ground, because the waters are only going to rise."

Gage sighed as he shifted his truck into gear. "Well, we can't get higher than the Hill."

With that, they cleared the last steep ridge and pulled into the wide circular driveway of Cabot House. Mateo still thought of it as Grandma's house—but as she'd said very clearly just before leaving town, now it belonged to him.

As Mateo jumped down from Gage's truck, he pulled the

heavy brass key to the mansion from his pocket. It clearly had been forged decades ago, if not more than a century. *Just like Grandma*, Mateo thought, *to be scared of everything but not invest in a dead-bolt lock.* He pushed the door open and turned on the light, then blinked.

"She didn't take anything?" Gage walked in just a few steps behind Mateo, looking around at the oil paintings in their gilded frames on the walls, the sumptuous furniture, and even the baby grand piano in the corner of the music room. "Wow. As of today, you have the sweetest crib of anybody I know."

"This place has always creeped me out," Mateo confessed. The heavy drapes were in such a dark red that they looked almost black; each window framed a sliver of night, and every pane was spattered with droplets as the relentless rain continued.

"I thought it was your grandmother who creeped you out. Now that she's gone, you can make this place your own, right?"

Maybe Gage had a point. But Mateo couldn't quite envision him and his dad living someplace like this, with marble tile and velvet rugs. It didn't matter anymore. "Come on. We need to clear a room. Any room will do."

Gage turned around; he was framed by the arching doorway, with its elaborate plaster scrollwork. "Why do we need to clear a room?"

"No specific reason," Mateo admitted, "but I'm gonna guess that battling the forces of hell makes a mess."

They decided on the living room, or parlor, whatever he ought to call a room with a bunch of fancy couches that nobody had sat on in the past twenty years. As heavy as the couches were, and as much swearing as he and Gage did, it beat trying to move the grand piano.

As they walked the longest sofa into the hallway, Mateo sweating as he tried to walk backward with it, Gage said, "So—you and Elizabeth—that really wasn't a thing."

"Right. The one time we made out, she'd cast a spell that made me think she was Nadia."

"You were trying to warn me the entire time," Gage said. They never stopped edging the sofa out of the room, never once looked directly at each other. "You just couldn't tell me the whole truth, because I would've thought you were crazy."

"Yeah. I should've tried harder, though."

"I wouldn't have believed you."

The heaviness in Gage's voice reminded Mateo of how much the guy had always adored Elizabeth from afar; nobody could be genuinely in love with a person they hadn't even talked to much, but Gage had come as close to it as anyone could. For a few weeks there, he'd really believed Elizabeth loved him back. Learning the truth had shocked Gage, even repulsed him—but a broken heart didn't mend in a day, or a week.

Quietly, Mateo said, "You still love her."

Gage just kept inching the sofa forward. "I still love the girl I thought she was. Just a dream I made up, I guess. Some kind of stupid, falling in love with a dream."

"Elizabeth's powers made almost everyone love her. I mean, I wasn't in love with her, but I thought she was the best friend I ever had. When Nadia tried to tell me who and what she really was, I shouted her down. Walked out on her. I could've lost someone real for the sake of an illusion."

That wasn't even the worst part. The worst was that, anytime Mateo tried to call up a happy memory of his childhood, the first images that came to mind were the false ones Elizabeth had slipped into his mind. Climbing trees, making cookies, doing cannonballs off the pier in summertime: Every single memory was clear, bright, and beautiful. And every single one of them was a lie.

He thought he'd miss the childhood friend he'd never really had for the rest of his life.

Look on the bright side, Mateo thought. *If we lose this battle, the rest of your life won't actually be that long.*

Finally they were able to set the couch down in the center of the music room, which was now crowded from wall to wall like a furniture store having a closeout sale. "Okay," Gage said, flexing his hands in relief. "We've cleared a room, created a playing field. Now what?"

Mateo knew they wouldn't talk about Elizabeth again tonight, and maybe not for a very long time. That suited him fine. "Now we wait and see."

"You don't sound as confident as you did at the house."

"I believe in Nadia," Mateo said. "But—you've seen what we're up against."

They'd lost the last two times they took Elizabeth on. He had to face the fact that they could lose again.

Gage ventured, "So, in the worst-case scenario—which is not gonna happen!—what comes next?"

"You get out of here. You do whatever you have to do to make your family get in the van, then swing by Verlaine's to pick up her dads and Cole, too. Then La Catrina—" Mateo's throat tightened, but he kept going. "Tell Dad I told you to go get him, okay? He'll go with you then. After that, you step on the gas and get as far from Captive's Sound as you can, as fast as you can."

Although Gage kept nodding, taking it in, he said, "Is that going to do any good? I mean, can you outrun the apocalypse?"

"I don't know. But if you guys can have any chance at all, I want you to take it." Mateo breathed deep, got his focus back. "Okay. You ready?"

"Yeah. Are you?"

"Yeah," Mateo said, and tried to believe it.

From the depths of her walk-in closet, Verlaine called, "You know, the time for arguing about this is over."

Uncle Dave called back from the hallway, "Do you mean it's time to admit that magic is real? Is it also time to check for chocolate from the Easter Bunny every morning?"

"You have no sense of timing." Uncle Gary's voice was distant, probably from the kitchen. "It's December, Dave. We should be waiting for Santa, not the Easter Bunny."

"We're not waiting on either one!" Uncle Dave sounded like he wanted to start thumping his head against the wall. "Just like we're not going to start believing in witchcraft!"

Verlaine didn't pay too much attention to any of this. She'd told her dads only that she was going to help Nadia tonight, leaving out the whole "actually descending into hell" bit. If Uncle Dave knew about that, his freak-out could probably be measured on the Richter scale.

Heels or no heels? The dress won't look right without them, but what if I have to run? What am I talking about? I'll already be in hell. Can't run away from that.

Normally Verlaine only wore Converse—or, lately, rain boots. But she owned a few pairs of size-10 modern shoes for dressy occasions, those moments when tennis shoes simply wouldn't do. If the end of the world didn't count as a special occasion, nothing did.

Black patent heels on her feet, she sat at her vanity and put the final touches on her makeup. She'd gone all out this time, even studying the tutorials on YouTube for liquid eyeliner. Maybe she was being silly, but fixing up felt like . . . putting on armor. Getting ready for absolutely anything that might come next. Besides, if they were successful, soon she'd see Asa again. *Gotta look pretty for that, right?*

Of course she knew it wouldn't matter what she looked like. Asa loved her regardless.

What about you? Are you going to love him no matter what? Verlaine knew that in hell she would see Asa without Jeremy Prasad's body. He might look like the person he'd been during his long-ago mortal life, whether that was fat or thin, handsome or ugly, well-made or deformed. Maybe he'd had leprosy. People used to get leprosy.

The thought of any regular human problems wasn't nearly as bad as the idea that Asa might be in his pure demonic form. Verlaine had no idea exactly what that might look like—classic Judeo-Christian demon with horns and tail? Something tentacled and baroque, straight out of Lovecraft? Whatever it was, she felt sure demons didn't look good.

Could she love something that wasn't even human?

Verlaine leaned her elbows against her vanity, breathing in the scent of powder and perfume. Her mind filled with thoughts of Asa—flirting shamelessly with her at the *Guardian*, daring her to call him out as a fake in class, desperately fighting to keep her above water during the flood, burning with unearthly heat as he drew her close to give her back all the love she'd missed for so long . . . and kissing her that first, perfect time, snowflakes floating in the air all around them.

I love him no matter what.

She took a deep breath, pulled herself together, and just had time to fiddle with her hair a moment longer before she heard the doorbell. Then Verlaine pulled on her bulkiest raincoat and headed to the door.

The Caldanis stood in the living room, all three of them; Verlaine had announced to her dads that they'd be babysitting Cole tonight. Nadia's father looked slightly dazed, like he was still fighting to take it all in, but Cole grinned as he said, "My big sister can do magic!"

"That's just a metaphor," Uncle Dave said.

"Is it?" Uncle Gary smiled at Nadia, who stood there in black sweater and leggings, smiling more easily than Verlaine had seen from her in a long time. "Verlaine tells us you're the baddest witch in town. Except Elizabeth, who is baddest in the literal sense of bad. True or false?"

"True," Nadia said.

To Verlaine's surprise, Nadia's father smiled, too. "I've seen her cast spells. It's pretty amazing."

"Oh, cool," Uncle Gary breathed. "Can you do one of those floating pink spheres that takes you anywhere you want to go? Like Glinda in *The Wizard of Oz*?"

Nadia shrugged. "Never tried it."

"Wait. Hang on. Are you all serious?" Poor Uncle Dave had to lean against the wall.

Verlaine announced, "No time to prove it tonight, but I'm sure Nadia won't mind showing you some spells when we get back. Or tomorrow."

"Tomorrow," Nadia repeated. Her eyes looked haunted, and from the way her father put his arm protectively around her shoulders, he knew exactly what was at stake. Then Mr. Caldani looked at Verlaine for the first time since she'd come in the room—really looked—and his whole face lit up. "Verlaine. You look lovely."

"Like a fairy princess," Cole whispered.

All the extra love was warping their minds, too. Verlaine laughed nervously. "Oh, just did my makeup for once."

"No, it's more than that." Mr. Caldani seemed to catch

himself. "Gary, Dave, forgive me if this is inappropriate, because I'm being totally sincere—have you ever introduced Verlaine to modeling agents? She could be on the cover of *Vogue.*"

If Uncle Dave's eyebrows had gone any higher, they would have merged with his hairline. "Well. Huh. Nobody has ever suggested that before."

"Thanks for the compliment," Verlaine said hurriedly, "but I'm going into journalism. Come on, guys. Let's head out."

"Hang on, sweetheart." Uncle Gary pressed a Tupperware container into her hands; inside were—

"Chocolate chip cookies?" Verlaine wanted to cry. Maybe that was because her dads were so sweet; maybe it was because she knew she might be seeing them for the last time, but couldn't tell them so. "I can't believe you made these."

"Just the rest of the slice-and-bake. I thought you guys might need a sugar fix."

"Chocolate actually makes magic stronger," Nadia said. She went on tiptoe to kiss Uncle Gary's cheek, then ruffled Cole's hair. "Hey. Verlaine says they have a Wii. Why don't you ask Mr. Dave if he'll show you the games?"

Cole brushed her hand away as he tried to smooth out his hair. "Okay. Will you wake me up when you come in?"

Nadia's chin trembled, and Verlaine put her hand on her friend's shoulder to steady her. It must have worked, because Nadia's voice was steady when she answered. "You bet."

They snacked on the cookies the entire way to Mateo's

house—even Mr. Caldani, who probably needed a comfort-food fix as badly as any of them. All around them were orange reflective cones or barricades, cutting off the flooded roads that shone like dark rivers around all the houses. Some houses had plastic tarps on the roofs or windows, trying to patch leaks and breaks; the rain alone had nearly torn Captive's Sound apart.

"Are you sure it's going to be tonight?" Verlaine asked. "The apocalypse, I mean."

"The near-apocalypse," Mr. Caldani said stubbornly. The windshield wipers beat at their fastest rhythm; the rain had intensified to a downpour. "Because we're going to stop it from happening. Right?"

Nadia nodded between bites of her cookie. "Right. And I know it's happening because Elizabeth is calling me. She wants me with her, helping."

"Don't you have to go to her?" Verlaine asked.

"No," Nadia said. "I can resist. The penalty would be terrible—but what we're doing is so much worse for Elizabeth, she's going to forget all about this. Trust me."

Mateo's grandmother's house—correction, Mateo's house—seemed to glow white amid all the darkness. They dashed inside, umbrellas held overhead or in raincoats, to walk into the grand foyer. Nadia went right into Mateo's arms, and they embraced so long that Mr. Caldani clearly felt awkward.

Faye Walsh, who'd been standing in the hallway, came forward to break the weird moment. Her lilac jeans and deep coral sweater seemed to defy the winter gloom. "Mr. Caldani. I see you've been brought into the loop."

"Yeah. But isn't that against the laws of witchcraft? Or something like that?"

Faye nodded. "I have a feeling the whole rulebook's going to be rewritten tonight."

Verlaine shrugged off her raincoat, and instantly, everyone in the room was staring at her. *Good. People ought to stare at a red vintage designer gown.*

"Wow," Mateo breathed.

Nadia wasn't even jealous. "Wow is right. Where did you get that?"

"My greatest eBay victory of all time," Verlaine squared her shoulders. "If I'm going to see the devil, you'd better believe I'm wearing Dior."

"Damn straight," Nadia said. Her black outfit made a sharp contrast to Verlaine's as Nadia came forward to take Verlaine's hands—Nadia sleek and ready for action, Verlaine in red satin that billowed out into a full skirt, and her hair pulled up to the crown to give her ponytail a retro look. Yet Verlaine felt closer to Nadia than ever before.

"Are we ready?" Mateo asked. Faye nodded. Mr. Caldani looked like he wanted to object, but he said nothing. Verlaine just squeezed Nadia's hands, trusting her to understand. However, Nadia didn't move. After a moment, Mateo said, "Is it not time yet?"

"It's time." Nadia's gaze had turned inward, as she "listened" to whatever magical currents and forces she could sense. "Elizabeth's at work. She's going to cast her final spells any moment."

After a silent few seconds, Verlaine prompted, "So this is where we swing into action, right? Batman and Robin?"

"Not yet," Nadia said.

What are we waiting for?

The foolish child would not come.

How ridiculous of her. Nadia had sworn herself to the One Beneath, first as any other might, then again to deepen the vow and make it permanent. Why fight it now?

Deep in her heart, though, Elizabeth was glad of Nadia's stubbornness, her stupidity. This work would be more difficult without her—but that meant Elizabeth alone would be responsible for bringing the One Beneath into this world. His love and gratitude would be hers alone. Never again would she have to feel that terrible jealousy when the One Beneath longed for Nadia; from now on, He would know the strength of Elizabeth's adoration outweighed any of Nadia's inherited gifts.

For you alone, my beloved lord.

Elizabeth did regret the demon's absence, however. She stood on the beach, rain beating down, her feet half-sunk into waterlogged sand. Had Asa been here, she could have used his pain to hurry this final step. Already she was so impatient to see her lord before her, to truly share a world with Him for the first time.

The demon suffered already, of course. Perhaps, in the

future reign of hell, she would be able to watch Asa's torment for herself. How sweet to see him writhe, and to share in the laughter and triumph of the One Beneath.

Within her she felt a strange rending, as though she were being torn at the seams. Nadia's magic, Elizabeth realized—the girl wasn't only hiding, she was trying to fight this.

Elizabeth laughed out loud. The rain on her face pounded down hard enough to ache.

Does she want to fight? Then we'll fight. Let her see what we truly are. Let Nadia Caldani learn the truth about magic at last.

She reached out toward the water, and at her command it began to roil. The waves churned in a dozen directions at once, and foam spiraled higher and whiter. Beneath the surface, a rich and strange orange glow brightened, glowing more and more strongly until it might as easily have been the sun.

Elizabeth's breath caught in her throat. She realized—for the first time in centuries, she was crying. Not for sorrow. For joy.

Everything she'd fought for. Every sacrifice she'd made. All of it was being redeemed, here and now.

She held out her hands, all the rings around her fingers shining from the rain, as she cast the spell that tore the world in two.

15

THE WORLDS BEGAN TO SHATTER, TO MERGE.

Nadia's eyes widened as she hung on to Verlaine's hands, panic rising inside her until it stifled her breath, tightened her throat. So far this was no more than a tremor within the ground; soon it would become far stronger, and unmistakably supernatural.

"So should we maybe get going to hell around now?" Verlaine said.

"I can open the portal," Nadia answered. Normally that would have been beyond her powers—but now that the mortal and demonic realms were so close, the journey would be easier.

But Nadia knew they were doomed if she entered hell unarmed. She'd gambled everything on creating the perfect weapon—everything, based on the slimmest of hopes—and now it looked like she'd been hoping in vain. How could she have been so stupid as to hope?

A heavy knock thudded against the door. Everyone jumped.

"Don't let anyone in," Faye said. Dad stepped forward, like he wanted to put himself between the rest of them and whoever was out there.

But Nadia knew who it was. "Open it. Now."

Although Mateo's eyes searched hers, unsure, he didn't hesitate. He went to the door and opened it, to reveal a woman standing there, unshielded from the rain. She walked inside, water running from her soaked sweater and skirt, trickling from the long hair plastered to her head, neck, and shoulders. She might have been the survivor of a shipwreck. Really she was the survivor of something far worse.

The worst part was seeing her father flinch—one hand to his gut, like he'd actually been struck. Nadia felt a moment of guilty relief that she hadn't been able to see his face; just hearing his voice was bad enough when he said, brokenly, "Kim?"

Somehow Nadia forced herself to smile. "Mom. You came."

"I said I would." Mom didn't even seem to get that Nadia would have doubted her; she walked by Dad as though he were just some object in the room, like a table or a chair. "It wasn't easy to get here. Most airports are closed all over the East Coast. I had to fly into New York, rent a car, and drive from there." She sounded ticked off, like saving the world was too much trouble for her.

But she couldn't help that, Nadia reminded herself. Mom

had given up all the love in her heart to save Nadia's life. The bitter, empty shell in front of Nadia now—that was a reminder only of how much love Mom had given up. That emptiness was the shadow of the love before, equally vast.

Verlaine squeezed Nadia's hands, offering comfort. She whispered, "Should I let go?" Meaning *Don't you want to hug your mom?*

Mom wouldn't want a hug. But that wasn't the main reason Nadia gripped Verlaine's hands as tightly as she could. "Don't let go," she said. "Whatever happens, whatever you see, you can't let go until I tell you to. Do you understand? No matter what, Verlaine."

"No matter what." Verlaine's face was even paler than usual, but Nadia didn't doubt she could handle this. Her friend was a lot tougher than the rest of the world had ever seen.

Dad tried again, "Kim, you came here because of—what—the spells?"

"You told him, I see." Mom's laugh was harsh; she only spoke to Nadia, never even glancing at her ex-husband. "Breaking the First Laws right and left."

"If that's what it takes," Nadia said. Then she felt it—a deeper, more terrible sundering of the world below than she'd ever felt before. It was like a cramp in her gut, all the magic that existed being poisoned and bent all at once. "We have to do this."

"Then let's do it," Mom said.

Mateo came closer; she could tell how badly he wanted

to hold her, to shield her through all this. But he only said, "What's going on?"

"The ultimate weapon is forged from hate," Nadia said. "And where we're going, I need the ultimate weapon. Nothing less could ever destroy the One Beneath. That means I need pure hatred—completely untouched by love."

Mom's smile was a crooked mockery of what it had been before. "I gave away everything that made life worth living to keep my daughter safe, and the One Beneath tricked me. Tricked her. Made my sacrifice meaningless. And you know what? It pisses me off."

Nadia nodded once at her mother, who put her hand on Nadia's shoulder. The emptiness Nadia sensed within her—the utter lack of any ability to care—seemed worse, in that moment, than the evil she was trying to fight.

The earth trembled again, stronger this time. Even as Faye cried out in alarm, and Dad braced himself against the wall, Mom just kept smiling. She said, "I can't love anymore. But I can damn sure hate."

Nadia closed her eyes and called upon a spell she had never tested before. The very first spell she had ever created herself.

A spell for forging a weapon of the spirit:

One who does not fall to cruelty.
One who does not fall to sorrow.
One who does not fall to danger.

The memories came to Nadia, fuller and richer than they had been even when she lived them.

Verlaine, ignoring the sneers and disdain of everyone around her as she walked through Rodman High in her vintage clothes and unwavering smile.

Dad, trying to cook dinner for his kids even though he had no idea how, and making jokes for them just like his heart hadn't been broken.

Mateo, diving into the sound where Nadia was trapped underwater, taking her in his arms, pressing his mouth to hers, and breathing the air from his lungs into hers.

Nadia didn't see the weapon. It wouldn't be visible here, in this world; it was made out of stuff truer and realer than the regular world would show. But she felt it, a weight settling on and around her, yet making her stronger. Mateo's nearness enhanced her power as it always did—he was a part of this, part of every spell she cast. The purity of her mother's hatred flowed through her, terrible in every way, and yet Nadia could feel it taking shape. Sharpening. Coming to a point.

"We're ready," she said. "Let's go."

This was glory manifest.

Elizabeth threw her head back in exhilaration. Every crack in the world's foundation felt like silk against her skin. Every quake of the earth's crust shuddered through her like pleasure.

The water in the sound was boiling away before her eyes.

Not boiling exactly—there was no heat to temper the wet, bitter cold—but bubbling up, surging away, revealing the first breach between the mortal and demonic realms. This was His doorway, His portal. He was coming closer to all places on earth now, surging up from below to turn this entire world into His possession, His playground.

"At last," Elizabeth said. She had fallen forward onto her hands and knees at some point; she didn't know when, and didn't care. Wet sand was caked in her long hair, and the grit was rough on her legs and palms. Her body shook with barely repressed laughter. "At last—"

And then a tremor. An interruption. As though the destruction whirling upward and outward were a symphony, but at the center of the music was a single off-key note growing louder and louder.

Nadia.

Elizabeth's eyes narrowed. The girl was free to destroy herself through her arrogance if she liked. None of her magic could avail her against the One Beneath now. But she was ruining the perfection of Elizabeth's greatest triumph and that—that, she would not endure.

She pushed herself to her feet and walked steadily into the water. The waves surged around her, through her, splintering her into a thousand pieces and putting her together again.

Screams and shouts of alarm welcomed her. Elizabeth pulled the waters around her like a cloak, then let them splash down around her as she stood within a vast empty room—the Cabot family home; she knew it from eras past. The few people huddled near the stairs gaping at her were not her concern. Not while Nadia Caldani stood before her. Mateo Perez was here, too, her old toy and future slave, and the gray-haired girl who . . .

Elizabeth recognized the glow of love around Verlaine, the glow that was rightfully her own but had been stolen by Asa before he was cast down. Her fury only grew.

"Oh, my God," said Nadia's father, the one Elizabeth had attempted to seduce. That failure had mattered little to her before, but now it was just one more reason to loathe everyone in front of her.

"Is this the Sorceress?" This was spoken by a lanky woman of adult years, bedraggled and wan.

"Yes," Nadia said. She pulled the gray-haired girl to her. "But she's too late."

And then—

The magic was one that Elizabeth herself had never worked, yet she recognized it instinctively. Nadia was taking advantage of the thin barriers between the realms; she was leaving this world. As the portal between the worlds widened, Nadia intended to leap through it.

Elizabeth reached for her, but already Nadia and the gray-haired girl were—not vanishing, but somehow becoming thinner, as if they could be folded up within the air itself. In a flash, they were gone. The air popped softly, rushing in to fill the spaces they'd left behind. Nadia's father swore under his breath, and the woman at the edge of the room, with her dark skin and bright clothing, gasped out loud.

It didn't matter. Nadia was too late now.

But how dare she see the One Beneath's true face before Elizabeth herself had the chance? How dare she steal this one last thing?

Elizabeth would follow her there.

It's like the world turned inside out, Verlaine thought.

At least, that was as close as she could come to thought. Fear and confusion gripped her as though in a powerful fist, and she was sure of nothing except Nadia still hanging on to her, and the need to hang on to Nadia in return.

She'd envisioned the demonic realm as looking like something off a death-metal album cover: fire, lava, caverns, the works. But she'd been thinking of it as just another place she could go, a place like any other. The demonic realm existed on a completely different plane from anything Verlaine had ever known—from anything she might recognize as reality.

When she opened her eyes, she saw visions that looked like the time someone had pushed her off the playground swing set, and when she fell hard on the ground, for a moment she'd only been able to see the pattern of veins behind her eyes. Or was it like a photographic negative? Whatever it was, it changed and writhed and pulsed . . .

Like we're inside something alive, she realized, her gut clenching.

That explained why she could only smell blood.

"Nadia! What's happening?" she shrieked over the roar of wind, rushing water, and screams.

"We're okay!" Nadia shouted back.

Apparently they had very different definitions of okay. "What do we do?"

"Not yet. Hang on! You're protecting me!"

That is NOT what this feels like.

Verlaine opened her eyes again, meaning to plead with Nadia to get them out of this before they went any farther. (But they weren't descending, of that Verlaine was sure; it was less that they were going down, because up and down didn't exist here, but they were getting deeper. Getting to the center.) Then she realized that a strange bluish light clung to her and to Nadia, so pale and filmy that it reminded her of cobwebs. "What is that?"

Nadia called back, "The love Asa stole for you! It's more than anybody should have—strong enough to carry us here—"

Had Asa known he was shielding her? Had he guessed this would happen?

Verlaine wasn't sure. She only knew that, even as she watched, the soft blue light tore. Shredded. It seemed to rip apart and go dark, thread by thread.

Even love could only protect her for so long.

Mateo had been raised to never, ever hit a girl.

Obviously Elizabeth didn't count.

He didn't swing at her. He lunged, ready to tackle her against the floor and knock her senseless—but even as he moved, something jerked him back so powerfully that he flew across the room and thudded into the wall. The breath knocked out of him, he had to gasp for air as he slid onto the floor.

"You think you can hold me," Elizabeth said. "You forget that I hold you, my future demon."

"You forget that I'm standing right here," said Mrs. Caldani.

Before Elizabeth had time to react, Nadia's mom cast—some spell, Mateo didn't know what, but whatever it was looked like fire and made Elizabeth scream. But Elizabeth threw something back at her that made Mrs. Caldani stagger and fall to her knees. Mr. Caldani went to her, his arm around her shoulders, but Mrs. Caldani didn't even seem to notice.

"And you," Elizabeth said, wheeling on Faye Walsh. Faye stood there, fists at her sides, obviously wanting to do something but—like Mateo—not knowing what. "Your Steadfast powers are withered, like the witch who linked herself to you."

Faye flinched. Mateo knew that the witch in question was her elderly mother, who had Alzheimer's. It was cruel of Elizabeth to throw that in Faye's face, but what about Elizabeth wasn't cruel?

Elizabeth continued, "Still, two Steadfasts in the same room will give me the power to follow Nadia. I will kill her before the eyes of the One Beneath, and when we ascend to this world, we will be wearing her blood."

Mateo's stomach turned over, but he lifted his chin and said, "Okay. Try it."

She stared at him, and he knew she'd sensed that his defiance wasn't just bravado. Maybe she hadn't thought this far ahead yet.

The thing about chaining a future demon to you was this—You were also chained to him. Elizabeth couldn't leave this realm, not while her bonds to Mateo were intact.

Her jaw tightened. Her gaze darkened, and the strange powers rippling around her seemed to intensify. It was all Mateo could do not to laugh in her face. "Guess you'll have to let me go."

Elizabeth cocked her head. "It will be quicker to kill you."

She lifted her hand, something brilliant flared all around them—

—and the water started rushing in.

How can water be flowing uphill? That was Simon Caldani's first thought. But why was he even questioning what was possible in a world with magic? Everything was possible. Anything could turn against them, at any moment.

Waves gushed through the doors. Water broke the panes of the windows. Trickles of water ran across the floor, finding each other and becoming puddles. Simon grabbed Kim and towed her to her feet. Still dazed, she fought him at first, then sagged against his shoulder.

He held her tightly. *God, she feels like skin and bones.* All this time he'd spent angry with Kim—trying to make himself hate her—and really she'd given up everything to protect their daughter. *We'll fix this,* he swore to her silently.

First they had to live through the night.

"Simon!" Faye shouted. She had run to the front door, which was shuddering in the lock, water spurting through the smallest cracks at the hinges. "Help me!"

He picked Kim up in his arms, took her halfway up the staircase, and set her down. She hardly seemed to notice. Then he ran to Faye's side. Together they put their backs against the door, trying to keep the water from gushing in so fast they would drown. But no. That couldn't be possible.

Could it?

"We're in a two-story house," he gasped. "Elizabeth could flood the whole thing?"

"She could drown us in this house and set it on fire at the same time," Faye said. "Welcome to witchcraft."

"We can't let this happen. If Nadia's hurt—"

"She won't be. I believe in her. We're not letting it happen."

Faye couldn't know that, not really, but it helped him just to hear it.

The door bucked against them so hard it seemed to hit Simon in the back of his head. Although the world went fuzzy for a moment, he braced his legs and pushed back harder. Next to him, Faye spread her arms wider, attempting to balance.

He could just see into the great room, the floor of which was already covered in water a few inches deep. Mateo sat on the floor, letting the water flow around him as he stared up at Elizabeth. "What's the matter?" Mateo said, a smile on his face. "Your magic isn't working as well as you thought? Nadia said even your powers had a limit, and breaking the worlds to bring the One Beneath here—that's as much as you can do."

"Not for long," Elizabeth said, so flatly, with such certainty, that Simon shuddered.

Nadia could sense the One Beneath all around them. Literally—this realm both enclosed Him and was Him. She imagined she could hear blood rushing through great veins, or the heavy low pumping of an enormous heart. But those were illusions, her mind trying to make sense of something completely outside human experience.

Her only comfort was Verlaine, who held on to her with all her might. That was an act of will, not of strength; physical effort meant nothing here. It was Verlaine's determination and courage that bound her to Nadia—that and the incredible depth of love around and within her.

Not all that love was the result of Asa's spell, either. Here, in the absolute darkest place anyone could be, Verlaine's goodness shone more brightly than ever before.

I hope I can be as strong for her, Nadia thought.

She looked upward—again, an illusion, but her spirit sought Mateo and would find him if he were here. They'd talked about the bonds of his oath; the same power that condemned him should be enough to hold Elizabeth in place. If Nadia was wrong, or if Elizabeth had simply struck him down, Mateo would soon be here in hell alongside her, without any hope of escape.

Yet Mateo wasn't with her, not yet. Nadia would have felt relieved if the strangeness whipping around her, reverberating within her, were not becoming more chaotic and violent by the second.

To Verlaine she shouted, "When I tell you to, let go of me. And scream for Asa as loudly as you possibly can."

"I don't want to let go of you!" Verlaine's face was just in front of hers, her silver-gray hair twisting and floating in the unearthly winds.

"You have to." For the last terrible moment, Nadia would have to stand alone.

At that moment, the darkness around them shifted. Took form. It seemed to Nadia that she was staring into a face—expressionless, blank, more like a mask than anything human, and yet more hideous than anything she'd ever imagined.

The One Beneath.

Nadia wanted to close her eyes. She didn't. Staring directly into that terrible face, she reached inward, drawing upon her mother's hate—pure hatred untouched by even the slightest suggestion of love. It blazed like a furnace.

That hate spiraled within her, taking a form that could only have existed here in the demonic realm.

The ultimate weapon is forged from hate. The ultimate weapon.

"Now," Nadia said, pushing Verlaine away. "Now!"

16

NOT YET, NOT YET, I WANT TO FIND ASA, BUT I DON'T *want to be alone in hell, and this is definitely hell, not yet—*

"Now!" Nadia shouted, and Verlaine let go.

It felt less like being pushed away by Nadia, more like being yanked back from her in a dozen directions at once. Verlaine tumbled head over heels, sideways, and for a moment she thought the forces might pull her apart until she was only so much sinew and bone.

She stayed in one piece, or she was too dizzy to even tell she'd been ripped apart. Verlaine flung her arms out in an attempt to steady herself. There was nothing for her to brace herself against, no way for her to know up from down; Nadia was invisible to her, lost in the twisting chaos of this realm. And yet, when she opened her arms, Verlaine knew somehow she was more balanced than she'd been before.

It's really not because of anything I did physically, she realized. *It's because I'm doing something, instead of letting this place toss me around.*

I have power here if I act.

The surge of hope she felt was visible—a kind of white electricity burning along her skin, and it was the only light Verlaine needed. She drew in a breath (*Oh, hey, hell has air*), let herself want and hope with all her strength, and screamed out her love's true name.

"ASAEL!"

The waters surged higher around Elizabeth, forming a whirlpool with her at its vortex. From all around the room, the few items remaining were drawn into the currents—a china vase, the golden rope tassel of a curtain, even an oil painting in a gilded frame.

Mateo Perez hung on to the crown molding around the archway between this room and the foyer. His body was now suspended in the water, on the verge of being torn away from his handhold. Then the currents would bring him to her, and she would . . .

How best to kill him? Angry as she was, Elizabeth saw no need for spite. Only for speed.

Even now, Nadia Caldani had descended to the depths of hell, armed with hatred so pure that she could destroy the bridge between the worlds. Elizabeth had to protect the One Beneath's path while the worlds were merging. Once the earthly and demonic realms were one, all Nadia's weapons would be useless. This moment was the last moment of danger the One Beneath would ever know. She would defend Him. But first she had to follow Nadia—and she couldn't, so long as she was tethered to Mateo Perez.

Once Mateo died, he would become a demon. Her slave.

Maybe she would bring him into hell with her, make him watch Nadia die.

Elizabeth raised her hands, quickening the current. Mateo's hands were torn free, and she smiled in satisfaction as he floated toward her.

But he grabbed her hair and shoved her underwater.

She clutched him down with her, and for a long moment they struggled together, each trying to hold the other under. The powerful currents tossed them both back and forth; when they popped to the surface, Elizabeth couldn't stop Mateo from sucking in a breath, because she was as desperate for air as he was.

There were spells to help her breathe underwater, but she had no time to cast them. No strength or focus leftover from defending herself against Mateo—this would not be settled by magic, but through brute force.

Mateo coughed water from his lungs. The smile on his face was terrible. "Together just like we were when we were kids, huh?"

Elizabeth clutched the collar of his shirt; he grabbed her shoulders so hard that his fingers felt like they could press through her flesh. She realized he would drown with her before he would let her go.

That meant he was willing to die. Good. The advantage was hers.

"Friends to the end," he said, and dragged them both back down.

"ASAEL!"

The word reverberated through the entire dimension around Verlaine; she could feel it as surely as she could feel heat on her skin. A demon's true name had power, Nadia had said—but only to the servants of hell. Within hell, where everyone was a servant, the word alone could start something like an earthquake.

Verlaine strained for an answer, hoping to see Asa appear in front of her. Or to hear his voice calling her name. Nothing. She was more alone in this creepy, warped void than before, and she thought, *That's it. I'm lost.*

Then she felt the faintest, softest brush against her palm.

Another, against her belly.

Another, in the curve of her neck.

Was someone touching her? The sensation was more like a silk scarf drifting next to her skin—ethereal and lovely. Here, amid all this ugliness, the softness was as welcome as it was strange.

Verlaine's eyes widened as she felt the next brush along her arm, and for the first time saw the shadow. Even in this twisting darkness, she could tell the shadow was different— black on black, but a kind of smoke that turned and swirled and sought—sought her.

"Asael," she whispered. Although she wanted to call him Asa, the name she thought of as his, she remembered what

Nadia had said. Here, nothing but Asa's real name could be spoken.

The smoke continued to darken as it finally took shape. These two wisps became legs; the cloud near her chest became a torso. And resting against her cheek was an oval cloud that had no features, but Verlaine knew it was a face.

This was what was left of him: spirit, not flesh. Only the outline of a human being. But whatever Asa was now, whatever he had endured for her sake, he had heard her call. He had answered. He'd found her, and she'd found him, and now maybe they could get out of here.

But he was in so much pain. So confused and afraid. More than anything, Verlaine wanted to comfort him. *Hold on, I'm here, I'm with you, not much longer.*

Saying any of that would damn him forever.

Her skin still glowed slightly with the blue light that Nadia had said was all that stolen love. However, Verlaine could tell the light had dimmed considerably since this journey had begun. It was like—like hell was burning it off. Consuming it.

Which meant soon it would consume her.

"Asael," Verlaine whispered. His name would have to say everything she felt. She put her arms around the shadow—a gesture she thought was futile—and was startled to feel Asa there. He had some kind of substance, then. Maybe he really could get out of hell in one piece.

That should have reassured Verlaine. Instead it panicked her. Before this, she'd been willing to dare anything. The

315

fate of the world was in the balance, which meant it was time to suck it up. And Verlaine had found it easy to risk it all for her friends and for love. But now that she had Asa back, she had something to lose.

She held him tighter and prayed for Nadia to come.

Nadia heard Verlaine calling to her—not with her voice, with everything else that she was—but couldn't answer. She was too busy forging her weapon.

The hate built and built within her, like a volcano bubbling with lava and on the verge of eruption. It was so tempting to give in to her anger, to add her loathing of Elizabeth and the One Beneath to the fire.

She didn't. Nadia knew that if she did that, she could only add normal human hate. Her hate would be tempered by all the other emotions she could feel, especially love. That meant the weapon she was creating would be weakened. For this, purity was the key.

It was her mother's hate she felt. All the venom that came from knowing herself tricked, realizing her empty, meaningless life was for nothing.

By now the One Beneath's face had become clear, and more malevolent—like He was becoming infinitely vaster in front of her eyes. Now that she could see Him more clearly, Nadia thought His face looked less like a mask, more like a skull.

A skull seen from the inside.

Imagine it as a sword, Nadia thought. She came from a

world of tangible things, so she needed to believe she had a tangible weapon. That was her only chance. If she could destroy that bridge, hurt Him, make Him turn back—that would be enough. Maybe that would undo Elizabeth's plans, or delay them long enough for her to come up with a real way to defeat them.

The darkness mocked her. No sound, no change in the still, dead face that spread across the entire void—and yet Nadia knew the One Beneath was laughing, to show her His contempt.

She also knew He wouldn't do that if she had no chance.

I'm sworn to Him. If I strike Him down, I may die along with Him.

That wasn't a reason to hesitate. Just a moment to think of her dad, and Cole, and even her mom. And Mateo.

I love you.

Nadia envisioned the blade, put all her force behind it, and struck.

The roar deafened her. Surrounded her. A cry of the greatest rage and pain she had ever known—beyond anything she had imagined—and for a moment she thought the force of it could tear the flesh from her bones. Maybe that was how the One Beneath would take her down: killing her with the power of His own fury.

But Nadia stayed alive, while everything around her began to collapse.

Darkness turned into nothingness—it wasn't a difference she could describe, but she could sense it. The spiraling chaos all around her became even more disordered as it slowed. It was like a great machine was breaking down, shedding gears, and stopping. She'd done more than destroy the bridge to the mortal world; she'd hurt the One Beneath . . .

No. The One Beneath wasn't merely wounded.

He was dying.

That's impossible, Nadia thought wildly. Wasn't it? She'd never even tried to figure out how to do it, because she'd believed it couldn't be done. Surely the unearthly din around her had confused her, was making her imagine things that weren't true.

And yet she could see it happening all around her. The One Beneath was collapsing, dragging the whole dimension of hell down with Him.

He took my mother's ability to love, Nadia thought in a daze. *He made her able to hate perfectly. He forged the weapon I used to kill Him.*

He's dead.

*He's **dead**.*

She felt one split second of triumph before she realized: *If we're still in hell when the One Beneath dies, the chaos will be more than we can survive.*

Mateo's lungs burned with the need for air, but he refused to come up. If he came up, Elizabeth would come up, too, and killing her was more important than staying alive.

They were tangled up with each other now, clothes torn, eyes open underwater as they stared at each other in mutual fury. Her fingernails had gouged deep cuts in his arms, and by this time his blood had mingled with the water.

Last time we surfaced, the water was chest-deep. Soon there won't be any air left in the house. Soon I can stop fighting and just let her die.

Somehow it seemed almost right to die with Elizabeth. His mind knew all those childhood memories of them playing together were fake; his heart couldn't put them aside as easily. Mateo felt as though he'd lived his entire life by her side, and now he'd end by her side, too.

After that—he'd be made a demon. He'd be a slave to the One Beneath, or some other Sorceress. He'd be controlled as severely as Asa had been controlled, and punished as cruelly. Mateo didn't care anymore. All he cared about was making sure that Elizabeth died, and Nadia lived.

Elizabeth writhed in his grip, and he felt a moment's elation at the thought that she was finally weakening—

—when two strong arms seized him by the shoulders and pulled him to the surface.

"No!" Mateo shouted. But it was too late. Faye Walsh, behind him, was already trying to tow him to safety, and Elizabeth's head was above the water.

Shoulder-deep.

"Let me go," Mateo protested.

Faye shook her head. "You can't die to defeat Elizabeth. She's not worth it."

"Someone has to!" Then it hit him. "Not you."

"No. Not Faye." Mr. Caldani managed to get through

the water to them, so that he stood between them and Elizabeth, who was already struggling through the current back to them. "This is my job."

"Simon, don't." Faye's voice shook with effort and fear. "You have children who need you. Me—I've got no one anymore, not anyone who'll miss me—there's no reason you should—"

"Nadia's my daughter," Mr. Caldani said. He took Faye's hand, like he was trying to thank her even as he pulled her back. "That makes this my work."

Mateo intended to fight this out if he had to, but that was the moment when Elizabeth began to scream.

Nadia cried out, "ASAEL!"

Instantly Verlaine appeared in front of her, cradling a frail shadow that must have been what was left of Asa's soul. As Nadia had hoped, Verlaine's love had bound Asa to her so tightly that summoning him had brought them both.

"Nadia! What happened?" Verlaine's hair wreathed out around her, as if it were floating. "It's all falling apart!"

"Hang on!" With that, Nadia reached upward, outward, envisioning the world she knew in every detail.

The big oak tree outside her bedroom window.

The sound of Cole's giggling.

The smell of hot cocoa.

Winter wind in Chicago, sharp enough to cut through a down jacket and make her shiver.

Dad's arms around her when he'd welcomed her back home.

The scent of sunblock lotion on her warm skin as she walked along the beach.

Mom at the doorway, suitcase in hand, saying, "It's better this way."

Bolognese sauce warm and rich on her tongue, but still needing just a touch more oregano.

Trying to laugh about the pictures her friends drew on her cast when really her broken arm still hurt terribly.

Verlaine asking if Nadia was an alien, and welcoming her to planet Earth.

That time some guy on the "L" inexplicably decided she was Selena Gomez and tried to get her autograph.

Her very first memory, laughing and kicking out her little toddler feet while Mommy pushed her gently, and asked if she wanted to swing even higher.

Mateo framing her face in his hands, looking at her with all the love she could ever have imagined someone could feel for her, and bringing his lips to hers.

They were the ingredients for every spell Nadia could ever have cast. She could draw upon her whole life, all the richness and pain and weirdness and love, and use all of it to draw her back to the world she knew.

It was like making that world all over again, even more beautiful than before.

They were arguing over who would die by Elizabeth's hand. They would all die by her hand, this moment, because now she was free of Mateo's battering and able to collect herself.

Now she would be able to cast a spell to destroy them—

Elizabeth screamed.

The pain was like nothing else she'd ever known. She had seen men burn, watched women starve. She knew death both fast and slow, had memorized the way each anguish worked, but Elizabeth had never once sensed anything as terrible as the pain that had her now.

The worst wasn't the intense, crushing pressure upon her whole body. It was feeling her magic dry up and leave her.

No, she thought, staggering one step forward through the water. *That's impossible. I am sworn to the One Beneath, and His fury and His power sustain me.*

Elizabeth sought the One Beneath in her mind, and found only silence.

This could not be true. It could not. His darkness underlay the entire world; He was mightier than any earthly force. How could she call for Him and hear nothing in return?

Only one answer arose in her mind, a terrible slow kindling like the bonfire around a stake. Elizabeth tried to hold back the knowledge—to turn away from what her witchcraft told her, for the only time in her life—but she could not. She knew.

Her beloved lord had been destroyed.

Every spell Elizabeth had ever cast with His power— the waters to flood this house, the curse against the Cabots, the binding of Mateo to her with the chains of demonhood—the spell to extend her own life—

All of them were burning out.

The water began to drain from the great house so quickly

that Elizabeth almost instantly felt her feet make solid contact with the floor. As the water went down to her waist level, she looked toward her opponents to find them staring at her in horror; only then did she realize she was still screaming.

She wanted to claw at them, to take Mateo Perez's eye, or the other Steadfast's throat, as some small measure of vengeance—but as Elizabeth held out her hand, she saw that it no longer looked like her own. Before her eyes, the flesh withered, exposing bones that became weaker by the moment. Her wet hair against her shoulders paled from chestnut to a dull, brittle white. Spots and blotches marred her skin, and her voice changed from one scream to the next, becoming more feeble. She even felt her teeth loosening in her gums, falling out with every shriek, until she could taste blood.

The water fell beneath her hips. Only then did she realize it had been holding her up.

Elizabeth fell forward onto her knees. The fragile bones shattered, sending pain spiking up through her legs. That didn't matter, though. Worse was the pain of knowing that the One Beneath was gone forever.

Mateo took one halting step toward her. Apparently the rapid aging of her body had shocked him out of hatred into unwilling pity. "Elizabeth?"

Better to be dead than to be pitied.

Elizabeth let herself fall forward into the shallow water, thinking she would drown.

But her skull shattered against the floor, and everything she'd ever been or known floated away. Lost in the flood.

❧

Shaking, Mateo leaned down and turned over Elizabeth's body. If he hadn't watched her transform in front of his eyes, he would never have been able to recognize this ancient crone as the girl she'd been moments before. Now she was old—older than human beings ever actually got, wrinkled to the point of obscuring her features. Toothless. And very, very dead.

She looked more like a mummy than a corpse.

What could kill Elizabeth from within like that? And make the waters go down? Mateo had an idea, but he almost didn't dare to hope.

He looked over his shoulder at Faye. "Does this mean what I think it means?"

"I'm not sure. But at least Elizabeth's dead."

Faye's smile was weary; she'd braced herself against the wall, and was visibly trembling with exhaustion. Only once he'd seen her did he realize he was shaking, too. Fighting in the water had taken more of his strength than he'd realized. Without his anger at Elizabeth to fuel him, Mateo felt emptied out.

Mr. Caldani had already gone halfway up the stairs to check on his semiconscious ex-wife. "Did Nadia win? This means she won, right?"

"I don't know." Mateo looked down at Elizabeth's dead body—crumpled up like so many wet rags—then walked away from her without looking back.

Faye cocked her head. "Do you hear that?"

"Hear what?" Mateo could only think, *What now?*

"It's not so much what we do hear as what we don't." A slow smile dawned on Faye's face. "It's stopped raining."

The enormous room was still draining water, which welled and puddled in strange ways. Elizabeth had broken the laws of nature to get it in here, and the last evidence of her magic was the strange way the water flowed out again. Mateo's side of the room was completely clear, while the far corner was still a couple of feet deep. Falling fast, though . . .

And as he stood there watching, the water went down just enough to reveal three forms huddled together in the corner.

Mateo's eyes widened. Hope stole his voice, so that he could only stare.

That was enough, because that let him see Nadia—and Verlaine and Asa, too—all of them, gasping as though they'd been underwater a very long time.

"Nadia?" he whispered. She tugged her wet hair away from her face, saw him, and smiled.

Then he was running toward her, and she rose to meet him so he could swing her into his arms. They were both soaking wet, with their clothes stuck to them and their hair in their faces, but Mateo thought he'd never felt anything better. Never seen anything sweeter than Nadia smiling again.

"You made it," he said. "Oh, my God, you made it."

On the floor, Asa seemed completely dazed. He still looked just like Jeremy Prasad. "Did that just happen?"

"Did we just kick supernatural ass?" Verlaine grinned as she helped him sit up. "Yeah, that happened."

Mateo never wanted to let go of Nadia again, but then Mr. Caldani was there, too, and suddenly they were all sort of hugging one another at once.

"It worked?" Faye said through tears. "Your weapon was able to stop the One Beneath?"

"We didn't just stop Him." Nadia shook her head, as if in disbelief. "We—we killed Him."

"More like annihilated," Verlaine said cheerfully.

Asa, who had one hand on Verlaine's shoulder and another against the wall, looked like he was ready to fall over again. But his smile was as devilish as ever. "The demonic realm collapsed. Completely. That hasn't happened in millennia."

"Does that mean it's gone for good?" Mr. Caldani said. "The, uh, 'demonic realm'?"

"Oh, hell will restore itself. It always does." Asa managed to stand on his own, and started to wring water from the tail of his shirt. "And eventually there will be another lord of hell. But that's going to take a long time. Eons. I mean, literal eons. The forces of darkness will be fighting among themselves for quite a while now."

"Which means they'll leave us alone?" Verlaine said.

"It also means all the bonds, oaths, and other verbal contracts with the One Beneath are null and void." Asa frowned. "Maybe I should go to law school."

Relief washed through Mateo. "You mean—we don't have to become demons anymore?"

"That's what it would mean. Maybe your curse is gone, too." Nadia took his shoulders and leaned close, her joy seeming to flow into Mateo along with her touch. Then she went tense. "Elizabeth—where is she?"

Mateo didn't bother pointing; he just looked at the crumpled form on the floor. What remained of Elizabeth looked like a pile of rags on the wet parquet wood.

Although the sight of Elizabeth's corpse clearly shook Nadia, she didn't look at it long. "A mirror. Mateo, we have to find a mirror."

"Why?" Mr. Caldani asked.

Mateo knew why. He looked around the room, cluttered with debris—bits of broken vases, a waterlogged curtain torn free from its rod and a lamp that lay halfway through a window. Near the stairwell, on the floor, a cracked mirror was tilted on its side against the wall.

He ran to it, Nadia by his side. When he lifted it with shaking hands, he saw his reflection, splintered by the cracks in the mirror glass.

His Steadfast abilities let him see magic, and had always shown him the curse as a black halo of thorns—twisting and terrible, as much a part of him as his skin. Now the halo was gone.

"The curse is broken," he said, turning to Nadia. "It's gone. Everything Elizabeth did to all of us—it's over."

Nadia's eyes welled with tears, but he knew she was crying for joy. She whispered, "We're free."

17

AS HE STOOD IN THE BROKEN, WATER-LOGGED ROOM, Simon Caldani thought he'd put together the basics. Elizabeth Pike had been a bad witch, in league with something very like the devil. Nadia was a good witch. There had been an epic battle, during which his daughter had managed to destroy Elizabeth's black magic, plus the devil.

This definitely called for an increase in her allowance. More to the point, it meant everything was going to be okay. All the old scars would be healed. Which meant . . .

He looked at the stairs, where his ex-wife sat, rubbing the side of her head. As thin as she'd become, as strange as this whole scenario was—even knowing Kim had lied to him throughout their marriage about being a witch—all Simon could think was, *She's come back.*

While everyone else hugged and talked, and Nadia and Mateo made out in a way that made Simon think they'd have to have A Talk soon, he walked toward the stairs. Kim's eyes flicked toward him for a moment before she closed them and went back to rubbing her head.

"Hey," he said softly. "You all right? Do we need to take you to a doctor?"

Kim shrugged. "I never actually went unconscious. So I guess not."

"You were pretty out of it for a few minutes." It was all Simon could do not to brush back her wet hair and check for himself. He wanted to take her to the hospital, have them make her well, so that they could go back home together.

"I feel fine," she said. "Just pissed off I didn't give that Sorceress the beat-down she deserved."

Simon had spent most of the last year of his life trying to cast his wife out of his heart. Every memory they'd made together—even their wedding, even the births of their children—had been changed for him. Every proof of their love now seemed like an illusion; every word Kim had ever spoken to him seemed to have been translated into another language, one he didn't know.

He'd done well at moving on, but now he had to try to come back to her again.

"Then we'll go home," he said to her gently. "You'll like the house here. And Cole—he'll be so glad to see you."

Kim frowned. "I'm going back to Chicago."

"But the black magic ended. That means this thing you did—giving away your ability to love—that's over, too. Isn't it?"

She smiled at him, but that smile had none of the warmth he remembered. "It's not like the One Beneath put it in a safe-deposit box and hid the key. He consumed my ability to love. Destroyed it, for good."

At first Simon couldn't make sense of the words. "That can't be undone now? Or—or we could bring it back in some other way—"

"You don't understand how magic works." Kim got to her feet. Although she was slightly unsteady, she never reached for him for support. "When I gave it up, I gave it up forever. That's why we call it a sacrifice. Why sacrifices have power in the first place. Because they do what can't be undone."

Simon nodded, because he was unable to speak. Why should it be so much harder to watch her leave the second time?

Kim walked toward the door, and Simon couldn't even tell her not to go. But Nadia called out, "Mom! Wait!" She jogged toward her mother, but she didn't try to hug her, like Simon had expected. She didn't even ask Kim to stay. Nadia said only, "Thanks for coming when I called. You made the difference. Your sacrifice—it really did save me after all."

"Good to know," Kim said. There was that strange smile again, the one harsher and colder than Simon could ever have imagined. "I'm going to go. I can drive out of town, fly home in the morning."

Nadia nodded. Now Simon could see how moved his daughter was—the faint glistening of tears in her eyes—but he also saw that she knew nothing would do any good, that the mother she'd known was gone forever.

As Kim opened the door, Simon said, "Can I say one thing?"

"Sure." She didn't even seem interested to hear it.

But Simon had to get this out, not for Kim but for himself. "Thank you for protecting our daughter."

It was the single most important bond between them: the children they'd created and loved, and put before anything else. All this year he'd been so angry that Kim hadn't lived up to her end of the bargain spouses made to each other—but he'd been wrong. Kim had come through after all, and in the long run, it would help to remember that.

"Okay," Kim said. Then she walked out of the house, and their lives, for good.

Simon sank back down onto the stairs and put his head in his hands. After a moment, Nadia sat beside him, and he slung one arm around her. He didn't know if he was comforting his daughter or she was comforting him. All Simon knew was that they'd made it through the worst. So they'd make it through the rest.

Asa slumped in the passenger seat of the land yacht; after the Caldanis had dropped them off at Verlaine's house, she'd immediately gotten him into her car and started to drive him home.

The Prasads' home. Not his. But it was the only place he had to go.

"Are you all right?" Verlaine kept looking over at him,

like she was afraid he'd disappear at any moment. "What you went through down there—"

"Let's not talk about it. Not now." He put his hand on her knee and managed to smile. "Right now I just need to know it's over."

"Okay." Verlaine bit her lower lip, then blurted out, "How are you still alive?"

"You rescued me. Remember?"

Asa would never forget it. Hearing his true name, seeing Verlaine appear in the darkness, impossibly beautiful, made of light—and suddenly being in this body again, wet and cold but instantly free from pain: It was the single most glorious moment of all his centuries.

Verlaine persisted. "I mean, black magic put you in Jeremy's body to begin with. So when Elizabeth died, you should have . . . left it, I guess?"

"The demonic realm still exists. So do my powers." Though at the moment, Asa was too tired even to stop time. "Elizabeth put me here, but I keep myself here. For now, anyway."

"What do you mean, for now?"

"I can't live this lie." Asa thought again of Jeremy's mother smiling at up at him. "The Prasads lost their son. He was murdered. They deserve the truth."

Verlaine was silent as she considered his words. The only sound in the car was the soft splash of tires through puddles. Asa was grateful that he didn't have to hear rain anymore.

Then, very quietly, Verlaine said, "You can't tell them."

"I have to. They'll be upset—they'll hate me for it—but at

least I won't be cheating them any longer."

"Think about this." Verlaine pulled the car onto the gravel shoulder of the road, put it in park, and turned to him. "Are you seriously going to tell the Prasads you're a demon who's moved into Jeremy's body? They're not going to believe you. They're just going to send you to a psych ward."

So many people in Captive's Sound had learned the truth in the past few weeks that Asa had almost forgotten that everyone else still had no idea how the supernatural worked. "Maybe—maybe Nadia could cast a spell."

"Then you'd leave Jeremy's body? Can you even do that?"

"Yes," Asa said, but already he could see the problems. "I don't have the power to put myself in another body, though. I wouldn't do it even if I could. I'd have to return to the demonic realm."

Which now was pure chaos. Which would be riddled with the battles of evil versus evil, the struggle to be the new lord of hell, for eons to come. Not anyplace he wanted to be.

Verlaine took his hand in both of hers. "I know it sucks, lying to the Prasads. But I feel like they'd be happier with you as their son. If you take care of them, and love them, and see them through old age and all the rest—that's really the only way you can pay them back."

Like anything made up for the murder of their child. Elizabeth was the one who had murdered Jeremy, but Asa was the one who'd benefited from it. If he deceived the Prasads about this, he would keep feeling terrible about it, probably forever.

Maybe . . . maybe that was the price he had to pay for

taking over Jeremy's body. The rent, so to speak.

He imagined the Prasads finding their son's dead body, mourning him—no. They deserved to be spared that pain. There was nothing else he could do for them any longer, and nothing else he could do for the late Jeremy Prasad, to whom he would always owe a debt.

So he would bear this terrible knowledge alone, and be the best son he could possibly be.

"Besides," Verlaine said, "if you went away, I'd miss you like crazy."

"I'm not going anywhere." Asa pulled her into his arms.

"You mean—you're staying with the Prasads?"

He nodded. "And I'm staying with you."

She breathed out, a sigh of exhaustion and relief. For a while they simply held each other, as Asa tried to wrap his mind around the idea of . . . a future.

He'd go on from here. Graduate from Rodman High, go to college. Finally find out what it was like to grow up, grow old. He could think ahead to days and months and years to come—the luxury of it stunned him.

Best of all, he could stay with Verlaine as long as she still loved him, and he intended to do whatever it took to keep her in love with him forever.

"So it's over," she murmured. "You gave yourself away to avenge your sister, and now you got yourself back again."

That was correct, as far as it went, but Asa wasn't able to tell her so. Instead he was overcome by a flash of memory— another moment from his first mortal life, given back to him at last. His eyes widened in wonder, and joy.

"Not just to avenge my sister," he whispered.

"What? I thought that was why you said you'd become a demon."

"It was. But that was only half of it." Slowly he started to smile. "I asked for my sister to be avenged, but I also asked—I asked to be there on the day darkness fell. My sister was killed by the One Beneath's black magic, so I wanted to see Him fall. To witness His death. He made the deal, probably because He thought He couldn't die until the end of time."

Verlaine grinned. "Instead, it's today. The joke's on Him, huh?"

For a moment, Asa could almost imagine his sister's face again. His love for her came back to him, and he thought he'd never known a moment more beautiful than this, when he knew she'd been avenged—and Verlaine was here with him. This was as good as it got.

After as much kissing as Asa could manage, exhausted as he was, Verlaine dropped him at his house. He tried to come in quietly, but as he trudged up the stairs, Jeremy's mother appeared on the landing. "Jeremy! There you are. You haven't been answering our texts."

"I lost my cell phone," Asa said, which was technically true, if you considered burned in the fires of hell as lost. "Sorry, Mom."

Mr. Prasad walked out of his bedroom, too, knotting the tie of his bathrobe. "Did everything go well at Mateo's house?"

"Everything went great. It's stopped raining, too." Asa reached the top of the stairs. No doubt his parents could see how exhausted he was, but they'd chalk it up to his helping with sandbags and such.

Mrs. Prasad's smile grew mischievous. "That pretty girl who came by for you—Verlaine, with the lovely silver hair—she seems to like you quite a lot."

"I like her, too." Asa thought of Verlaine's lips against his. "You'll be seeing her around."

"Oh, will we?" Mr. Prasad shared a pleased glance with his wife.

Dad, Asa thought. *Mom. That's who they are to me now. That's who they'll always be.*

Despite the guilt he still carried, he couldn't help but be glad.

On an impulse Asa said, "Hey, can I ask you something?"

"Of course," Dad said. Now his parents both looked worried.

Hastily Asa said, "It's not a big deal. It's just—Verlaine, and my friends at school, they've given me a nickname. Asa." He thought fast. "From the middle letters of Prasad. I like it, so I was wondering—would you guys call me that?"

"These phases you go through!" Mom giggled. "It's just like when you were five and wanted me to pretend you were a dog, and you'd only eat when I put your food in a bowl on the floor."

"Not exactly like that," Asa protested.

"If that's what you want," Dad said. "Come on, let's all get back to bed. Good night, Asa."

"Yes, Asa. Good night." Mom was still giggling as his parents went to their bedroom.

Asa smiled at them as he quietly said, "Good night, Mom and Dad."

Mateo helped his dad with inventory all morning. Since the rain had stopped a few days ago, the water had subsided, and now finally trucks could get into town. Which meant La Catrina would soon be open for business again.

"Glad to see people acting like normal," Dad said as he double-checked the manifest. "Can you believe it was just one week ago they were talking about witches?"

"Weird." Mateo shook his head, like, *Those idiots.*

Dad folded his arms as he leaned against the storage room wall. "By the way—the sheriff told me he's dropping the charges against you."

His life had become so bizarre that Mateo had almost forgotten about getting arrested. "Whoa. Okay. Good to know."

"Mass hysteria was setting in. The sheriff knows that as well as anyone else. So you got lucky this time, buddy."

"Dad. Come on. I jumped in there because those guys were harassing Verlaine."

With a raised hand, Dad said, "I know. I know. Let's just hope we never have to deal with anything like that again."

Mateo turned back to the crates of diced tomatoes to hide his smile. "I have a feeling we won't have any problems like that for a really long time."

"Hey, have you decided what to do with the house on

the Hill?" Dad got back to work, too. "It's your place, so it's your decision. But I warn you, property taxes are a bitch."

"I'm going to put it up for sale." The misery of all his cursed ancestors seemed to cling to the place. "Which means you don't have to worry about paying for college anymore."

"Oh, you're Mr. Moneybags now. Well, *jefe*, does the place need fixing up before it goes on the market?"

Mateo thought of all the broken objects, the curtains ripped from the walls. He'd gone back there just once, with Gage, to bury what was left of Elizabeth—but by then her corpse had turned to so much ash. In the end Gage vacuumed her from the floor, and then they'd burned the bag in an alley.

"Yeah," he said. "Mostly cleaning up. But we already took care of the worst of it."

It would have been ideal not to run into anyone while she was breaking into Elizabeth's house, which was why Nadia had hauled her butt out of bed so early in the morning. Instead, just as she got to Elizabeth's front door, Kendall came jogging past. "Oh, hey, Nadia!" she called. "Isn't it, like, great to be outside without getting rained on?"

For once, Kendall seemed truly friendly. Nadia might've been happy to see her, except for the awkward questions that had to be coming. "Yeah, it's great."

"Also, you know, humidity makes hair look incredibly gross. It's way better now." Kendall kept running in place, iPhone strapped to her upper arm; her pink track suit stood out brilliantly against the brown leaves scattered across Elizabeth's lawn. "So you can start fixing yours again if you want to."

Nadia thought she already had. Frowning, she put one hand to her ponytail.

Oblivious to having hurt any feelings, Kendall added, "So, do you think she ran away?"

"Elizabeth?"

"Well, duh." Kendall rolled her eyes. "She was always so skanky and weird. Like how she wouldn't shower and came to school without shoes on, when she showed up at all?"

The luster Elizabeth had carried around her had disappeared from people's memories as well. "Yeah. Seriously strange."

"My mom says Elizabeth probably hitchhiked out of town when it was flooding. I'm like, how would you hitchhike out of here when nobody from out of town could drive in to begin with?"

"Good point," Nadia said. Already she had begun to relax. Kendall wasn't going to ask awkward questions, because she already had her own theories about what had happened to Elizabeth. Probably everyone in town would come up with their own story, but Nadia doubted anyone would even go to the trouble of filing a missing persons report.

Elizabeth Pike had slipped out of this world without even a ripple. Soon she would be forgotten by everyone who hadn't learned who and what she really was, and this town could start to heal.

Kendall said, "Personally, I think she ran away. Can you blame her? Who would want to live in a run-down old house like that?" She wrinkled her nose. "I hope she's okay, though."

"I don't think you have to worry about her," Nadia said. She jammed her cold hands in the pockets of her coat. "Elizabeth always could take care of herself."

"Except for that hair. Ugh." Cheerful again, Kendall slipped her earbuds back in and waved as she began to jog away. Over her shoulder she called, "Hey, if I don't see you in the next couple of days, Merry Christmas!"

Nadia waved back, smiling, but she waited until Kendall had rounded the corner out of sight before she opened Elizabeth's front door.

The house looked even more forlorn now. Before, the little stove had cast a strange orange glow that—however creepy—at least warmed the place up a bit. Now the rooms were purely derelict. As Nadia walked toward the back room, she noticed how often she could see through gaps in the floorboards to the ground below. Probably this house would collapse in a few years if the city didn't condemn it and tear it down first.

She pushed open the back room door slowly, every muscle tense. The last time she'd broken in here, she'd been attacked by hundreds of spiders at once. Yeah, this time she had protective spells ready, but she would just as soon skip the whole spider thing, if possible.

This time, though, nothing happened. Elizabeth's Book of

Shadows sat in the center of the room, closed, as if waiting.

Nadia kneeled beside the book. With one hand she reached out to touch it; still, nothing happened. No helpful guidance to spells; no attacks by spiders; nothing.

Books of Shadows gained power as their witches grew older. As Elizabeth had lived longer than any other witch in history, that made this the most powerful Book of Shadows that had ever existed. It could be malevolent—Nadia had experienced that for herself—but she also suspected that, with Elizabeth dead, the book could be changed. Cleansed, maybe. If so, it would teach Nadia things about magic that perhaps no one but Elizabeth had ever known.

"I'm taking you with me," she said.

Nadia felt vaguely stupid talking to a book—but then it moved. She jumped back, but the Book of Shadows simply flipped itself open to an early page.

Tentatively, she leaned forward to read what was written there. The ink was old, and Elizabeth's handwriting the thick flowery cursive that had been popular hundreds of years ago. But slowly Nadia made out the words. The spell was for cleansing magical items of any black magic they'd been used to cast.

That, she figured, was the Book of Shadows telling her it accepted her as its new witch.

"Come on," she said, hefting it into one arm. "Let's go."

"Come on, you two!" Verlaine called as she slipped on her winter coat. "How is it possible for me to fix my hair and put on makeup faster than you two can put on nice sweaters?"

"Talk to Mr. Hog-the-Hair-Dryer," Uncle Dave said. "Don't blame me. And look at that dress!"

It was only a Dior knockoff, and deep green instead of red, but Verlaine was wearing it as a tribute to the fallen designer gown that would never, ever recover from its trip to hell or its subsequent dunking in floodwater. Besides, the narrow waist and the full skirt were festive enough for a Christmas Eve party, even if they were just hanging out at the Caldanis'.

"Okay, okay," Uncle Gary said, coming out just a few seconds behind. "Let me grab the plum pudding, and we're out of here."

As they stood at the front door, listening to Uncle Gary do battle with tinfoil, Uncle Dave said, "There's not going to be any—*you know* at this party, is there?"

Verlaine batted her eyelashes innocently. "You mean eggnog?"

"No."

"Fruitcake?"

Uncle Dave gave her a look. "Magic. I mean magic."

"Not anything major." Who knew what Nadia might have gotten up to in the kitchen? Verlaine knew that if she could cast a spell to wash the dishes, she would. "Nobody's going to be talking about it, okay? This is just a Christmas party. The end."

He sighed. "Just as long as there are no surprises."

Verlaine waited for Uncle Gary to walk back to them before she said, "Actually, there is one surprise."

Her dads looked at each other. Uncle Gary's eyes narrowed. "And what's that?"

She put one hand on the doorknob. "You get to meet my boyfriend."

Then she opened the door and hurried down the steps before they could even start asking questions.

There was a brief interrogation in the SUV, but once they got to the Caldanis', her dads were both on good behavior. Neither of them threatened to kill Asa even once. It helped that Asa was being his most charming, and that his parents were so thrilled to see her. Within moments, they were fully into the swing of the party.

Nothing fancy, Nadia had promised. The only decorations were a few strands of twinkling lights around the room. Cole and his best friend, Levi, were watching *A Charlie Brown Christmas* in the living room, while Faye Walsh and Mr. Caldani chatted with each other, plastic cups of wine in their hands. *Huh, they're sitting kind of close,* Verlaine thought. *Maybe something's getting started there.* Mateo's dad was telling Levi's parents a story that made them laugh. Nadia still had on her apron as she walked in and out of the kitchen, obviously in a baking frenzy. However, Mateo was in the kitchen with her; maybe that was the real reason Nadia was in no hurry to come out. Christmas carols played softly on the stereo system, and everything was basically perfect.

Or at least it was once Asa embraced her from behind.

"Hey," she said, leaning back. "Our parents are getting along well."

"Almost too well. Be afraid. Be very afraid."

Verlaine laughed, and he hugged her tighter. Against her neck, he murmured, "How are you feeling?"

"Amazing. When I go out, people treat me like anybody else. I can actually make friends now. I can even get my teachers to rewrite my college recs." Verlaine paused, then made a face. "I wish I'd thought to do that back when I had all the crazy love vibes. Those would have been the best recommendations ever."

"You're going to get in on your own merits, now that the world can finally see them."

"Thanks to you."

Asa shook his head. "I couldn't make them see everything beautiful in you if it hadn't been there to begin with."

Verlaine turned in his embrace, intending to kiss him—but when she caught a glimpse of herself in the mirror, she gasped.

"What is it?" Asa said, his hands on her shoulders. "What's wrong?"

"Nothing. Just—in the mirror—"

How had she not seen it before? Maybe it hadn't been visible until this moment. Lips parted in wonder, Verlaine walked to the mirror and leaned close to it. "My hair," she whispered. "Look!"

At the very roots, right next to her scalp, her hair was no longer silver. Now that she had back everything Elizabeth had stolen from her, Verlaine's hair was turning brown again.

"A shame," Asa said. "You'll make a stunning brunette, of course, but—the silver is so beautiful."

Verlaine started to laugh. "I think I'm about to become the first person who ever dyed her hair back to gray."

"I can do more in a kitchen than slice pound cake," Mateo said, even as he brought the knife down through each curve of the crust. "Grew up in a restaurant, remember?"

"You get your chance to prove it with the crab dip." Now that Nadia could finally think about her future, about becoming a professional chef someday, she took more pleasure in cooking than she ever had before. "I can't believe we never really cooked together before."

"We have plenty of time to practice now." He grinned at her, and something about the way he stood there, with his black apron around his waist and a daub of flour on one cheek—it made her want to drop everything and kiss him. "We might be able to practice something even more interesting."

"Stop it," she whispered. "Dad's only a few feet away."

"Oh, no, not that! Well, I mean, yeah that, definitely that, but I was talking about magic."

"Okay. That, too."

Nadia suspected that Mateo probably was too old to learn the Craft, at least anything beyond a few basic spells. But she intended to find out. From now on, she wasn't bound by old laws, or accepting every legend as truth. She and Mateo would learn the true boundaries of the Craft—and expand them—together.

After the sandwiches were done, Nadia finally took off her apron and joined the party. Everyone was laughing. Talking. Happy. Even Dad finally had a smile on his face again. It wasn't like everything in their lives had been fixed—they hadn't gotten over losing Mom yet, if they ever would. Asa still turned moody when his parents slipped up and called him "Jeremy." And while Mateo had recovered from the curse, people in town still looked at him funny. They didn't know he'd changed his fate, that he'd be the first Cabot in hundreds of years to lead his own life instead of being Elizabeth's plaything. They only knew he'd been blaming witches for it a short time before.

So it's not perfect, Nadia thought as she leaned down to ruffle Cole's hair. *It's still pretty good.*

Mateo caught her hand in his and drew her toward the corner of the room, where—instead of the real thing—Cole's crayon drawing of mistletoe had been taped on the ceiling.

"Like you need it." Nadia drew him close and kissed him as warmly as she dared with both their fathers in the room.

Mateo touched his forehead to hers, smiling softly. When Cole began laughing at something Snoopy had done, he glanced over and asked, in a low voice, "Does Cole still believe in Santa?"

"Yeah, I think so, or at least he pretends to," Nadia whispered back. "He probably thinks he'll get more presents that way."

"Smart kid. What are you giving him?"

"A toy pirate ship, complete with toy pirates. Cards for his battle game. A tablet for kids, so maybe he'll leave Dad's iPad alone. Some pajamas, some books, and a white Christmas."

Mateo looked back at her. "What was that last one?"

Nadia pulled Mateo closer. "Cole's always had white Christmases before. You know, we lived in Chicago. I wouldn't want to disappoint him this year."

"You really can do anything, can't you?"

Between soft kisses, Nadia said, "No. But I can do this."

As she snuggled into Mateo's embrace, Nadia looked past him at the window. Right now the night sky was so clear that the stars shone as brightly as Christmas lights. She'd kept any hint of precipitation far away for the last several days, to give the town a chance to dry out and get ready for this.

Late tonight, after midnight, once Cole was fast asleep, Nadia would go outside in her coat. She'd try the second spell she'd created herself, calling on her very best memories, and she had a hunch it was going to work. She would look up at the night sky, gather the clouds, and cast a spell for snow.

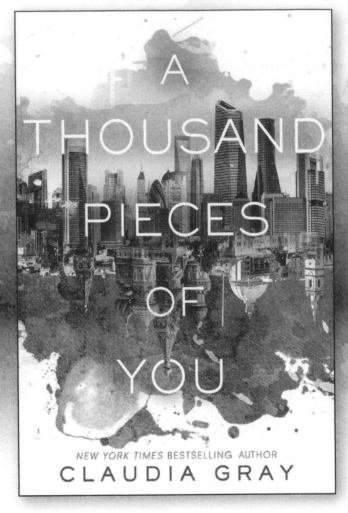